Mystikos

Casie Tabanou

TSD Books

Contents

CHAPTER ONE

There's never been any air conditioning on Maybelle, the old school bus my mom, Eteri, and I converted into our home on wheels, but that means the windows are always down in warm weather and I'm very good at predicting all kinds of things based solely on the smells in the cross breeze. I can tell you the political leanings of a community by how much fabric softener is in the air (the stronger the scent, the more conservative the town. Eteri says this is because Republicans are trying to hide something). I can tell you almost immediately how far away the nearest hospital is because the scent of antiseptic and fear mixes into something that tickles the back of my throat. I can tell you if there is a snow cone to be had in a 5-mile radius (especially if they have root beer float flavor because that's my all-time favorite). But at that particular moment, I could tell it was definitely going to rain.

"It's gonna be dark soon. We should stop for the night," Eteri said from behind Maybelle's big steering wheel.

Eteri does not look like your average mom. She's more of a cross between Stevie Nicks and those Victorian drawings of pressed fairies. She adores color, has never met a scrap of fringe or lace she didn't like, and almost always has a wildflower or spray of clover tucked behind her ear.

"Look for a solid spot. I'm not trying to jack this thing out of the mud again," I told her with a bit of sass that she didn't register. It's hard to ruffle Eteri's feathers.

"The weather's been gorgeous. There's no mud," she answered.

"There will be," I retorted.

Eteri knew better than to argue with my prediction, so she slowed down to find an appropriate spot not too far off the black top road we were traveling. As Maybelle came to a stop and her hydraulics made that familiar hiss, my body went on autopilot. There was a list of things to do when we were camping for the night and since Eteri was usually off foraging for mushrooms or connecting to "the energy of the landscape," those things often fell to me, but I didn't mind the routine, because it was pretty much the only one in my life.

Eteri said her spirit guide once told her she suffered from wanderlust because she was not of this world. I was fairly certain my mom had just picked up the habits of her hippie parents who had raised her on a series of communes in between short stints with the forestry service counting beavers and penduline tits (and yes, she was somehow able to tell me that with a straight face). In all of my sixteen years, the longest we had stayed in one place was a month, and that was because we got snowed in and had to wait for the spring thaw.

It was just the two of us. Eteri told me she found me inside an olive where the pimento should have been, but once I got a handle on basic biology, I figured out it could have been any one of several of my mother's "beautiful memories" who gave me life. The year she got pregnant, Eteri had been picking olives to save up for her first VW van and apparently, the crisp air made her fall in love easily and often. I wasn't mortified by this lack of patriarchal specificity. I respected

Eteri's fierce independence and honestly wished she had passed her total absence of fear when it came to tackling anything new onto me.

I unhooked the latch that held up the murphy bed in Maybelle's bedroom. The feet of the bed touched the floor with a satisfying click, and I briefly entertained allowing myself to fall into the soft quilt I had sewn together with Eteri from cut up dresses we found in thrift stores. It had always been one of my favorite belongings and being wrapped in that quilt was a suit of armor against any and all doubts and concerns. But in the end, I decided dinner would taste better than a nap and moved into what served for Maybelle's kitchen.

I'm a vegetarian. Eteri is not. Neither of us came to this decision with any political agenda, but we're solid in our choices. Despite the fact meat hasn't touched my lips since the age of five when I became convinced the braised rabbit we had for dinner was going to hop out of my stomach while I slept, I am willing to cook it for others.

Raiding the solar-powered bus fridge, I found a red pepper, some mushrooms, a near past its prime zucchini and a block of tofu and placed them on the butcher block countertop, then reached back in for a piece of chicken I'd left marinating in a Ziploc bag. I decided to shift from the shish kabobs I'd planned to grill that night to a stir fry because of my rain prediction.

"Mom, do we have another bottle of soy sauce under the bus?" I called out with my head still stuck in the refrigerator.

No answer came, so I wandered down Maybelle's steps and hung my head out the door for a look around. I caught a last bit of lacy skirt disappearing into the woods as Eteri escaped on one of her adventures. I smiled and shook my head. Eteri always brought me back a treasure from her woodland excursions. Sometimes it was the tiniest pinecone in the forest, or a perfectly smooth rock, or maybe a sparrow feather for our last name, Sparrow. It was no big deal. I'd finish setting up for the night and start dinner while she was gone.

Although it was nearly September and the sun was setting earlier every day, there was still enough daylight for Eteri to explore. In any case, it wouldn't be her first time coming back after dark. Eteri has a sixth sense about direction and is never lost.

***

The sky went from gray, to navy, and then to a deep black speckled with stars. I'd finished eating, made Eteri a plate, and packed away the leftovers for lunch the next day. Eteri still wasn't back, but I didn't feel panicked. I decided to crawl onto the bed and read for a bit before my mom came home with a million stories to tell.

I've always loved to read. Our first stop in any new town is the local bookstore (used if we can find one). Used books just have more soul in them. I imagine that the pages steal a little bit of energy from every set of fingers that flip through them. My taste in books is based primarily on whether or not the cover speaks to me. This is rarely about the artwork and more often about a frayed corner or an interesting crease. I'm particularly drawn to paperback novels with the title partially torn away. Far from being a snob about books remaining pristine, I think all these little bits of destruction give a book life.

That night, I was re-reading a Terry Pratchett book with the cover torn clean in half from top to bottom. I imagined someone still using the other half of the cover as a bookmark and wondering where the rest of the story had gone.

A soft breeze blew through the windows, and I toyed with opening the emergency door at the back of the bus, but I didn't want to risk another raccoon sneaking in like the last time we camped. That was an interesting but exhausting night, and there were still tiny handprints on one of the windows in the kitchen where the bandit had tried to steal all our snacks. I let my head fall on the pillow and opened the book, taking a deep breath in. It would only be about five more minutes. The rain was close, but I could tell it would start with a drizzle, so Eteri still had time.

When I'm reading, it's like I'm sleepwalking. I can do a multi-stepped task, move from point A to point B without injury, and carry on a semi-coherent conversation with zero memory of it once I return to the "real world." After many hard lessons learned over the years, Eteri takes whatever book I'm reading away and holds onto it until she's done speaking to me if there's any information I actually need to retain. And so it goes that drizzle turned to pitter patter and pitter patter turned into something like a deluge without me noticing I'd made it through a couple hundred pages of my book and it was close to midnight.

Thunder snapped me out of my literary induced trance, followed immediately by my nose alerting me that something wasn't right. I sat up quickly. The scent was dizzyingly strong, and I couldn't tell if it was coming from inside or outside of the bus. I took another deep breath of a mixture between singed meat and chlorine. My gag reflex kicked up and I pressed my fingernails into the palm of my hand to stop myself from throwing up all over the bed.

Maybe lightening had struck near Maybelle! I'd need to make sure there wasn't a fire.

Fighting the urge to puke my guts up, I placed one foot on the floor and was immediately thrown back into bed as the bus tipped onto its side, hovered for a moment, then slammed back down again. A horrible metallic crunching noise came from just outside the bedroom and I yelled, "Mother!"

Eteri and I used to share Maybelle's one bedroom, but when I got older, she decided I needed my privacy and started sleeping on the futon in the front of the bus. Whatever was attacking us would be out there with her. I ran from the tiny room and tried to get my bearings inside the dark bus.

"Mom, are you ok?"

I felt around where the futon should be, but it was empty.

Suddenly, a terrible shriek pierced the night, Maybelle was struck once more. This time something landed on the roof, forcing me to crouch as the ceiling buckled.

"Mother!" I screamed again and army crawled towards the front of the bus.

It sounded as if something or someone was being torn to shreds above my head and I silently prayed it was anything but Eteri. I slipped into Maybelle's driver's seat and felt around for the keys. There was another thud, and the windshield cracked into an intricate spider web.

Thankfully, the keys were in the ignition as usual, but just before I followed my knee jerk reaction to start up Maybelle and speed away, I remembered I couldn't leave until I found Eteri. I grabbed the closest weapon I could find, a walking stick with a lamb's head carved into the top. It didn't look menacing, but it would do the job. I took a deep breath and pulled back the handle that opened the bus doors.

I flew out the door swinging my pseudo staff. Rain pelted me in the face, but I didn't even feel it. I turned and swung the stick towards whatever was on top of Maybelle, but the only thing I could see were stars and black night. I ran to the other side of the bus with a battle cry and slashed the walking stick into the empty darkness once more.

Where had it gone? It was just here! And did whatever "it" was take my mother with it?

"Mom, answer me, please!!" I screamed, but there was no response, only the sound of the rain.

Suddenly, something glowed from inside the forest. I turned and ran towards the light, but a hot gust of air pushed me back onto the muddy ground. Thunder clapped and instantly the rain became golf ball-sized hail. I ran back towards Maybelle, my only shelter, wincing as the hail pelted against my body. I could already feel bruises exploding underneath my skin. I jumped for the stairs but stupidly risked one more look towards the trees for my mother, and in the same moment, a piece of falling ice struck my temple sending me crumpling into the bus.

CHAPTER TWO

I came to with my nose pressed against something cold and hard. My eyes popped open, and I slowly rolled over to find myself sprawled out on Maybelle's floor, just inside the door. I had no idea how long I had been out, but I could see sun shining through the bus windows and I couldn't hear any rain. When I sat up, a fireworks display went off inside my head. I instinctively put my fingers to my temple and that's when I felt the swollen lump near my right eye.

All at once the memories of the night before came flooding back to me along with the panic. Adrenaline took over and I bolted out of the bus. I looked all around, taking in the damage. Maybelle had a couple of flat tires, was crushed in on one side, and the roof was buckled. A portion of her front grill had been ripped away and wiring poured out of the gaping hole. Half-broken limbs hung on the trees around her and a younger sapling lay on its side with its roots sticking in the air. I didn't know what damage had been done by the storm and what might have been ravaged by the shrieking mystery monster from my memories. I took a breath. The horrible burning, chemical smell was gone but so was my mother.

"Eteri!"

I took off running towards the forest- the last place I had seen my mother. Every step sent fire piercing through my skull, but I couldn't and wouldn't stop. As I broke through the trees, I called out once more, "Eteri, where are you?"

It took a second for my eyes to adjust to the darkness under the dense tree cover, but I kept pushing my way through looking for footprints, broken tree limbs, and (terrified to even think it), traces of blood.

Eteri has a way of dancing through the trees as if she were made of air. When I was little, it was hard for me to keep sight of her when we would hike together, so I quickly learned to see the holes in the forest and rush through them. This talent serves me well when I'm only a few steps behind, but there was no knowing which way Eteri had taken the night before or how far she had wandered.

I needed to stop and think. This forest went for miles in every direction. Which way would my mother choose? I tried to calm myself with a couple of deep breaths and let my instincts show me where to go. I noticed the Christmassy scent of pine and let my eyes wander to a hulking tree with one branch that had grown into a loop on itself. I knew Eteri would have considered this important. I stepped beneath the curved branch and looked up at a patch of sky breaking through the tree cover. Two black crows flew across the brilliant blue, and I followed their direction. That's when I saw a tiny tower of three rocks balanced on top of one another and purposefully set upon a decomposing log, another sign that Eteri had passed this way. Just beyond that, I spied the familiar bits of fur and shredded leaves of a rabbit's burrow and knew Eteri would not have been able to resist watching for baby bunnies. I rushed towards the rabbit hole, accidently sending mama rabbit and her little ones scurrying. Startled by the motion, I lost my footing in the leaves. I tried to claw at a branch but missed and fell backward.

When I recovered from the shock that rocketed through my already sore skull, I found myself in a small clearing. Densely packed dandelions released clouds of white tufts which danced around my face. It was otherwise perfectly still inside the circle of white, not even a mosquito buzzed. For a moment, I was so taken that I even forgot about Eteri.

"It's beautiful," I whispered, launching a single piece of dandelion fluff from where it had stuck to my lip.

I stood slowly. I didn't feel afraid inside this circle. In fact, I felt like my feet wanted to spring roots into the ground and stay here forever. I was seriously considering this option when I noticed another tuft of dandelion fluff rising towards the sky.

Rushing in the direction of the commotion, I sent a storm of ivory filaments afloat. It was like being inside a snow globe. And that's where I found her. Eteri lay sleeping peacefully on a bed of dandelions, her fingers laced beneath her cheek for a pillow.

"Mom, are you ok?" I shook Eteri awake and rolled her over to check for damage.

"Good morning my sweet Sparrow." Eteri smiled and pulled me into a hug which I quickly wiggled out of.

"Where were you? I thought you'd been eaten by a wild animal! And how did you sleep through that storm? Mom, we have to make some new rules. I can't have you staying out all night." I spit it all out at once, sounding angrier than I meant to be.

"I love you too. I'm hungry. Aren't you? We should have pancakes for breakfast!" Eteri returned, understanding what I meant, instead of what I said.

I helped Eteri up and dusted the dandelions from her hair. "How did you even find this place?"

"Maybe it was my spirit guide," Eteri theorized as she took my hand and let me lead her back towards our camp.

"Sometimes I think your spirit guide just gets you into trouble, AND ruins all your best skirts," I said, eyeing the mud around Eteri's lacy hem.

"My spirit guide keeps me safe," promised Eteri.

"Well next time can you ask it to hide me from the danger too?" I wondered, half seriously.

The way out of the forest didn't seem nearly as far as the way in had been. Eteri's eyes grew into saucers upon seeing the damage to Maybelle.

"What happened?" she asked, registering concern for the first time all morning.

"There was a pretty bad storm. Check out what the hail did to me." I pointed to the purplish egg below my eye and pulled up my sleeve to show her some of the bruises dotting my arm.

"Hail doesn't have claws." Eteri pointed out the claw marks streaking down one side of the bus. "I guess it could have been a bear. They're getting ready for the winter. Poor hungry thing."

"Poor hungry thing tried to eat your child!" I said indignantly.

"Don't take it personally." Eteri gave me a teasing wink and once again I knew that everything would be ok.

"I've got to get in there and see if I can find my phone. We'll need to call someone to take a look and see if there's any saving Maybelle." I said as I climbed back inside.

Outside the bus, Eteri patted one of the many new dents. "Maybelle will recover. She always does."

***

"I'll have to tow her into town to get a better idea." But despite what he said, the mechanic, who I knew was named "Dave" from the embroidered patch on his denim coveralls didn't look optimistic.

"Can we grab a ride with you? Might as well take in the local history while we're stranded." Eteri, on the other hand, always felt the glass was half full.

"Sure." Dave said with a friendly smile. "It'll just take a couple of ticks to get her ready to go." Then he set about pulling chains from the back of his tow truck and Eteri found a rock to sit on and watch.

"Mom, aren't you even a little bit upset about this?" I asked quietly.

"It's all journey, my sparrow," Eteri said as she squeezed my hand and pulled me down onto the rock with her.

"Do you remember the story of how I came to your grandmother and grandfather?" Eteri asked.

"Of course I do but tell me anyway." I loved this story. I never believed all of it, but I believed my mom did, and that made it magic.

"I was a foundling, and I came in a rain drop. My mother and father were living on a commune in Oregon. There was a rainstorm the night before and their tent was flooded. They were wringing out their sleeping bags when my mother heard a laugh. She asked my father if he was trying to trick her, but he had heard it too. They thought maybe it was a mockingbird, but when they heard the laugh again, it wasn't coming from the treetops. They put down their sleeping bags and started searching for the laugh, getting closer with each giggle. Finally, they found me. I was wrapped in a giant leaf tied with a vine of morning glory, and on that vine was a piece of paper with one word scribbled in charcoal- Eteri, so they knew that was my name.

They asked all around the commune about a missing baby. Town was a couple of hours down the mountain and would have been a near impossible drive in the storm, so they decided the rain must have brought me to them. And that's how I became the daughter of Vonda and Benjamin Sparrow."

"Well, if you came in a raindrop, it's no wonder you found me in an olive," I teased. "By the way, why didn't you just name me Olive?"

"My spirit guide told me your name before you were born," Eteri answered. "Soara means sky."

There was a last crunch of metal locking into metal and Dave waved us over. "She's ready to go."

We left our perch and climbed into the cab of the tow truck. Before Dave joined us, I leaned over and whispered to my mom. "Isn't it weird that he never even asked us what happened?"

"I guess they get a lot of bears around here," Eteri answered with a shrug.

Dave's lanky legs magically accordioned beneath the steering wheel as he started the truck. "You're going to love Mystikos. It's a beautiful place," he told us as we pulled back onto the blacktop with Maybelle creaking behind us.

CHAPTER THREE

I was already going to have to unbutton my jeans and there still seemed to be way more pancake sitting in front of me than plate. It was clear they believed in healthy portions at The Wistful Willow Café. Despite the depressing sounding name, the interior of the restaurant Dave recommended was contagiously cheerful. All the tables were covered in bright, floral, oilcloth tablecloths and topped with carnival glass vases filled with cheery plastic flowers. It should have been tacky, but instead, it gave the feel that it was always spring inside. A train track had been put up along the perimeter of the ceiling and every 10 minutes on the dot, a miniature locomotive steamed around the restaurant, tooting its hellos. There were velvet curtains on the windows with fringed roller shades and the walls each had a theme. One wall was covered in coins. Pennies, nickels, dimes, quarters, and the occasional silver dollar had been glued from top to bottom and although today it was pouring rain, I could imagine it gave off a warm glow when there was sun shining through the windows. A second wall was filled with framed paint by number canvases of every subject imaginable. Altogether, it managed to look like a fine art installation. Another wall was broken up by the kitchen pass-through and counter, but on the bits you could see, various cooks over the years had tacked up recipe cards, making their dishes immortal. On the final wall was a large cabinet filled with small cubbies. Inside each compartment was a coffee mug. They were all different shapes, colors and sizes and I had seen several customers walk in and remove a cup from a cubby to take back to their table. The floor was all black tile, but it sort of tied everything together and gave one's eyes a chance to rest.

"These are the best pancakes I have ever eaten, and I do not make that statement lightly," Eteri gushed to the waitress wearing jeans and a sweatshirt upon which she had lovingly hand painted the words "The Wistful Willow Café." The bright bandana tied around her hair framed her happy smile.

"Fred does all the cookin and I do all the fraternizing." The waitress leaned into the table, "Cuz if it was the other way around, all the food would be burnt, and all the jokes would be knock knock."

"I can hear you," Fred piped up from the kitchen.

"Then you aren't working hard enough," the waitress shot back, but it was clear they were only teasing one another. "I'm Roselyn, by the way." Roselyn stuck her hand out to shake Eteri's.

"Eteri Sparrow, and this is my daughter, Soara," replied Eteri with a smile.

"Welcome to Mystikos. Are you here for a long visit or just a lookey lou?" Once the question was out of Roselyn's mouth, I noticed the rest of the customers lean in to hear the answer.

"Our bus is getting fixed across the street," I responded.

Roselyn nodded her head knowingly. "Oh yeah. I heard about that. Bear attack. Gotta be careful this time of year."

"If you leave even one crumb of food out, the bears will think it's Thanksgiving," Fred yelled from the kitchen.

"You don't know anything about it, Fred." Roselyn leaned in again. "He's allergic to nearly everything outdoors: trees, fur, dust, bees, blueberries."

"It's blackberries not blueberries!" Fred yelled back. He seemed to have only one volume.

"Are you finished with that special for table five?" Roselyn called back.

She was answered with the clanking of a metal spatula hitting the grill top and seemingly satisfied that Fred was out of her business, she decided to take a seat with us two newcomers.

"Sorry about all this rain. It's not really the season for it." Roselyn looked out the window and gave a tsk.

"Into each life some rain must fall. Some days must be dark and dreary," I quoted. "That's Longfellow."

Roselyn blinked at me once or twice as if she was mulling over this unexpected piece of wisdom. "Well, that sounds depressing!" Then she burst out laughing taking me by surprise.

"You don't like poetry?" I was genuinely curious about anyone who wasn't charmed by words.

"Well, the kind I like usually rhymes a bit more and ends with something dirty." Roselyn slapped the table and let out another guffaw.

I wasn't sure if the waitress was laughing with me or at me, so I let Eteri take over the conversation.

"What do you recommend for a rainy afternoon in Mystikos?" Eteri asked.

"Galoshes," Roselyn answered, slapping the table again at her joke.

"Do you have a bookstore?" I asked hopefully.

"The library sells books to raise money, but they're closed today."

"Oh," I said, unable to hide my disappointment.

"But I've got a bunch of magazines laying around in my office if you'd like to take a few," Roselyn kindly offered.

"Oh...that's..." I didn't imagine Roselyn read the kind of magazines I would find interesting.

"That's so sweet of you! Of course we'll take them," Eteri interjected.

Roselyn pushed back her chair and asked me to follow her. I attempted to bore a hole in my mother's head with a dirty look, but all I got in response was one of Eteri's patient smiles.

As we made our way back to Roselyn's office, I got a closer look at the cabinet of mugs. Each little cubby had a name under it that had been burnt into the wood in a lovely cursive.

"Do all of your customers get their own mug?"

Roselyn stopped and turned, staring me dead in the eye. "You have to earn your spot on that wall. That's just for regulars." And the way she said it made me think earning that spot possibly involved completing the tasks of a dangerous quest.

Roselyn turned back around and kept moving, so I followed. We passed a large picture window where from the inside, "The Whispering Willow Café" was painted backwards, so it could be seen by passersby. There weren't many folks out on the sidewalks in the rain, but I noticed a yellow rain slicker moving towards the restaurant. Whoever it was had the hood up and their head down, but they were moving with definite purpose.

"There's a bunch of fishing magazines. Those are Fred's, but I know there's some fashion ones in there too." Roselyn waved me towards an open door. I gave another glance out the window before following her, but Mr. Rain Slicker had ducked out of view.

When we stepped inside Roselyn's office, I wasn't sure what I had expected, but it wasn't what I saw. A row of hair dryer chairs was against one wall. There was a beauty sink in the corner piled high with what looked like old menus and a desk sat in front of a leather barber's chair, the kind that could be pumped up or down to get the best angle for a haircut. A big, lighted mirror was hung on the wall behind it, and I gave Roselyn a confused look in the reflection.

"This place used to be a beauty parlor back in the day. They called it the Dine N Do, like hair do, get it? Ladies could come in and get a curl and set, then meet their friends for lunch in the café. When my Aunt Linda took it over in the 70's, she turned this space into storage and changed the name of the restaurant to the Wistful Willow Café.

"Why did she name it that?" I asked, genuinely curious.

"You know what? I never asked her and too late now, she's dead." Roselyn shrugged her shoulders and disappeared through a curtain that hung across a supply closet door.

I took advantage of the moment to check my reflection in the large mirror. Most of the swelling had gone down on the lump near my eye. The bruise had fanned out onto my cheek in a rainbow of purples and greens. I probably could have covered it with a crafty application of make-up, but I rarely wore the stuff. The current humidity had increased the volume of my curly chestnut hair by about half, so I quickly swept it back into a braid and pulled a hair tie off my wrist to finish it off. Green eyes and a light dusting of freckles stared back at me. No matter that I have had those "angel kisses," as Eteri likes to call them, since birth, my first instinct every time I see them is that I need to wipe the dirt off my face. I rubbed my knuckles across my nose and shook my head a little letting the tiny gold moon and star earrings I never took off catch the light. Eteri had gifted them to me during a brief jewelry making phase and I loved them dearly.

"Some of these are pretty old. My aunt never threw this stuff out." Roselyn plopped a stack of magazines on the desk.

Far from being the country crafts and family recipe mags I expected, these were beautiful high fashion magazines from the forties. A starlet in a satin evening gown looked over her shoulder on one of the covers.

"Thank you! These are amazing." My eyes lit up as she spread out the magazines.

"There's a whole bunch more back there if you want em," said Roselyn.

When we emerged from the back office, we were each carrying a box of magazines. I needed to re-adjust my load, so I set my box on the café counter and that's when I saw Mr. Rain Slicker again. He had pulled down the big yellow hood revealing sandy brown hair that nearly reached his shoulders. He seemed taller and maybe more muscley up close, and when he turned to see who was standing beside him, I looked into the darkest brown eyes I had ever seen beneath a pair of thick eyebrows that some model would probably be willing to commit murder for.

"Excuse me," Mr. Rainslicker said and reached past my box to grab a handful of napkins.

I tried to smile at him, but he didn't smile back.

"Here you go, Dell. I put some extra rolls in there for the boys. They deserve it after last night." Fred placed three large bags on the counter.

"Thanks." Mr. Rainslicker (well actually, Dell, now that I knew his name) stuffed the napkins into the bags, pulled his hood up, and trudged back into the rain.

Not everyone in Mystikos is as friendly as Roselyn, I quickly realized. Then I took the box to show my mom.

***

We spent most of the afternoon going back and forth between Dave's garage and the café. Nearly all the shops in town were closed on Mondays (some odd, local quirk), so we spent the day hanging out and drinking coffee while drooling over vintage fashions, then checking on Maybelle, who we were about to learn was on life support.

"Well, here's the deal," Dave said, twisting an oily rag between his blackened hands. "I think I can save her, but it's gonna take a lot of work and some parts that I don't have."

"That sounds expensive." I winced as I started calculating the damage in my mind.

"It isn't going to be cheap, but I promise I'm fair. You can ask anyone in town." Dave looked almost embarrassed that he'd expect to be paid for his work.

"Of course you're fair! I knew it the moment I saw you." Eteri patted Dave on the arm. She was trying to comfort him when we were the ones whose house was up on blocks.

"I guess we could stay in a motel for a few days?" I looked at Eteri to see what she was thinking.

"It might be more than a few days," said Dave. "I'll have to call around. They don't produce the parts for these old buses anymore."

"Well, when the rain lets up, we can tent camp," I suggested.

"Oh no. I don't think that's such a good idea. What with the bears and all," Dave cut in.

"We'll just be more careful this time and stay closer to town," said Eteri.

"Closer to town won't make you any safer," Dave returned solemnly.

"Well, what do you suggest?" asked Eteri.

"Listen, I've got an apartment above the garage. I used to rent it out to a real nice couple, but they decided to move away last-minute, and I haven't found anybody else. You can stay there as long as you like," offered Dave.

"We'll pay you to stay there, of course," insisted Eteri.

"We can figure it out as we go."

"Thank you." I really was grateful, but I also felt weird about this whole arrangement. Life on the road meant we often made fast friends of strangers, but we didn't usually move in on the first night.

"It's getting late. The sun will be setting soon and town pretty much boards up after dark. Why don't you grab whatever you need off the bus and we'll get you settled," said Dave, eyeing the horizon out the window.

"Um, yeah, sure." I stumbled over to Maybelle and stepped inside, wondering if I'd ever sleep in her again.

***

Dave went around turning on some lights and Eteri and me put our hastily packed bags down on the 1980's brown floral sofa in the apartment's living room. I noticed a rotary phone set into a niche on one wall and tried desperately to think of a reason to call someone on it. The whole apartment looked like a mish mash of garage sale finds and items left behind by past renters. I picked up a handmade ash tray shaped like an anatomically correct human heart from the decoupaged coffee table and gushed. "This is perfect."

Every place you looked was the ideal reading nook with a blanket, embroidered pillows, and a warmly lit table lamp. There was a record player on top of a giant old console television, but the glass and wiring had been pulled out and shelving put back in to hold a collection of albums. The wood burning stove in the corner had a kettle on top waiting to brew tea, and there was a tomato plant growing out of a single cowboy boot that snaked up a trellis on the wall beside the small card table and folding chairs that served as the dining room.

"I dabble in botany," Dave explained when he noticed me reaching towards a red ripe tomato. "They're organic. You should try one."

"Maybe later," I responded, internally wondering if dabbling in botany was code for "I grow hydroponic weed in the back of the garage."

"The kitchen's fully stocked. I like to keep it ready up here."

Dave proved it by opening the refrigerator doors so we could see the groceries inside.

"Let us cook you dinner to say thank you," Eteri offered with a smile.

I tried not to shoot Eteri a dirty look because I had already planned to spend the evening snooping through the apartment's treasures.

"Thanks, but I really should get home. It's nearly dark and I need to get my dogs in," Dave said with a glance out the window at the approaching dusk.

"Well, you can have a literal rain check," Eteri replied as she pointed to the droplets running down the windowpane and winked.

"Yeah. It looks like it might get worse. But don't worry, this place is watertight. You're fine as long as you stay inside," Dave responded.

I let out a chuckle. "And what if we don't?"

"I'd just hate for anything else to happen to the two of you in Mystikos. We'd like to make a good impression," Dave said seriously.

"She's only teasing. We'll be snug as bugs here," promised Eteri.

"Snug as bugs." I saluted to show I wouldn't do anything foolish, even though I was still sixteen, and thus my views on the value of authority were elastic at best.

"Ok, well, I'll see you two in the morning. Be sure to lock up," Dave said as he shut the door.

I followed Dave, sliding the chain and turning the deadbolt. Then I watched him go down the apartment stairs and back into the garage to shut down for the day.

"Oooh, capers! Let's have pasta tonight!"

I turned to find Eteri standing inside the fridge door holding a tiny jar and a stick of butter. I immediately felt a comforting warmth sweep over me. Eteri could be at home anywhere, and anywhere with Eteri was home.

***

Eteri offered to do the cleaning up after dinner and I had every intention of spending my evening uncovering the wonders of the apartment. Unfortunately, my quest didn't last very long because as soon as I saw the cushy reading chair with a perfectly nubby, hand-knitted afghan thrown over the arm, the previous night's adventures immediately caught up with me. I promised myself I'd just take a rest but as soon as I curled up and closed my eyes, "a minute or two" turned into a full-strength nap.

I woke up scratching. The afghan's cheap, acrylic yarn felt like hay against my skin. I yawned and sat up picking at the blanket's knitted flowers. I wasn't sure how long I had been asleep, but not a single one of all the interesting things in the room was a clock.

The rain had stopped, and the complete silence made the little apartment seem impossibly cramped and stuffy. I unlocked the door and stepped out onto the narrow balcony. The porch light was out, but the moon was nearly full and from my vantage point, I could see the streetlights all the way down Mystikos' main street. Dave was right, everything was shut up tight. All the storefronts even had those metal accordion gates pulled across them, secured by padlocks. Seemed kind of odd that they would need that much security in such a sleepy little town. but so far, nothing had really been "normal" in Mystikos.

I breathed in the crisp air. The storm was coming back- from the east and moving quickly. I was glad we were on the second story because parts of town were going to flood. I knew that I should probably go back inside, but I love that feeling when a storm is rolling in. I closed my eyes and raised my palms towards the sky to let the air tickle my palms. It felt like I was floating on electricity.

I took another deep breath in and choked as my lungs filled with the same horrible stench I had smelled in the forest the night before. I instantly felt woozy and grabbed onto the balcony railing to keep myself upright as my body was wracked with ragged coughs. My eyes darted around searching for the monster. I wouldn't be able to protect myself if I couldn't get a breath. I heard a deep rumble as a dark shadow glided overhead, blocking out whatever light the moon provided.

I looked up and saw two great claws descending out of the darkness. I wanted to run, but I could barely catch enough oxygen between hacking convulsions to keep from passing out. I needed to get back into the apartment or I'd be carried away by the monster in the sky. I let go of the railing and fell towards the door. Luckily my hand caught the knob instead of my head. I tried to push the door open, but when I turned the handle, it was locked. I pounded on the door with what little bit of strength I had left, praying Eteri would wake up and hear me. I felt my skin rip as jagged talons tore into my shoulders. The pain was unimaginable, but I couldn't even scream. The last thing I heard before passing out was the monster's triumphant shriek.

CHAPTER FOUR

"Soara. Soara, wake up! You're sleepwalking. You'll hurt yourself," warned Eteri.

I finally truly snapped awake. I was still beating on the front door of the apartment, but from the inside. "We have to open this door!" I yelled.

"Ok. Ok, honey. Hang on a second. Just calm down." Eteri turned me towards her and put her hands on both sides of my face. "Look at me. Take a deep breath."

I tried to focus on my mother's green-yellow eyes and reality finally started to trickle back into my brain.

"Mom, there's a storm."

"I know. It's been raining for hours," responded Eteri.

"And there's something else out there," I said digging my fingernails into Eteri's arms.

"Come on little sparrow. I need you to land. Come back to me. There's nothing out there," Eteri said gently.

But I didn't listen. I pulled away from Eteri and tried to throw the door open. It was locked just like in the dream.

"It won't open! I can't get it open!" I was starting to panic again.

"You're just upset. Let me give it a try." Eteri moved me aside to turn the knob, but the door truly was locked. She checked the chain and flipped the deadbolt again...Nothing. The door wouldn't budge.

"I guess it's really stuck. I'll just call Dave." Eteri patted at her pockets and pulled out her phone, then let out a sigh. "Shoot. I never got his cell number."

"Mom! He locked us in here. We have to break a window!"

I started looking around for something that would shatter glass. Eteri grabbed my hands.

"We most certainly are not breaking the window." Eteri rarely used a "don't argue with me" tone, but this was one of those times.

"What if there's a fire?" I desperately tried to appeal to my mother's sense of self preservation.

"There's not going to be any fire," Eteri answered, and steered me down the hallway.

"You had a nightmare. It's no wonder after what happened last night. Let's just get you undressed and into bed, and I'll do some reiki on you. We'll pull those bad thoughts right out of your mind."

"It was so real."

My mouth was sticky, and I still felt half asleep. I was no longer certain what was real and what was a nightmare, but Eteri was my true North, so I leaned against her and let her lead me down the hall to the bathroom.

***

When I opened my eyes the next morning, Eteri was asleep beside me. She was facing me with her fingertips barely touching my arm. I imagined that connection was the magical anchor that had kept both of us from floating off the bed last night. It was a game we used to play when I was little if Eteri wasn't ready to get up. If that didn't work, she'd sometimes lazily recite some of her poetry for me. Her verses were my childhood lullabies. I missed hearing my mother practicing her poems, but she hadn't written anything new in almost six months. Eteri said the words would come back to her at the right time, but I knew she was impatient to feel the spark again. Eteri stirred and rolled over, falling off the twin bed and hitting the floor with a squawk.

"Are you OK?" I leaned over the side of the bed trying not to laugh.

She popped up with a smile on her face. "It's good luck to fall off the right side of the bed!"

"How can you tell which side is wrong, and which side is right?" I responded.

"No, the RIGHT side, like left hand, right hand. It means your day is going to be free from hindrances," said Eteri, standing up and smoothing out her nightgown.

"Did you just make that up?" I asked suspiciously.

"I would never!"

Eteri's playful grin told me that she was doing one of her favorite things- speaking the day into existence. I had tried this technique myself with lackluster results, but Eteri swore that the only reason it didn't work for me was because I didn't truly believe in it.

My stomach grumbled. I'd only picked at dinner the night before and the blueberry pancakes from the Wistful Willow had worn off hours ago. I was just about to suggest cinnamon toast for breakfast when I heard a machine start growling in the garage downstairs and all at once the nightmare, the locked door, and the fact that I was furious with our new landlord flooded back into my mind. Most of the time, I'm the quiet type and prefer to ignore the stupidity of the general public, but when I get angry, Eteri tells people to hide all the sharp objects.

I whipped out of bed and threw open the window putting my face right up to the metal screen. Before Eteri could stop me, I screamed, "Hey Dave, It's Soara Sparrow, and here's the deal. If you don't get up here and unlock this door in exactly ten seconds, I start yelling for the police. 10, 9, 8, 7..."

"Soara, what are you doing?" Eteri snapped.

"Getting us out of this prison! 6, 5, 4, 3..."

Eteri ran to the living room, undid the deadbolt, and tugged at the door with all of her might, which sent her flying backwards, because the door wasn't locked anymore.

"For the love of Pete, stop! The door's open!" Eteri yelled across the room.

I didn't take a breath before whipping out the door and down the apartment stairs. Eteri flew out behind me in her nightgown and bare feet.

By this time, Dave had stepped out of the garage to figure out what all the hub bub was about.

"Hi, Dave. Good morning!" was all Eteri managed to eek out before I cut in.

"Exactly what the hell were you thinking locking us in that apartment last night? Are you some kind of weirdo who wrecks people's cars and lures them to your garage so you can sell their kidneys on the black market? Or do you just get off on being a creepy pervert and imprisoning women in your kinky sex den?" I screamed about an inch from Dave's face.

"My what?" Dave stuttered as he turned a million shades of red.

"You heard me!" I leaned in even closer for effect, but Eteri pulled me back and stepped between us.

"Don't worry. I can translate," said Eteri calmly. "What Soara means is, good morning, Dave. The front door of the apartment was stuck last night, and we were just wondering if you knew anything about that?"

Eteri's sweet voice eased Dave out of fight or flight mode and he could finally answer, "I'm so sorry."

"Oh, you bet you're sorry!" I interjected but Eteri put up a palm so Dave could finish.

"I was hoping you all just went to bed and didn't notice. I've got computerized locks on all the doors here. They're on a timer and you ladies moved in so last minute yesterday that I forgot to turn the apartment lock off. I didn't figure it out till I opened up this morning and I feel so bad if I scared you," Dave answered looking like he wished he had a rock to crawl under.

Eteri turned around to give me an "I told you so" look.

"See, Soara. It was just a mistake."

I hate being wrong and it is never easy coming down from one of my furies. I didn't answer right away because I was afraid I might still choke Dave out.

"I can translate again," Eteri offered, "Soara is also sorry she jumped to conclusions, and she'd like to pretend this whole thing never happened if that's ok with you."

"Oh, that would be great, really," Dave said with a relieved sigh.

I puffed back up. "Yeah, well it better not happen again or I'll..."

"I'm so glad we figured it all out," Eteri interrupted before I could make things any worse.

"Sure, me too," Dave replied, smiling back at Eteri.

"Now, is that library Roselyn told us about within walking distance of here?" Eteri asked.

“Oh yeah. It’s just a couple of blocks up that way, then take a right and you can’t miss it,” Dave responded.

“Let’s go to the library!” Eteri happily chirped and started towards the front gate.

“Mom, you’re in your nightgown,” I pointed out.

“Oh, you’re right. I need earrings.” Eteri skipped up the apartment stairs and I followed, making sure to give Dave one more “mess around and you’ll find out” look before going inside.

***

In the end, I managed to convince Eteri that we should both put some regular clothes on before hitting the town. Once we’d had another batch of pancakes at the Wistful Willow and Eteri was assured I had been restored to a normal temperament, she decided I could handle going to the library by myself.

Eteri really wanted to collect some rainwater for a bath (which she swore was the best way to re-align your chakras). On our way out of the garage that morning, Dave had asked forgiveness again for last night’s locked door debacle and offered to help her put some buckets out in the clearing behind the garage to catch the rain as a sort of apology. I was also pretty sure it was his way of thanking Eteri for not letting me remove his arms from his body and beat him with the bloody ends of them that morning.

There had been a break in the rain for the past several hours, but I knew if I didn’t hurry, I was going to get wet. Dave said I couldn’t miss the library, but I wasn’t exactly sure what that meant. I was scrutinizing the signs on the various shopfronts in town when I heard voices coming from somewhere nearby and decided to ask for more detailed directions.

I crossed the street to an old stone and beam building with a large wooden carriage gate that was standing open. It looked like something out of a history book, and I half expected to peer inside and find a group of colonists strategizing for the revolution. What I found instead, was a group of men and women, most of them dressed in matching shirts and sweatpants, lined up in formation and doing calisthenics. Toward the back of the group, I noticed a familiar face. Dell the rainslicker guy was dropping in and out of burpees, and unlike most of his cohorts, he was not wearing a shirt. His arms roped with muscle in that way people get strong from actually doing things instead of lifting weights in a swanky gym. He had washboard abs (I could literally imagine scrubbing a wet soapy towel across them). I realized I was holding my breath. I was also standing right in the middle of the large gateway staring. One of the t-shirted dudes, a fatherly looking man with a beard and mustache, jogged over to me.

"Can I help you, miss?"

This friendliness snapped me out of my sexy wash day fantasy with Dell, and I felt a blush creep across my cheeks. "Um, can you tell me how to get to the library?"

"Oh sure. You just go up another half block or so, turn right and you'll run right into it," the gentleman explained.

"Thanks." I glanced down at the insignia on his t-shirt. It said Mystikos Volunteer Fire Department with some kind of intricate crest. So, Dell was a firefighter. Maybe he got those abs pulling people out of burning buildings. Maybe one of those fires had burned off his shirt.

"I could walk you over if you're worried you won't find it."

"Oh no. I'm totally fine. Just taking in the historic architecture of this building," I lied.

"This is one of the oldest buildings in Mystikos. The library's even older if you're interested in that stuff," he responded proudly.

"Oh, cool. Well thanks again. And thanks for your service," I said, pointing to his shirt.

"It's my honor and pleasure to protect Mystikos," he responded with a bow then returned to the ranks.

I happened to look up just in time to catch Dell watching me. We locked eyes and my heart stopped for a second. He should really put on a shirt. I decided I might as well go all in and gave him a big smile. He immediately scowled, grabbed his water bottle, and went into the firehouse. So much for trying my hand at flirting. I hoped no one had noticed the moment and swiftly turned towards my destination.

***

The fireman and Dave were both right. I couldn't have missed the Mystikos Library. It took up the town's whole center and its tall, white steeple shot through the rain clouds like a magnificent jousting lance. Towering columns guarded the front of the building and framed banks of windows. The firehouse had been quaint and antiquey. The library could only be described as grand. I reverently made my way up the carved marble steps to a pair of intricately embossed brass doors that might have sparkled if the sun were shining. Stars and planets floated across the door tops, moving through nature to man, and finally to the fiery magma of the earth's core at the bottom. Mesmerized, I ran my hands over the artwork, thinking that the settlers of Mystikos must have given all their talents and treasures to this special place.

There were no handles on the doors, and I wasn't exactly sure how I was supposed to get them open, but when my hand swept across the center seam, the doors made a soft click and slowly swung outwards. I gasped and stepped back, feeling like a magician.

What lay behind the library doors absolutely took my breath away. More beautiful marble covered the floor. Deep green veins on a lighter background gave the illusion of grass moving in a breeze. There building was at least three stories and two immense wooden staircases climbed opposite walls. When I stepped inside, the air felt charged with the power of thousands of stories and I knew I could be happy here forever.

"You must be Soara." It was barely a whisper, but the acoustics carried the sound to my ears clearly. I turned, a little sad that my moment of solitary veneration was already over.

Standing immediately behind me was the perfect prototype of a librarian. She wore a cream woolen, knee length skirt and matching cardigan with a peter pan collared blouse peeking out. Her hair was swept into a neat French twist and the corners of her tortoise shell glasses came to a perfect cat eye point. A pair of pearl studs decorated her ears, but she wore no other jewelry and her fingernails were painted a most modest shade of pink.

"My name is Julie. I'm the Mystikos Librarian. Dave called and told me to expect you," she said with a smile.

"The library is beautiful," I whispered, not wanting to disturb the quiet.

"We are exceedingly lucky to have it. It's the heart of our little corner of the world," Julie responded. "Dave said you'd like to see our used book shop?"

"I want to see everything," I gushed like a giddy teenager at a Harry Styles concert. I felt like a complete dork, but I didn't care.

Julie responded to me with one of the warmest smiles I'd ever seen. I imagined it was because she knew a kindred enthusiastic reader when she saw one and the card file in her mind was clicking through book suggestions.

"Follow me. I'll give you a short tour," said Julie, moving past me towards the stairs, looking as if she was gliding along on an invisible escalator.

I had never been someplace so incredible, and I had been almost everywhere.

"On our back wall, you'll notice the stained-glass windows," said Julie.

Rising up before me on the second floor of the library were four glorious glass mosaics. Each illustrated one of the four Elements: Air, Fire, Earth and Water, and at the center of every window was a figure with arms outstretched like a saint.

"This was originally a church," Julie explained. "The settlers of Mystikos came here seeking religious freedoms, and to show their gratitude for the utopia they felt they had been divinely gifted, they built this chapel before they even started their permanent homes."

"When did it become a library?" I asked.

"It just happened over time. Books were precious in those days and as this was the only solid stone building for many miles, and unlikely to burn if fire broke out. The settlers stored their books and important documents here. Eventually, there were more bookshelves than pews. It's still technically a house of worship but it's very rarely used that way anymore," Julie answered.

A bit of sun broke through the clouds and shone through the stained-glass windows. I suddenly found myself at the center of a kaleidoscope of color and once again gasped.

"As you can see, when the sun is just right, the effect is dazzling."

I held up my hand and let the color dance on my arm. "It's like magic."

"I get used to it. It's nice to be reminded how special it is by someone seeing it for the first time," Julie responded with a smile. "Now, let's move on to the third floor."

I followed Julie up another set of stairs.

"Our used book shop is at the end of the stacks. It's really just a couple of extra shelves, but our selection is quite diverse. There's a money box and we operate on the honor system. I'll be in the basement doing some paperwork. If you need me, just pull this cord and it will ring a bell."

Julie pointed to a velvet cord that ran along the wall, and I pictured a complicated system of bells and levers delivering messages to the library's inner sanctum.

"Thank you. Is it ok if I stay and look around after I find a book?" I asked hopefully.

"The library is open until just before sundown. Until then, consider it your home." Julie gave a little wink then headed back downstairs and out of sight.

I took a deep breath and soaked in the delicious smell of perfectly vintaged pages. Some of these books were very old indeed. I ran my hands along the book spines as I weaved between the shelves. Many of the titles were familiar but most I had never seen before. Several were bound in leather and didn't even display a title. I imagined what it must be like to be in charge of so much history and the hairs on my arms stood up in excitement. I wondered how many days we had left in Mystikos before Maybelle was fixed and we were back on the road. If I spent every single moment here from sunup to sundown, I knew I would barely make a dent in all the books.

At the end of every row of shelves was a sitting area and a jar of bookmarks beckoning a reader to stay. I noted a particularly perfect spot and promised the fluffy, pink, velvet, wing backed chair I would return.

It took me a while to get to the last two bookshelves. On my way, I couldn't resist taking a few books down to thumb through their pages. One was a hand illustrated catalogue of moths. All of the descriptions were in German, but the realistic pictures almost flew off the pages. An epistolary novel from the 18th century and a book which showed a map of the original phone lines laid in Mystikos in the early 1900's was also extremely interesting. It didn't seem like this library was organized on the Dewey Decimal System, but I enjoyed the surprises.

The "book shop" sold mostly modern faire and I decided on a paperback novel with its back cover missing and a hardback book that someone had played tic tac toe on with a marker. Slipping some cash into the lock box, I continued my exploration.

Back on the second floor I found a display of antique astronomy equipment. Several telescopes were pointed out the windows towards the sky, but because the library closed at sundown, I wasn't sure what use they ever came to. I peeked into one of eye pieces, aiming it downwards towards the town. A few cars meandered along the streets and in front of a picket fenced house an elderly gentleman pushed a reel mower across a compulsively tidy lawn. I shifted my view and found myself focused on the firehouse. The big wooden gate was now closed, and all the windows were shuttered, making the whole building appear to be sleeping.

On the first floor of the library, there was a small room with a settee and a fireplace. I expected it to be too hot for a fire, but the room was perfectly cozy. There was a round wooden table up against one wall with a half-completed jigsaw puzzle covering it. I sat down and started picking up pieces, turning them around in my fingers to find a fit. The next thing I knew, the puzzle before me was nearly complete and the fire had mostly burned to ashes.

"It's nearly sundown. Time to close up shop, but you're welcome to come back tomorrow," said Julie with a friendly twinkle in her eye.

"It went so quickly." I glanced out the window and noticed the approaching darkness. "Oh my gosh! My mother is probably wondering where I am! Thank you!" I said as I gathered my books and rushed to the front entrance. But when I got there, Julie was somehow already waiting for me, and the brass doors were standing wide open.

I'm so glad you came to Mystikos, Soara. I have a very good feeling about you."

I stepped through the threshold but when I turned to thank the librarian, the brass doors were already closing with a soft click.

I rushed back to the garage, both to assure Eteri I was safe and sound, and to make it to the apartment before the unofficial town curfew locked everything down for the night. I was annoyed with myself that I was already caught up in the weird ritual, but as dusk settled around me, I had this bizarre feeling someone was watching to make sure I followed the rules. I expected Eteri to ask me where I had been all day when I walked through the door, but she wasn't even home. I thought about trying to call her, but Eteri could never be convinced to keep up with a cell phone. Instead, I decided to take the uninterrupted time to do a little of the exploring I had planned for the night before.

The apartment seemed both absolutely random and entirely curated. All of the drinking glasses were the kind they used to hand out at fast food restaurants with the cartoon characters painted on the side. There was a collection of souvenir spoons in a glass front case hung on the wall and a box of assorted toilet plungers in the hall closet. Everything in my room was blue: bedspread, sheets, lamp, carpet, stuffed bear, curtains, and a painting of the sky on the wall-just blue sky and clouds. Was Dave a hoarder or one of those people addicted to garage sales? Collections are a luxury people who live on a bus don't have, and I was fascinated. Looking up from a drawer filled with random pairs of vintage prescription sunglasses, I noticed it was completely dark outside and Eteri still wasn't home, but there was a light on in Dave's garage.

The storm had settled into an endless drizzle, and I could feel the moisture coating my curls as I approached the garage door. My mother's tinkling laugh filtered towards me and the mystery of where Eteri had gone instantly solved itself.

At night, Dave's garage was almost homey. I hadn't noticed the day before, but he even had a little kitchen set up with a table and chairs. Dave was at the stove tossing something in a frying pan and Eteri sat at the table drinking a cup of tea and still laughing at an unheard joke.

"I thought we all had to be locked up tight in our houses by dark," I said, shutting the door behind me.

"The gates are chained and padlocked. NOT because I'm trying to trap you in." Dave was certain to make clear. "I have to do it to keep my insurance with all the equipment and cars and such."

"Don't you have to get home to your dogs?" I asked suspiciously. Maybe I had caught Dave in a deception after all.

"Brought 'em with me today." Dave gave a loud whistle, and two dogs ran in from the back of the garage.

I expected hunting dogs or bloodhounds, Dave just seemed the type, but what came around the corner were two coal black greyhounds with coats so shiny they reflected the light. The graceful pups practically danced across the floor on eight delicate, spidery legs.

"This is Watcher and Sentinel," Dave said as both dogs seated themselves at his feet.

"Can I pet them?" came out of my mouth before I could stop myself. I had always wanted a dog, but that was another thing there was no room for on Maybelle.

"Sure. They really like it if you rub their ears between your fingers." Dave illustrated, and the dogs gave happy little moans. "Go see Soara," he told them, and they immediately switched to guarding my feet.

I took one ear between each thumb and forefinger. They felt like velvety violet leaves.

"Dave said he'd make us dinner. He feels so bad about scaring you last night," said Eteri.

I still wanted to feel mad, but how angry could a person be while sitting at the center of a puppy sandwich? "It's ok. I know it was an accident. I shouldn't have freaked out on you like that," was my olive branch.

"I gave your mom a copy of the emergency clicker that undoes the locks just in case it ever happens again," he promised. "I'm really glad you two have decided to stay for a while."

My head whipped back towards my mother. What was Dave talking about?

"I got a message from my spirit guide today!" Eteri gushed with a smile.

"When did you see your spirit guide?"

"You know I never see them, I just hear them, like an intuition, but clearer," Eteri explained, more for Dave, I think, than me.

"Well, what did they say?" I asked. The spirit guide's ideas were kind of a mixed bag in terms of their negative/positive effect on my existence.

"They said that Mystikos is very special, and that my writer's block will unlock if we stay here long enough."

"How long is long enough?" Staying was new ground for me, and I was starting to feel wobbly inside.

"Could be days, could be months, could be years. They didn't know," Eteri returned with no idea of the baseball bat her words were to my equilibrium.

I started to sway a little bit, and the dogs pushed in to hold me steady. "Years? But I don't understand," I said, trying to contain my emotions. "You hate staying in one place. You say you start to feel the earth spinning without you."

"Sometimes we have to be open to a new opportunity." Eteri sat on the floor in front of me. She gently pushed the damp curls away from my face with her long fairy fingers. "I was thinking that you've never been to real school before, and wouldn't that be an incredible adventure?"

"Our whole life is an adventure. I just don't understand why here? It's weird and we don't know anything about these people," I tried to whisper the last part so Dave wouldn't hear.

"We know Dave, and Roselyn and Fred and we know where we'll live. Dave said we can move into the apartment permanently." Eteri said reassuringly.

"But what about Maybelle?"

"She's our bonus house if we get tired of each other and need a little break." Once again, Eteri was very good at presenting even shocking news as a benefit. "I'll find a job in town and we're due another royalty check from my last book of poetry. We can finally build up a little nest egg. Maybe we'll find out we're small-town girls!"

Dave was trying to clank around the dishes loudly enough that he wasn't eavesdropping, but he was running out of plates and bowls to go through.

"Can we talk about it some more after dinner?" I asked.

"Of course." Eteri gave me a quick kiss on the nose and got up to help Dave with the drinks.

***

When the meal was done and Dave had decided to bunk up in the garage with Watcher and Sentinel for the night, Eteri and me squished ourselves onto opposite sides of the apartment couch. I held a pillow in front of me as an extra barrier against my mother's assaults of positivity.

"You get why this is a whole lot, right?" I asked.

"Of course I do. But I think it's important. I don't know why it is, but I wouldn't ask you to do anything I didn't think was right for BOTH of us." Eteri answered.

"Did your spirit guide talk about me too?" I wanted to know if I had suddenly popped up on the spirit guide's radar.

"They said you need to be here. It's the right time." said Eteri.

"But you didn't ask them why?" I was really trying to understand my mother's unerring confidence in the spirit guide, but sometimes it was hard.

Eteri scooted across the couch so she could put her hand on my knee. "You are my treasure, Soara. The most precious thing in my life. If you tell me you can't be happy here, we'll have to leave, but I'm asking you to give Mystikos a chance."

I was always a sucker for my mother's eyes. There were galaxies inside them, and they held wisdom that was often overshadowed by her free spirit. In that moment, Eteri's eyes were telling me it was all right to stay.

"Ok, we can try it."

Eteri's face erupted into a huge smile. She threw her arms around my neck, "This is so exciting! Dave said we should get you registered for school ASAP. They start the day after tomorrow."

"Wow. That's fast," I said trying to keep my breathing normal.

"Do you want to get a backpack?" Eteri jumped off the couch and started listing all the fun things I might need.

But I had already dipped inside myself. I had sometimes dreamed of whatever "normal" was, but it happened in the way people sometimes wonder what it would be like to fly. As in, something that was never actually going to happen. The pros were that I liked the apartment and was certain I hadn't unearthed even a tenth of its surprises. Dave seemed nice, kind of too nice to be true, but nice. Watcher and Sentinel were a real plus, and the thought of unlimited access to pancakes at the Wistful Willow made my stomach growl immediately. There was also the library. If we stayed, I could go there whenever I wanted. But then there were the cons: the whole shutdown at sundown thing was completely over the top, not to mention what did they put in the local water supply to make everyone comply? The only person I knew of even close to my age already seemed to hate me and we hadn't even had a conversation, and of course there was the possibility that everyone was lying about the bear thing and a terrifying monster (who with my luck had an insatiable appetite for the blood of virgins) was on the loose.

"I'm not sure if they'll have vegetarian options in the cafeteria, so we better pack your lunch," chirped Eteri, who was still compiling her back to school list. She looked so incredibly happy and excited.

I was still stuck on the thought of all my virginal blood being sucked out of my body. I wondered what was scarier, death or public school.

***

I couldn't sleep that night. my mind was racing with all the possibilities. I was in a real life choose your own adventure book and I was about to turn the page. I thought I might try a spoonful of peanut butter (one of Eteri's home remedies for a restless night) and set one foot on the blue bedroom rug. It was much chillier outside of the blanket, so I pulled on a pair of sweatpants with the sweatshirt I had worn to bed.

In the kitchen, I grabbed a wooden cooking spoon from a jar of utensils and dug a jar of peanut butter out of the cupboard. I served myself a giant scoop, eating it off the spoon like a lollipop. I sniffed at the air. It was raining again. I suddenly found myself wondering about Mystikos' local infrastructure. Did they have the drainage for this kind of weather, and if not, did Dave have an inflatable raft? I pushed aside the front curtain to check for any sign of flooding and dropped my peanut butter spoon on the carpet.

Someone was standing in the street watching the apartment. Whoever it was was tall, like freaky tall, and their frame took up a giant amount of space. I couldn't really make out more than a dark blob of shadow at first, but then the moonlight reflected back a pair of red, glowing eyes.

I jumped away from the window. Who was out there? And what were they doing? My startled energy was almost immediately replaced by the familiar tingle of my temper. How dare somebody try to creeper our new home! I'd give them a piece of my mind!

I wasn't even wearing shoes but I ripped the door open and flew outside. I miraculously managed not to slip and kill myself running down the wet, metal steps (probably only by sheer force of will). There were about five vehicles between me and the fence when I hit terra firma. I used them as cover to make my way to the spot where I had seen the peeping Tom. When I reached the car nearest the gate, I launched herself at the chain link with a yell intended to intimidate, but when I finally blinked enough rainwater out of my eyes to focus, I was hanging off the fence like a demented spider monkey and there was nothing on the street but a few puddles. The peeping Tom must have run away, but he couldn't have gotten that far. I scaled the rest of the fence and jumped down onto the street. It took a second to get my bearings, then I scanned the area for signs of which way the creeper had gone. There was nothing- not a sound, not a footprint, not even a ripple in a puddle.

I slowly stood up out the crouch I was in and that's when the words, "Danger! Go Back!" sprung into my mind. It would be great if this was my own sense of self preservation, but I was too mad for that. The words had just found their way into my brain by themselves. I turned quickly, convinced someone must have said the warning out loud, but between the rain and the darkness, I couldn't see anything except the outlines of the buildings on Main Street. The message blasted my skull again, "Danger! Go back!"

The voice in my head was so loud I instinctively covered my ears with my hands, but there was nothing to block out. It was all on the inside. "Who are you?" I yelled to whoever was playing this trick, but I didn't get an answer.

Instead of doing the smart thing and listening, I went with reckless disregard and took off running down Main Street. There was no strategy behind the direction I chose, other than perhaps I was running towards the moon.

"Danger! Go back!" My head felt like the inside of a church bell, and I stumbled, landing on my hands and knees in a pool of water. Loose gravel pushed its way under the skin of my palms, but the pain only increased my determination.

I thought I saw a flash of light and turned down a side street. It was much darker there. The few streetlamps in town were only on Main Street and I had to stop to let my eyes adjust, fearful I'd run into a wall and knock myself out. My guard was down just long enough, and a hand clamped over my mouth and dragged me into an alley.

CHAPTER FIVE

I tried to scream but it was impossible with a mouth full of palm. I remembered once being told to go limp like a rag doll in some rec center self-defense class Eteri and me had taken. I quickly liquefied every bone in my body and tried to slide out of my attacker's grip. Unfortunately, all this did was get my legs tangled up in theirs. They fell on top of me, smashing me into the mud, but it caused them to release their hold just long enough for me to kick myself away and sprint towards anywhere but there while screaming bloody murder. I quickly ducked behind another building and suddenly found myself in an empty lot.

The moon was brighter there, and I was totally exposed. The first thing I did was stop screaming. I still wanted someone to find me, but the likelihood of that person being a deranged rapist was pretty certain if I didn't shut up. My mind was reeling through my extremely limited list of options when I was nearly knocked over by a dizzying wave of nausea. It was that smell again. The monster was back and no matter what human danger was after me, I knew it would be exponentially worse. My only hope was that I could shift attention to my attacker and let them be ripped to shreds instead of me. I heard a deafening shriek, just like the night Maybelle was attacked. The sound of flapping wings filled the sky, and a gust of wind pushed me across the lot. A dark shadow covered the moon and before I could turn to look up at what nightmare was descending upon me, I was tackled and pressed against a brick wall.

"Let me go!" I yelled.

"Just shut up!" a deep male voice snapped back at me angrily.

I was about to unleash a collection of my best curses when I heard the shriek again and over the shoulder of my attacker, I saw what looked like a set of razor-sharp talons. The claws ripped at my attacker's back, and he let out a cry of pain but still didn't release me.

The creature shrieked once more in frustration, then started to rise back into the darkness. Wind swirled around us, and every flap of unseen wings echoed back as a clap of thunder. The smell felt thick in my nostrils. There was one last shriek as lightening set the sky on fire and then all at once, everything was silent. I pushed the attacker away and was preparing to take out his kneecaps with my bare feet when I realized I was looking into the face of Dell the rainslicker guy. This momentarily threw me off guard, but it didn't change the fact that sandy-haired Dell was very probably a mad rapist, so I lunged at him angrily.

"What the hell are you doing?" I screamed.

I expected Dell to be surprised at my bravery, but instead he was pissed.

"I was trying to protect you. Why are you out after dark?"

"Because I'm not prisoner and you can't keep me trapped like an animal. It's a stupid rule!"

"It's to keep dumb people like you safe!" Dell shouted back.

"Safe from who? Perverts like you? Why do you get to be out in the middle of the night?" I was not going to back down. It was a big mistake to call me dumb.

"It doesn't matter. We need to get you home." Dell grabbed my arm.

I saw Dell wince at the pain in his back as he started pushing me towards the street.

"Like hell it doesn't matter. What was that thing that came after us?" I said, planting my feet in the mud.

"We have to move!" Dell insisted.

"Answer me!" I demanded.

Dell let out a sigh. I obviously wasn't going to give up.

"It was a hawk. It's breeding season and some of them are really protective of their nests."

Dell started to pull my arm again, and I was so stunned by his ridiculous answer that I let him take me this time. We were already to the street before I could gather my words again.

"You really DO think I'm dumb, don't you?"

"I think you're ignorant and reckless."

I tore my arm away from Dell once more. He let out another growl of pain. We were both dripping wet and his t-shirt clung to every ripple on the washboard beneath his jacket. Dell was out of breath, and I caught myself watching his chest move up and down, looking like it might bust through his shirt at any moment. I felt like an absolute waste of womanhood for letting my hormones change the subject in my brain and forced myself to snap out of it by pinching my arm.

"That wasn't a hawk, Dell"

"How do you know my name?"

"It's a small town. Why were you watching my house?" I was determined to keep control of the conversation.

"I told you. I wasn't watching your place. I was in the middle of a zone check on Panola Avenue when I saw you."

"What's a zone check?"

Dell didn't immediately have an answer for me. I could tell he was figuring out how to pave over the hole he had accidently dug with his mouth. "It's like a thing we do...for the volunteer fire department. We watch for fires."

"What kind of fires happen in the pouring rain?" I asked incredulously.

"Lightening can be very dangerous. And we patrol every night. It's a neighborhood safety thing."

"Well, you might want to tell your fellow fire dudes to worry less about the imaginary fires and more about the flying wild animal that's attacking buses and teenage girls."

"Thanks. I'll be sure to pass on the information." Dell was trying to act as if his back wasn't on fire, but he had to lean over and put his hands on his knees to brace himself against the pain.

I suddenly remembered the terrible claws coming towards us and was able to muster a tiny shred of sympathy in the midst of my anger.

"How badly did it get you?"

"I'm fine." Dell lied and stood up straight again.

I could tell he was clenching his teeth to keep it together, so I stepped forward to try and get a look at the wound. Dell jerked away from my touch.

"I said I'm fine."

I wanted to rip into him. The only reason I didn't was because I suddenly realized we had reached the gate for the garage yard. Dell gestured for me to go inside, and that's when I remembered that I didn't have the clicker and my only way back in was going to be climbing over.

"I forgot my key," I mumbled under my breath.

Dell reached for his cell phone, "Do you want me to call Dave?"

"NO! Definitely not! I'll just climb back in."

I pulled my soggy sweatpants over my knees and started up the fence. I was hoping Dell would return to his "zone check" but clearly he wasn't going anywhere until he knew I was locked safely back inside the apartment. I threw my leg over the top of the fence and chanced a look down. Despite his injuries, Dell was definitely enjoying my humiliation, so I decided to show off a little by jumping off the top of the fence instead of climbing the rest of the way down. I stuck the landing like a champ, but then my feet slid in the mud and the next thing I knew, I was on my butt. Dell didn't even try to cover up his laughter.

"You know, some people are trying to sleep," I hissed.

"Are you ok?" he managed to eek out between chuckles.

"I'm great."

I jumped up and started back to the apartment. My entire backside was caked with mud and every body part was sloshy, but I still had enough dignity left not to look back. When I finally shut the door behind me, I carefully took off my clothes and carried them to the bathroom. I'd have to clean up all traces of the mud trail when I got out of the shower, because there was no way I was telling Eteri about what had just happened.

***

When I rolled over to pull the curtains closed the following morning, every muscle in my body screamed to remind me of the previous night's adventure. I sat up hoping to leave my embarrassment hangover on the pillow, but that tactic was unsuccessful. I needed to filter through some things.

First, I knew I wasn't crazy and someone or something had been watching the apartment last night. Second, I was pretty sure Dell was lying about patrolling for rogue fires. And thirdly, I was going to have to go to the library today and look up giant, angry, nesting hawks.

"Guess what I found?" Eteri breezed into my room and sat at the foot of the bed.

I held my breath. Had I missed anything cleaning up?

"A job!" Eteri grabbed a throw pillow and gleefully tossed it at me.

"How long did I sleep?"

"It's early. I just went over to the café to get some tea. We're out, by the way. Put tea on the grocery list. I was telling Roselyn about how we're staying for a bit, and she said she's been looking for a new waitress and I said perfect!"

"Mom, you've never waited tables in your life."

"But I love food, and I love people. I'm uniquely qualified."

I leaned forward and gave my mom a congratulations hug. She smelled like rainwater and roses.

"Did you take your rain bath?"

"It was glorious, and my chakras are all abuzz. I was thinking I could walk you over to the school to register and then this afternoon I'm getting my first training at the café."

"Oh no, mom. It's fine. I can register myself and I planned to go to the library this afternoon anyway, so I'll just walk there right after."

I was already nervous enough about "real school" without Eteri doing something like suggesting we cast runes in the school office to make sure I was fully aligned with my elective choices.

"Ok, well the offer still stands if you change your mind." Eteri kissed me on the forehead, then floated back out of the room.

***

The Mystikos School (it's THE school because there's only one campus for all grades) met the typical, red brick, academically reassuring standards of a well-kept, but un-updated since the 1950's, institute of learning. I paused before taking the first stair, then gave myself a mental kick in the pants to stop putting off the inevitable.

Inside, the school smelled like peppermint trying to cover up whatever industrial solvent they used to polish the floors to a reflective shine. The lockers were a muted green and lined the hallways, punctuated by classroom doors with cheerful "Welcome back to school!" messages taped to the outside.

I let the lockers blend together in my peripheral vision as I made my way to the office. My footsteps echoed in the empty hall, and I was tempted to yell a curse word to see if it would ricochet back to me but decided that had all kinds of potential for bad first impressions. I noticed a woman with a stack of folders speed walking past me with a sense of purpose and decided to follow her. It was a good guess. Another couple hallways and a turn to the left and we reached our destination.

Inside the main office, there were three or four other ladies milling around, but as soon as I walked in, they all stopped what they were doing and greeted me with a smile. They had heard there was going to be a new student this year and were very excited to meet me. I still wasn't used to everyone knowing what I did before I did it. It felt like constantly having to catch up with myself.

"We understand your unique educational history," said the attendance secretary, Mrs. Golden, with a pat on my hand. "Given that you don't have any transcripts, we assumed you'd like to be slotted into tenth grade with the other students your age."

"Yes, thanks." I hadn't considered what grade I was in.

"Do you want to be in athletics or regular P.E.?"

"What's the difference?" I asked, starting to feel overwhelmed, there were apparently going to be all kinds of new distinctions I hadn't thought about.

"Do you want to play sports?"

"Do you have a quidditch team?" I teased, but Mrs. Golden didn't seem to get the joke, so I quickly moved on. "Regular P.E. is fine."

"Art, Choir or band?"

"Couldn't I take an extra study hall or something?" I've never really understood the concept of electives. You can't force a hobby on someone, and the idea of grading artistic outcomes seems utterly antithetical to encouraging creativity. This feeling is my mother's training at work. Eteri says grading art is like "caging butterflies."

"Afraid not. We expect our students to graduate well-rounded citizens."

"Art I guess?" I liked to draw, and I'm decent at it, but then again, at that point, my mother had been my only critic.

"The rest of your classes are just the normal stuff: English, Science, Math, History, Foreign Language- we only offer Spanish."

"Son buenas las enchiladas aqui?" I asked using some of my best restaurant Spanish.

"Oh, well it sounds like we should definitely put you in Spanish II." Mrs. Golden added a comment to her notes.

I decided I should also check out a book on basic Spanish from the library and maybe stop acting like a smart ass.

"Well, I think that's it. You'll get your schedule tomorrow before classes. There will be signs telling you where to go. Just bring a #2 pencil and a smile." Mrs. Golden shut her notebook and winked at me to signal the conversation was over.

"Thanks for your help." I was about to leave when a door labeled "Principal" opened and Dell stepped out. The two of us locked eyes. He let out an annoyed sigh, then turned around and walked in the opposite direction, disappearing through another exit. Apparently, he hadn't expired from his injuries the night before. He also clearly didn't consider the ordeal a bonding moment between us.

"Does that guy go to school here?" I asked.

"Oh yes. That's Dell Percie. He's Principal Percie's son. You'll be in tenth grade together."

"Great." I faked a smile then trudged out of the office. Things were getting worse by the second.

***

I ran my hand over the seam on the library doors and took a step back for them to swing open. I was practically an old pro now. Julie was already standing right inside the doorway with a stack of books.

"Hi, Soara. I thought you might be back today. I gathered some books I think could be of interest to you. Don't worry about checking them out. I set you up with a library account and your card is right on top."

Julie held out the books and I took them, impressed I hadn't read any of the titles before AND that all the books were beautifully battered in the ways that intrigue me most.

"What would you like to explore today?"

Julie was wearing the exact same outfit she had on the day before, except today it was all a shade of peach.

"I'm curious about the local bird population?"

"Oh, that's quite an interesting subject. Did you know that Mystikos is on the migratory path of the yellow-rumped warbler?"

Julie had already started upstairs and I followed dutifully.

"I was thinking about something bigger. Like a lot bigger, that flies at night."

I noticed Julie wobble a bit on a stair, but she quickly regained her bearings and the helpful smile returned to her face.

"You may be looking for an eagle or a nesting hawk. They can be real rascals sometimes."

"Yeah, I've heard you have sort of a problem with that around town. Don't you have an animal control department or something that could look into it?"

"All things are part of the natural order."

I wasn't sure how Julie's reply answered my question, but before I could push any further, she stopped at a shelf and pulled out a book on ancient birds of North America.

"Try this. Just ring the bell if you need me," she tossed over her shoulder as she headed back downstairs.

The whole library was mine for the rest of the day. I assumed there must be other patrons sometimes, I just hadn't run into any of them. I took my growing stack of books to the fireplace room and plopped down on the tapestried settee.

I opened the ancient birds book and let myself relish the delicious crack a book makes when it hasn't been read in a very long time. The first page showed a photograph of a rock drawing. The silhouette of a great winged bird with a hooked beak was chiseled into a cave wall and rubbed with a reddish ochre to bring out the details. The book said that birds are essentially living dinosaurs and their ancestors were once grand rulers of the sky. That was great, but I wasn't hunting for dinosaurs. I needed to find out what kind of rabid, 21st century bird had descended on Mystikos and how to get rid of it fast if this was going to be my new home.

I gave up and decided to look through the other books Julie had checked out for me. There was a 700-page history of astronomy, a graphic novel about a female lab assistant that had been crossed with a raccoon in a botched experiment and morphed into a super dexterous art thief, a teen romance, and a tatty book of fairytales that seemed incredibly old. I was surprised Julie checked it out to me. The book seemed like it belonged in a special room where it would only be handled with white gloves, but I wasn't going to point out the mistake because I was instantly intrigued.

A little shiver ran down my spine and I stood to warm myself at the fireplace. I hadn't noticed the intricate carvings on its mantel the day before. Much like the windows, each carving represented the four Elements. Clearly nature was a big thing with the original settlers of Mystikos. I reached out to touch a carving of a broad-winged bird surrounded by swirls of wind. I wondered if it was just a weird coincidence like when you see a certain new type of car you've never noticed before and suddenly you see them everywhere you go? I had definitely never thought about freakishly large birds before, but lately they had been a theme. The feathers were carved with so much detail they looked real. I brushed my finger across one and instantly a frosty wind whipped down the chimney and completely snuffed out the fire in one go. I looked around for someone to tell me I wasn't going crazy. The room went ice cold. My skin suddenly felt paper thin, as if a single touch would rip me into a thousand pieces that would float up the chimney like confetti. And in that moment, I WANTED to float like that, to just rise into the sky with no weight and no worries.

"I brought you some hot cocoa."

Julie's voice snapped me back to the room. I was still standing in front of the fireplace and the flame was once again burning hot, but my teeth were chattering. Julie led me back to the settee and placed the hot chocolate in my hands.

"This should warm you back up."

"Thank you," I managed to say through my clicking teeth. "Is it ok to drink in here?"

"I don't usually allow it, but occasionally it just makes sense." Julie sat beside me placing her hands primly in her lap.

I took a sip of the cocoa and began to defrost. "That was the weirdest thing. It got windy in here."

"These old buildings can be quite drafty."

"It was less a draft and more a cold front."

"How strange." Julie cocked her head to the side but didn't offer anything further.

I took another sip of the cocoa, which brought me back to room temperature. It seemed like we were still the only two people in the whole library.

"Where are all the other people?"

"What people?"

"The ones that check out the books. Don't people like to read in Mystikos?"

"Oh yes. Knowledge is incredibly important to our citizens, but as I explained before, this library has always been more a receptacle of information than a lending institution."

"So, people store their books here, and then never come back to read them?"

"They can if they want to, but for most of our benefactors, knowing their stories are safe is enough."

"So why do you have the bookstore if no one ever comes here?"

"I had a hunch we would need it one day." Julie never completely evaded a question, but she also didn't elaborate.

I finished off my cocoa. I needed to set my mug down, but I was afraid I'd leave a ring on a priceless antique piece of furniture. Julie seemed to sense my concern.

"I'll take that. Is there anything else you'd like to see today?"

"I think I've got plenty to process for now." I stood and loaded up my books. "I start school tomorrow, but maybe I can drop by afterwards. If that's ok?"

"You are always welcome here." Julie walked me back downstairs to the entrance.

When the doors swung open, I breathed in deeply.

"I hope you have an umbrella. The rain is coming back."

"Have you always been able to feel the weather before it comes?" Julie asked.

"Since I was little. I can sense other things sometimes. My mother says I'm uniquely connected to the energy field because I had my first fever during a hurricane. I think I just have a wildly sensitive sense of smell. It's a weird superpower I guess."

"Well, whatever it is, you have a gift. I hope you appreciate it."

"I honestly don't think about it much."

"Perhaps you should." Julie smiled and the doors of the library swept closed.

I shifted the books onto my hip. What exactly did Julie mean by that? I briefly considered opening the doors again and asking but suddenly I was overwhelmed with the desire to get home, crawl into one of the reading nooks at the apartment and get lost in something besides my own confusion.

The rest of "First Day of School Eve" (as Eteri named it) went by without any hiccups. I spent the rest of the afternoon reading through my books. Unfortunately, I didn't make any revelations about the giant bird problem.

When Eteri got home from training at the cafe, Dave offered to make dinner again and we had grilled cheese sandwiches with tomato soup. I snuck a couple of bites to Watcher and Sentinel (mostly to say thank you for the fact they somehow slept through my shenanigans the night before). Eteri wanted to help me pick out a first day of school outfit, but I informed her that I would wear whatever I reached for first in the morning and begged her to stop making a big deal cuz she was making me nervous. Honestly, I was already nervous to the point of a stomachache, but I was also too stubborn to let a challenge scare me off, so I yelled at my brain to quit being such a baby and pretended I was fine.

When I finally pulled the fuzzy blue tassel on my bedside lamp that night, I said a little prayer that I'd have my first peaceful sleep in Mystikos. I really wanted to look out the window first to check for possibly imaginary creepers, but I decided to trust the locks on the door and try not to go vigilante for a night. That didn't mean I didn't grab the largest plunger from the hall closet, the one I could swing like a bat, and keep it beside the bed. I didn't trust the locks THAT much. I gave the plunger a quick pat, just to make sure it was in place, let my head sink into the pillow, and the sound of rain on the window sung me into a land of dreamless sleep where I blessedly stayed until morning.

CHAPTER SIX

I wasn't used to setting alarms, so when my phone went off that morning, I thought I was back on Maybelle and Eteri was playing the radio too loud. "Mom, turn it down!" I yelled and pulled the pillow over my head.

"Get up! Get dressed!"

"This can't be right," I moaned, beating at my phone alarm to turn it off.

"First day of school, little sparrow. Time for you to spread your wings and fly." Eteri snatched the pillow from my head and kissed my cheek.

I sat up fast, almost accidently clocking Eteri, and jumped out of bed. I groggily pulled a pair of jeans on under my sweatshirt and tried to decide if I'd just keep the same top on or switch for another sweatshirt. I ultimately decided, new day, new shirt, and added a bra for extra support. I was pretty sure I needed all the support I could get to make it through the coming day. Eteri followed me into the bathroom and watched with a goofy smile on her face while I brushed my teeth and threw my hair back in a ponytail. I tried to ignore her occasionally snapping pictures with her old school film camera.

When I trudged into the living room to find my shoes, I discovered a surprise. Eteri had gotten me a brand-new backpack. It was terra cotta brown, my favorite color, and beside it was a leather-bound journal with a clasp in the shape of a sparrow. My grumpiness instantly melted away.

"Where did you get these so fast?"

"Dave helped me with the backpack, and I was saving the notebook for Christmas, but it told me you needed it sooner."

"Thank you, Mom. It's great." I picked up the journal and ran my hand over the soft leather. Gifts were Eteri's gift.

"That's not everything. We're having a special breakfast at the café."

Eteri clapped her hands together and grabbed my boots. She dropped them at her feet and did a little dance of impatience. I pulled the boots on as quickly as I could. I was afraid Eteri was going to burst from excitement.

When we walked into the café, there were crepe paper streamers strung across the ceiling and bouquets of balloons tied to the vases on all the tables.

"A great day of learning starts with a healthy breakfast!" Roselyn gushed, then ushered Eteri and me into a booth laden with pancakes, bacon, scrambled eggs, biscuits, hash browns, strawberries, and a giant chocolate chip cookie.

"Don't forget the cinnamon rolls!" Fred yelled from the kitchen.

Roselyn rolled her eyes as she motioned for us to dig in.

"Hold your horses. I'm comin."

I looked around the café. The other customers were all staring at us with big smiles. Everyone in Mystikos had really tried to make us feel welcome (well, everyone except Dell Percie). I smiled back and gave a shy wave. I could tell they were all waiting for me to take a bite, so I grabbed a pancake and shoved half of it in my mouth.

"Delicious!" I warbled through a pound of butter and syrup.

With the assurance I was going to be satisfied with my breakfast feast, everyone went back to their own conversations. It briefly occurred to me that if Dell was telling the truth and he wasn't my peeping Tom from the other night, it could be any one of the café patrons, but since none of them were a giant with the shoulders of a lesser mountain range, I quickly crossed them off my list of likely suspects.

"Was this your idea?" I said, stuffing another bite of pancake in my mouth.

"Actually, Fred cooked it up. No pun intended." Eteri giggled. "He sounds grumpy, but he's really very sweet. Said they don't have a lot of young people in Mystikos, and that youth is the town's future, so they oughta let you know you're appreciated."

"Wow. Been here three days and I'm already the town's whole future." I took a big swig of orange juice to wash down the unexpected responsibility.

"Fred even packed you a lunch. He wasn't sure what kind of sandwiches vegetarians eat, so you've got peanut butter, tomato and cheese, and some kind of tofu salad he looked up on the internet." Roselyn plopped a big brown bag onto the table with my name written across it in marker.

"Tell Fred I said thank you."

"You're welcome!" He yelled from the kitchen. Apparently, Fred could hear as well as he could cook.

"Maybe the sun will peek out today to celebrate your first day of school." Eteri chirped.

"It better, or pretty soon we're all gonna float away." Roselyn chuckled, but I saw her eyes dart towards the window nervously monitoring the overcast sky.

"It's not going away for a while." I said without thinking.

"Did you two bring the rain with you?"

Roselyn was only teasing, but for some reason the pancakes in my stomach suddenly felt like rocks.

"I should go. Don't want to be late on the first day." I grabbed my lunch bag and stood.

"Are you sure you don't want me to walk with you?" Eteri gave me a hug that pushed all the breath out of my lungs.

"Yes, Mom. I'm positive."

Roselyn and Eteri followed me to the door. The little bell hanging from its handle tinkled as I walked outside, but to me, it sounded like an executioner's gong. I turned and looked at Eteri and Roselyn smiling through the big front window and wondered when things would stop feeling like a roller coaster in Mystikos. There was a dull crack of thunder in the distance, so I hoofed it to school, hoping I wouldn't be spending the whole day in damp denim.

***

Just as Mrs. Golden promised, there were signs all over the place and colorful arrows taped to the floor to direct each grade to where they should pick up their schedules. Teachers also stood at every classroom door to offer help if needed. I had been to stadium concerts with tens of thousands of screaming fans squeezed together, but this was much more overwhelming. It was also a little bit weird seeing 11-year-olds mingling with Seniors in the halls, but nobody else seemed bothered by it. I followed the green arrows up to the third floor where a card table was manned by two students handing out schedules from an index card box.

"Hi, I'm Soara Sparrow."

"We know who you are," said the first girl, wearing a Mystikos School t-shirt.

I was playing catch up again. "Oh cool. What's your name?"

"I don't give out my name to strangers!" The girl snapped back.

"But you just said..."

"Stop being an id, Zion," said the other girl at the table. "I'm Sierra."

"I'm not being an id."

"And this is my idiot sister, Zion."

"Screw you, Sierra. This is stupid." Zion pushed her chair back from the table and stomped away.

I wasn't sure what to do, so I stared at a chipped floor tile.

"Zion has rage issues. She probably just needs a candy bar." Sierra took my schedule out of the box and handed it to me. "We have four classes together. I checked."

"Thanks?"

I was pretty sure this had to be a privacy violation in at least 20 ways, but maybe class schedules were considered part of the public record?

"I mean, honestly, there's 25 of us in tenth grade. We all have a lot of classes together."

"And here I was, worried I'd never be able to learn everybody's name."

The nervous laugh that escaped my mouth sounded like an axe murdering clown. I decided to go climb in a locker as soon as no one was looking.

"Well, everybody's heard about you. New is a big thing in Mystikos."

"Yeah. I can tell."

"You get a tour before first period."

"With you?"

"No. I have to give out schedules. Hang on. Dell? "Sierra called over her shoulder.

"Never mind, I can totally figure it out myself." I started backing away, but unfortunately, I wasn't fast enough. Dell Percie walked out of a classroom looking annoyed before he even laid eyes on me.

"Soara's here for her tour. Be sure to tell her where we sit at lunch." She might have said more, but the next student arrived to get their schedule.

"Welcome to The Mystikos School, where learning is our pride and joy." Dell spit out the memorized script without enthusiasm.

"You don't have to do this."

"Yes, I do, or my mom will kill me. I'm the official school tour guide and you may be the only customer we ever get." He said as he started down the hallway and I dumbly followed.

"First and second floor are middle school. Third and fourth are high school. K-5 is in the primary building behind this one. We share a cafeteria, gym and auditorium." Dell stopped in front of a locker. "This is your locker. If you want to lock it, get a lock, if you don't want to lock it, then don't leave cash or your good drugs in there."

Dell's expression didn't change, but I was cheered to see there was at least a dry sense of humor hiding somewhere in his soul. He kept walking and pointed at the staircase.

"Those are the stairs."

"Yeah. I can see that."

"That concludes your tour of The Mystikos School. Congratulations. You are now officially an Elemental."

"What about lunch?"

"It's the meal that comes between breakfast and dinner."

"Sierra said there's a place where I should sit?" I was trying to keep it friendly, but Dell wasn't giving me much to work with.

"The cafeteria isn't that big. You'll see us." Dell started to walk away.

"Can we talk about the other night?" I said more urgently than I meant to.

Dell immediately stopped. He walked back to me and leaned forward to whisper in my ear. It felt intimate in a way that gave me a buzz I wasn't used to.

"This isn't the place or the time and don't talk to anyone about it."

Then he quickly disappeared around a corner.

"What the hell was that?" I said to myself.

I wasn't exactly dying to share the details of that night with anyone anyway, but that reaction was intense. Dell probably wasn't supposed to be out after curfew either and made up that whole neighborhood watch thing so he wouldn't get in trouble. I'd heard that children of authority figures tended to be the bad kids and Dell was playing up to the stereotype. The good news was I had potential blackmail material as a bartering tool. The bad news was, Dell had the exact same wrench.

***

The first three periods of the day were my favorites: English, History and Art. Despite my misgivings, my art teacher, Ms. Fields, won my respect right away with a presentation on pre-Colombian indigenous pottery and I made a mental note to ask Julie if she had any books on the subject. I had all three classes with Sierra, and somehow none with Dell, and I wondered if he had hacked into the school computer system to keep me out of his way.

Sierra was the easiest friend anybody ever friended. She did the majority of the talking (which was totally ok with me) and was a fountain of information on the entire school population. By the time we got to lunch, I could guess the names of everyone at the table based solely on Sierra's descriptions.

There was Zion, who I'd already met, so that was easy. Zion was sitting cross-legged on top of the table, throwing tater tots into the mouth of Noah, Ms. Fields' son. They shared the same dark hair, olive skin and dimples. According to Sierra, Noah was still technically a freshman, because he failed so many of his classes the year before, but the school was letting him make it up in some kind of independent study because his mom was a teacher.

Sitting next to Noah was Matthew. Everyone else was in baggy jeans and t-shirts, but Matthew had on a pair of skinny, cropped chinos and a button down with the sleeves expertly cuffed at the elbow. He also had undeniably perfect hair, and yet, managed to look entirely effortless. Sierra warned me not to fall in love with Matthew's beauty. He was openly gay and also, the only person on earth who didn't know Matthew had been in love with Noah since third grade was Noah.

"How do we know what they put in these hamburgers? They could be feeding us the souls of former students," said August Midwinter, which was the coolest name I had ever heard.

I knew it was her because she only had one hand. Sierra had told me August was born that way and that there was a whole story there, but that was the one instance where she didn't elaborate.

"There are no souls left in Mystikos. The monsters gobbled them all up," said Zion, casually lobbing another fried potato pellet at Noah's head.

I noticed everyone at the table instantly stiffen and August elbowed Zion in the ribs, knocking her off the table.

"Oh my gosh! Chill the hell out! I'm only kidding." Zion finally noticed me and Sierra. "Oh right. Don't be weird in front of the new kid."

Sierra gave Zion a dirty look. "Zion, don't you have lunch detention today?"

"It's the first day of school."

"Well don't you still have to make some up from last year?"

Noah stood up and grabbed his and Zion's backpacks. "Oh yeah. Me too. We should go check into that."

Any annoyance Zion might have felt melted into a mischievous smile. "Oh yes. We should DEFINITELY do that." And the pair exited the cafeteria to parts unknown.

"Are they together?" I asked Sierra as we took a seat.

"Officially, no. Between you, me and everyone else at this table, they're madly in love with each other and constantly looking for places to make out."

"But DO NOT tell Zion we said that," interjected Matthew.

"Truly. What do you think happened to my hand?" August held up the nubbed wrist where her hand should be and waved it around for effect.

"I thought Sierra said you were born without it!" I tried not to look too mortified.

"I was. I meant my prosthetic hand. Zion hid it the last time I accidently mentioned something about her and Noah being cute together."

"That's horrible!" I was scandalized, but August just laughed.

"Oh, she eventually told me she hid it under my bed. I hate wearing it, so I didn't miss it much, but still, power move."

"My sister's actually really fun, but only when she feels like it."

I opened up my specially curated, vegetarian lunch bag and looked inside. Did Fred think there were three of me?

"I don't suppose any of you would like a spare PB&J or a dozen brownies, would you?"

"I love PB&J!" Sierra took a sandwich and checked between the slices of bread. "Strawberry jelly is my fave!"

I pulled out a sandwich for myself and pushed the bag to the center of the table, where August and Matthew happily went fishing for treats. The making friends part of starting school seemed like it was going to be surprisingly easy for me, but then I looked up and saw Dell coming out of the cafeteria line with his tray. When he noticed me, he deliberately turned and picked a table on the other side of the room. Maybe I had spoken too soon about the friend thing.

***

The rest of the day wasn't terrible, but it wasn't great either. I could now ask where to find the bus station in Spanish. Math and Science were no big deal- academically speaking. I was way ahead in both subjects, but I also had both classes with Dell. I had to sit right in front of him in Math. Our teacher decided to seat the class in reverse alphabetical order for some reason and unfortunately, there wasn't a single Q or R between Dell's P and my S. It felt like Dell's eyes were boring into the back of my head the whole hour. I didn't dare turn around and I shot out of class the moment the bell rang.

P.E. was my last class of the day. The whole tenth grade had to take it at once (otherwise they wouldn't have enough people to split into teams). The first day was supposed to be super easy, so the coach just had us walk around the gym for the whole period. Sierra, Zion, August, Matthew, Noah, and I set our pace at a leisurely amble.

"You've really never been to school before? Sierra asked me. "I wish my Nana would let us do that."

"No, you don't. Nana would drive us nuts. She'd just spend every day trying to brainwash us with her political agenda." Zion snapped.

I had found out earlier that Zion and Sierra lived with their grandparents because their parents passed away when they were little.

"True, but I'd like not getting graded and sleeping in."

"My mom told me you guys were living in a bus." Matthew said it with genuine sympathy, as though he assumed it had to be a circumstance and not a choice.

"Well, it was a bus, but we rebuilt it. Maybelle's pretty much a regular apartment, except on wheels."

"How many states have you been to?" Sierra asked.

"All of them. Some more than once. My mom's a poet, so she can work from wherever."

"I've never really been out of New England," Sierra sighed. "I'd love to travel."

"We barely leave Mystikos. My grandparents don't like to leave the ranch unguarded," said Zion, rolling her eyes. "They're gun people. If you can shoot it, stuff it, or eat it, they'll kill it."

"Fun." The vegetarian in me tried not to be offended.

"What kind of poetry does your mom write?" Asked August.

"Um, mostly stuff about nature. She had one of her poems get kind of "poetry famous," I said, making air quotes with my fingers, "Because some movie star quoted it in a college graduation speech, and it went viral. But that was a few years ago."

"Nature writes her songs upon the wind and teaches the trees to sing them."

"That's really pretty, August." I said, impressed.

"It's something my mom says. But she says lots of things."

August's response was a little odd, but she didn't seem like she had any intention of embellishing, so I decided to gloss over it.

"Excuse me," said a voice from behind the group.

Our line split in the middle and Dell passed through. He was running at a sprint and kept having to dodge the other students.

"Why is he always so intense?" Matthew wondered aloud.

"So, he's like that with everyone?" I wanted to believe I wasn't the only person Dell despised.

Of course, Sierra had the inside scoop. "The Percies are all overachievers. How do you think his mom got to be principal? And Mr. Percie has won a bunch of awards for rebuilding vintage cars. He sells them too. Sometimes Dell works at the lot after school."

"I thought Dell was all busy being a volunteer fireman."

Before anyone could answer, Matthew tripped over his shoelace and went down hard, taking August with him. We spent the rest of P.E. walking them to the nurse's office to get band aids for their minor abrasions.

CHAPTER SEVEN

I was glad that Eteri brought home extras from the café for dinner that night. She only had enough for the two of us, so we'd finally get some time to ourselves. I thought Dave was super nice and a great cook, but I wasn't used to sharing my mom so much.

"Give me your highs and your lows."

Ever since I was a little girl, Eteri has asked me to describe the best and worst parts of my day to her. It's one of our special traditions.

"My high today was that I found all of my classes and didn't get a single tardy."

"That's a decent high."

"My low is that there's someone at school who I think doesn't like me."

"Who wouldn't like you, Sparrow?"

"His name is Dell."

"Is he a Capricorn? They can be very rigid."

"Oddly enough, not a single student gave me their astrological chart today."

"Maybe you have a connection he's trying to fight."

"We've barely said three words to each other. How could we be connected?"

"That's what you'll have to figure out. When someone doesn't like a person, it usually means they're afraid of something about themselves they see in that person."

"Well Dell must be terrified of whatever he sees in me. But I don't want to talk about him anymore. What was your high and low?"

Eteri never answered this question immediately. She would close her eyes and mentally play out her day to make sure she picked the right moments. I waited patiently. It was usually worth it.

"My high is that I learned how to use the milkshake machine at the café today."

"That's a delicious high."

"My low is that my spirit guide told me you're keeping something from me, and I hate thinking we have secrets from each other."

It was true. We didn't keep secrets. I remembered my recent, late-night adventure and my shoulders immediately tensed.

"There it is. I can see it all over you. Oh Soara, what is it? Do you hate it here? Did I push you into going to school?"

"No, Mom. I mean it does feel weird that we just suddenly decided to settle down and be regular people, but all the regular people have thought the way we live is weird for years. I just did something that I'm embarrassed about, so I didn't want you to know."

Eteri scooted her chair around to mine and put her arm across my shoulder. "You can tell me anything."

I took a deep breath, then I let the whole story out. "I thought I saw someone watching the apartment the other night, so I went outside, and I climbed the fence, and there was this weird, scary bird, and I got locked out, and then I fell in the mud, and it was probably just too much peanut butter."

Eteri's eyes were all sympathy. "Oh, Soara."

"I also didn't want to tell you because of the whole thing about how we aren't supposed to go out after dark. We promised Dave and he's been really nice to us."

"Who was watching the apartment?"

"Whoever it was, was gone when I went outside. Or I'm crazy and it was just a shadow."

Eteri nodded in understanding. "I used to see the shadows too."

"Mom, what are you talking about?"

"When I first started communicating with my spirit guide."

I had always believed Eteri made up the whole spirit guide thing to explain her wacky decisions. She had never said anything about seeing something concrete. In fact, she was very clear that she only heard her spirit guide.

"I was much younger than you. I think they were afraid I wouldn't believe if I didn't see them at first, that I'd think it was just a voice in my head or something."

And then I remembered the voice in my own head saying, "Danger, Go Back," and my heart started beating faster.

"What does the voice sound like?"

"I know I always tell you I hear it, but it doesn't actually happen like that. I just know what they're saying to me. It's as clear as a bell."

I stood up from the table. "I'm really full, Mom. I think I'm gonna go to bed."

"You don't have to be afraid, Soara. Your spirit guide wants to protect you."

"The first day of school was a lot and I think I just need to decompress."

"This is a wonderful thing. I promise!"

I let Eteri hug me, then I stumbled half-drunk with adrenaline down the hall and into my room. I was bombarded by a thousand thoughts. Maybe my mother had always been crazy, and now I was going crazy too. Mental health issues were often hereditary. If I was having some kind of breakdown, maybe it really was just a hawk that I had seen the night before, but my blistered brain made it seem bigger, more like a monster. No wonder Dell didn't like me. I'd gone full tilt psycho on him in the middle of a rainstorm. I told myself that if I had the same thing Eteri had, it wasn't the absolute end of the world. She had managed to have a whole career and life and raised me on her own. It wasn't as if I was about to be carted away to an institution, and some people turned mental illness into something incredibly beautiful, like art or music. Maybe that was what made Eteri such an amazing poet and I just hadn't discovered my gift yet but when I did, all of this would make sense. My heart rate slowed back to normal. I could handle this. I'd been too tired to go to the library after school, but I decided I would for sure go the next day and do some serious research on my alternatives. It was O.K. The library would have answers. It was still early, but I really was exhausted from the day. I crawled into bed and fell right into another night of thankfully dreamless sleep.

***

The next morning, I woke up with a new sense of purpose. I decided not to be afraid of possibly being delusional and instead to try to be more like my mom who had happily made friends with the voice in her mind. A clap of thunder cracked outside my window, and I jumped, hitting my head on the headboard. I rubbed the knot that was forming and realized I'd have to be more careful about rattling my brain if it was already prone to short circuits.

Sierra had explained yesterday that they did a lot of "spirit days" at Mystikos School. On those days, the students were asked to dress according to an ever-changing theme. It was supposed to help the student body bond or something. On the second day of school, the students were supposed to wear their favorite band t-shirts. I sifted through the pile of folded tops that was sitting on my floor. I was incredibly organized about a lot of things, but unpacking wasn't one of them. It was a real perk being able to drive my whole bedroom to my next destination. With Maybelle up on blocks for the foreseeable future, I'd have to turn my new collection of piles into a system at some point, but not this morning.

If anyone has a prolific collection of band T's it's me. I inherited all my mom's old shirts from her groupie days and have picked up more than a fair share of my own over the years during our travels. I decided on a Patsy Cline t-shirt I bought at a flea market outside of Nashville. I don't think of myself as a big country fan, but Patsy Cline is an exception. Her low, syrupy croon always soothes me, and although I don't dance much, I can never keep from swaying when Ms. Cline comes on the radio. In my recollection, New England wasn't well known for being a country music mecca, but I figured my teachers would at least appreciate me wearing something besides the latest pop diva or boy band across my chest.

Eteri had left me a note on the kitchen table saying she had her first early shift at the café that morning. I peeked out the front window. Despite the rain, things were bustling by Mystikos standards. It looked like some city workers were trying to set up safety cones around the more flooded spots on Main Street, and I was glad I owned a pair of tall galoshes. If this kept up, I wondered if I'd have to switch to a pair of those rubber pants that fly fisherman wear, the ones with the suspenders.

I looked over at the cuckoo clock on the wall. I had plenty of time before I had to leave for school, so I decided to run a little experiment. I stood in the center of the living room floor and closed my eyes. Then I tried to talk to the voice in my head.

"Are you there?" I whispered and waited for an answer, but nothing came. "I'm listening now. I promise."

I could hear a cricket hidden in some crevice in the kitchen, but no words. Maybe the voice was mad at me.

"I'm really sorry about the other night, but I've never heard you before and it was a little bit scary. But my mom, you know, Eteri, explained it to me."

I listened so hard I thought my ear drums might pop. I knew I couldn't be impatient with this kind of thing, but it was difficult. I took a deep breath and held my hands out in a position I assumed looked welcoming. After a moment, I could feel something like a gentle breeze tickling my fingertips. Maybe this was how it started! The breeze was so cool and light against my skin. I slowly lifted my hands over my head and the breeze began to pick up power.

"Cuckoo, cuckoo!!"

I was startled back to attention. I looked around the room and swore I saw the curtains swaying just a little bit. I assumed there must be a window open somewhere, but I'd lost track of time and now I'd have to hurry. I grabbed my backpack and an umbrella and darted down the stairs.

Outside, Dave was bent under the hood of one of the cars in the lot. He seemed oblivious to the fact he was drenched from the waist down. "Hey, Soara. Cool shirt."

I didn't really have time to chat, but Watcher and Sentinel were sitting under a makeshift shelter Dave had set up beside the car. Unlike their owner, they were cozy and dry as bones. I couldn't resist a quick ear nuzzle.

"Thanks. It's vintage."

"You like Patsy Cline too?" Dave asked with genuine enthusiasm. "There's some of her records in one of the closets in the apartment. She sure could make you feel what she was feeling."

By this time, the ear nuzzles had turned into full on belly rubs.

"Mom likes her too. She'll be excited."

"She does?" Dave perked up more at the mention of Eteri.

It was a fairly common occurrence for folks to go full crush on my mother. I usually didn't pay it much attention. Eteri was the out of sight, out of mind type when it came to romance, but we weren't leaving Mystikos anytime soon. Dave really was a sweet guy. Eteri would never break his heart on purpose, but either way, I didn't wish an unrequited love on him.

"Um, yeah, but now that I think of it, she's gonna be so busy at the café. I doubt she'll have time to listen." I hoped Dave would read between the lines.

"Maybe I'll drop by there this morning. Fred's pancakes are the best."

Dave's big smile and dreamy look told me that he had not cracked my code.

"I'm gonna be late. Gotta go. Bye, Watcher. Bye, Sentinel. Bye, Dave." I quickly called back then sprinted for school.

Dave called after me, "Make sure you're home before dark."

***

I made it to first period on time, but about five minutes into class we got interrupted by a fire drill. This was a totally new experience for me, but I had enough secondhand knowledge to know this was a standard occurrence at most schools. I expected everyone to feel pretty blasé about the whole thing, but my teacher seemed a little panicked, ushering everyone out of the room and quickly shuffling us to our class's assigned spot on the lawn. I wondered if it was like being on a plane and watching the flight attendants when there's turbulence. If they panic, it's always a bad sign.

"Why would they make us do a fire drill in the rain?" Sierra complained.

I looked around. Most of the students just seemed tired or annoyed. A few of the cute and perfect types were worried about their hair getting wet, but the teachers were all exchanging concerned glances. It didn't seem like they knew about this drill ahead of time.

"Where's Zion? She really didn't want to come to school today. Nana and Pops will kill her if she set the fire alarm off."

I could see Zion talking to Noah under a tree and she didn't look the least bit guilty.

"I don't think so."

I lifted the hood of my raincoat. At this point it was just going to keep the wetness in, but I did it anyway.

Sierra finally noticed the looks on the teacher's faces. Her skin went pale. "What if it's happening again?"

"What if what's happening?"

I looked around to try to spot whatever Sierra was talking about and noticed some movement back up by the school. It was Dell, climbing into a ground floor window. Had he declared himself a one-man volunteer fire brigade? I knew he took his "job" seriously, but this was just stupid and downright dangerous.

"Hang on. I'm gonna go check something out," I said as I started towards the building.

"What are you doing? You're gonna get in trouble." Sierra grabbed my arm and whisper yelled so she wouldn't draw too much attention.

"I just want to see if there's any firetrucks."

"There won't be if it's just a drill."

"Then we'll know there's nothing to worry about."

"Fire's not the only thing that can hurt you." Sierra was starting to tremble, but I wrote it off as her being cold from the rain.

"I promise I'll be really careful."

I gently untangled myself and casually made my way through the groups of students on the lawn, being careful to steer clear of any teachers. I didn't know why it mattered to me if Dell wanted to get himself killed out of some misguided sense of duty, or why it was my job to save him. I just knew I was going to go.

"Go back. Danger."

There it was again. The voice. It had super bad timing, as usual. I wouldn't do what it said, but I wouldn't ignore it this time.

"I'm just checking on Dell." I said it out loud, but I didn't know which direction to speak in, so I just looked up.

"Go back. Danger."

The voice wasn't changing its mind.

By now I had made it to the windows. If I crouched down just the right way, I'd be able to remain hidden by a shrub and shimmy through the opening.

"GO BACK."

This time the voice was so loud inside my head I thought my skull would crack open. I stumbled a bit, but instead of making me listen, the ringing in my ears made me mad.

"Shut up! You haven't said a damn thing in sixteen years and now you want to yell at me?"

I sprang through the window, but unfortunately, I hadn't put any thought into how high up it was or where I was going to land. I clawed at the air for a few milliseconds before I hit the cement floor. It was the second time I'd cracked my head that day. I made a mental note to look into getting a helmet.

Once my eyes adjusted to the lack of light, I found myself in a basement storage room. There were old desks stacked up everywhere. The kind of antique blackboards you could roll in and out of classrooms snaked a haphazard train through the space, making it impossible to see the exit. Dusty cardboard boxes were starting to accordion under the weight of other boxes, and the whole place was thick with a sour stench. I assumed the smell was a mixture of sweat and determination emanating from the vintage sports equipment piled around the room and tried not to breathe through my nose.

I quietly tiptoed into the darkness, not having any idea where I was going, but I was certain I would never reach that window again, so the only way out was forward. I made my way through an obstacle course of broken track hurdles, desks, and a big pile of dusty velvet that was probably an auditorium curtain in a previous life. I was trying to squeeze between two stacks of chairs when I heard a crash and something clattered across the floor. I bit my lip to keep from yelling and giving myself away. The sour smell was getting worse, or maybe it was getting closer. I could hear a clicking sound on the cement. It wasn't exactly rhythmic, but it didn't seem random either.

"You need him."

The voice shot through my head again. For some reason, I knew exactly who "him" was and I didn't like it.

"Why him?" I answered back silently inside my head so I wouldn't give away my hiding place.

"You must trust."

It was an unsatisfying answer, but there was not time to dwell on it. The taps grew louder as they closed in on my hiding spot.

"MOVE."

This time I listened to the voice without argument. I scrambled out from between the chairs just as something hard and thick smashed through a stack of boxes beside me. It was too dark. I had no idea where I was. I climbed on top of a rickety desk to try and find the path out. That's when I saw the thing. Its body was a patchwork of nightmares sewn together and covered in course, black fur. It was probably as tall as me, but that was standing on four legs. Yellowed spikes like rotting teeth ran down it's back and along a serpentine tail that whipped around, tearing through a pile of football pads. When the creature lifted its face, putrid drool dripped from hooked fangs that framed a set of needle-sharp teeth. Its mouth was wide, almost froglike, and a black tongue licked at its lipless mouth. But the creature's most terrifying features were its dead, milky white eyes. I was certain if I didn't throw up from the smell, I would from fear, but when I bent over and opened my mouth to wretch, the only thing that came out was his name.

"DELL!" I choked. Once I'd gotten it out, it was easier to do it again. "Dell, it's over here!"

I jumped to the next pile of boxes. They slid off balance, and I found myself wedged tightly against the wall. I could hear the creature change directions to follow my voice, and I knew that now that it had found its prey, it would destroy anything in the way of satiating its hunger.

"Be still."

I had no choice but to follow my inner voice's orders. The boxes pinned me tightly in place. I couldn't see anything, but I could hear the chaos all around me as the beast smashed through desks and something that sounded like metal being crumpled into a ball. If I called for Dell again, the monster would find me, so I silently asked the voice for help.

"You have to tell Dell where I am. Please."

"He cannot hear me." The voice answered softly and apologetically.

I'd have to do this alone. I tried to push away the boxes, but I had no leverage to move. The monster was getting closer. I could hear the slimy rattle of its breathing. I thought about Eteri. My mother had told me the voice wanted to protect me. I should have listened. Now I'd never see Eteri again.

I had never been afraid to die, but I'd always assumed it would be instant, and I'd be very old. I never thought about the hundreds of terrifyingly slow seconds I'd have to contemplate my actual death. It seemed strange that I didn't cry. I guess my body refused to spend its last moments bathing in salt water. A swampy scent wafted around the edge of the boxes. It wouldn't be much longer.

"If you can talk to my mother, please tell her I love her so much and I'm sorry," I said out loud.

There was no point in continuing to hide now. I kept my eyes open. I wanted to see the thing that would destroy me so that if there was an afterlife, I'd recognize it when it got there, and I could send it straight to hell. I felt something sticky and hot against my arm as the creature used its tongue to smell me like a snake. It clicked its teeth together excitedly. My adrenaline surged, but I forced myself not to pass out.

"Here, Fido. Look what I've got." It was Dell's voice! "Come on you stupid hell ox. Smell the steak."

The beast turned and smashed its way to its treat. I heard a scuffle and the disgusting sound of meat being swallowed whole. Dell's face appeared in the crack between the boxes and the wall.

"I'm gonna get you out, but we don't have long. They didn't have much meat in the cafeteria fridge."

I had about a million questions, but I also had enough wits about me to only ask the most important one.

"How do I help?"

"I'm gonna try to push the top box off. Hopefully that's enough for you to be able to pull yourself out. Just be ready."

I tried to nod, but I didn't have the space to do it.

"Yes. Just hurry."

Dell threw all his weight against the highest box, and it started to shift- I hoped not onto my head. He took a couple of steps backwards so he could get a running start. The second push was enough, and the box toppled down. I was free from the waist up. I tried to pry myself out, but it felt like something was caught.

"Can you do it?"

"No."

By this time, the creature had run out of snacks, and it let out a scream of frustration. I tried harder to release myself.

"You have to get the other box off me!"

"O.K. Hang on."

Dell wedged his shoulder against the box, but it didn't move. We didn't have gravity on our side this time. There were a series of crashes as the creature tried to find its way back to us.

"It's coming." I whispered.

"It can't hear you. It can just smell you." Dell yelled back as he charged into the box again.

"Do you know what that thing is?"

"Hodag."

"Hot dog!?"

I wanted to laugh and scream at the same time.

"I said Ho-Dag."

Dell hit the box again and it moved just enough for me to escape, but when we turned to run, we were face to face with the monster. It was way worse seeing it up close. It looked like a rabid zombie dog. The smell was overwhelming, and I started to gag again.

"Back up," Dell said as he slowly pushed me behind him.

I took two steps back and tripped on an old hockey stick. It spun me around and that's when I saw a clear path to the door.

"Come on!"

I grabbed Dell's hand and pulled him towards the exit. The hodag let out another hellish scream and whipped around, sending a set of metal risers skidding across the room. I knew that even if we made it to the door, the hodag would follow us. It was faster, more powerful, and basically covered in knives, but every creature had a weak spot.

"We have to kill it!"

I grabbed a metal flagpole leaning against the wall and prayed its sharp finial was strong enough to pierce hodag skin.

"No!" Dell screamed.

He ripped the flagpole out of my hands and threw me over his shoulder fireman style. I was screaming and kicking as we burst through the door into the school hall. The hodag was right behind us. I felt its sticky tongue against my cheek.

Suddenly, the hallway was jammed with Mystikos volunteer firemen wearing breathing masks. The wretched scent of the hodag was replaced by a chemical tasting fog that filled the space. The last thing I remembered was the voice in my head saying, "You are safe."

CHAPTER EIGHT

"Hi, Sparrow. Are you finally waking up?"

I could hear Eteri talking, but I couldn't open my eyes.

"Just take your time. I'm right here."

What if this was another dream or a trick of my mind, the last surges of my brain simulating my mother's voice before I was digested into Hodag fuel?

"It's O.K. It's all over now."

If it really was all over, did that mean I had survived? I used all the strength in my body to force my eyelids open. Everything was blue except Eteri's smiling face. I was in my bedroom in the apartment, and Eteri sat on the sky-blue bedspread holding my hand.

"Did they kill it?" As soon as I was certain I wasn't dead, I sprang up in bed, ready to run.

"Kill what?" Eteri asked.

"That thing, the hodag!"

I couldn't understand why my mother wasn't more upset. Her only daughter had been stalked and nearly eaten by a terrifying monster that was possibly still on the loose.

"What is she saying? Is she O.K.?" Eteri turned to Dave for an answer.

"They said she'd be a little mixed up from the gas, but that it would wear off. You're so lucky Soara. If Dell hadn't seen you go back into the school and called 911, we don't know what would have happened."

"But I saw Dell go back into the school. I followed HIM."

Eteri's eyes crinkled with worry. She turned her face up to Dave who put his hand on her shoulder. I couldn't help noticing the familiarity through my confusion. Dave sat down on the bed with Eteri to try and explain.

"Soara, you're disoriented. There was a gas leak at the school. They got everyone out, but Sierra told us you wanted to go back for something. Dell saw you climb in through the basement window and he knew you must have fallen, so he called the fire department. He shouldn't have gone after you. We could have lost you both. But luckily, they found you in time."

"You were on oxygen for a little bit as a precaution, but they said we could bring you home."

Eteri tried to get me to lie back down, but I refused.

"Is Dell O.K. too?"

"He's fine. Back with his parents. They closed school for at least the rest of the week to repair the leak and make sure everything is aired out."

Dave looked just as concerned about me as Eteri.

"There was something else in the basement with us. Something evil."

Eteri ran her fingers softly through my hair.

"They said you might have some hallucinations. I know it felt very, very real, but I promise that you're safe."

I tried with all my might to remember things the way Eteri and Dave told me they happened, but all I could see in my mind were those milky white eyes, and I was certain they had been real.

"Do you want to eat something? Or maybe a cup of tea?"

"Yeah, tea and toast sounds good. Dave, do you think Watcher and Sentinel could stay with me tonight?"

"Sure. I'll go get them right now."

Dave and Eteri left the room. I knew I wouldn't have much time to myself. Someone had put my backpack on a chair beside the bed. I jumped up to grab it and my brain started playing ring around the rosey. I had to hold onto the wall to find my phone without collapsing in a dizzy pile. I texted Sierra (the only number I had).

"I need Dell's cell number."

Sierra immediately video called me back. I sat on the bed to stop the room from swaying.

"Are you alive? Why did you go back in there? I was freaking out! I didn't know what to do. What did you see? Can you describe it?"

"They said it was just a gas leak, but I can't remember anything," I lied. "Sierra, listen, I really need to call Dell and thank him. Can you send me his number?"

"If you do remember ANYTHING that happened, will you promise to tell me?"

There was an unexplained urgency in Sierra's voice.

"I promise."

I could hear Eteri coming down the hall.

"Sorry, I gotta go. Text me his number."

I hung up just as Eteri walked back into the room with her cup of tea.

"It's turmeric ginger. That should help if there's any inflammation in your body from the gas. Drink it slowly. I'm gonna check on your toast. Just butter? Or do you want jam? I think Fred sent over strawberry and apple butter. Roselyn said preserves are his love language. If you don't want jam, I could use honey."

Eteri always talks a lot when she's worried.

"Mom, I'm ok. I just need to wake up a little bit more. I'm actually really hungry. Can I have one with apple butter and one with the strawberry and another piece with honey?"

Eteri smiled. An appetite was a good sign.

"I'm on it!"

As soon as she left the room again, I checked my phone. Sierra had sent the number. I clicked on it and opened a text to Dell.

"*We need to talk.*"

I hit send and waited, staring at the screen, but there was no response. Maybe Dell was still asleep from the gas. I took a sip of the warm, spicy tea and let it spill down my throat and tingle its way to my fingertips. Eteri always knew the right thing to make me feel better. With another sip, my mind began to clear. I wasn't crazy. There had been something very alive in the school basement, and when I tried to kill it, Dell stopped me. Was he trying to protect it? Had the firemen lied to Dave and my mom because they were trying to protect it too? Hodag- that's what Dell had called the horrible thing. As soon as Eteri would let me out of her sight, I was going back to the library. Now that school was closed again, I'd have plenty of time for research.

I heard the front door open and a thundering of paws running down the hallway. Sentinel and Watcher burst into my room and hopped on the bed without invitation. Each one did a few circles then curled into a ball at my feet. I had asked Dave for the dogs to get him out of the room, but I was honestly glad they were staying. I'd feel safe as long as they were close by.

***

After the toast, tea, and reassuring Dave and Eteri I was fine a million more times, my energy was completely exhausted. Dell never returned my text. There were tons of good reasons why he might not have been able to answer, but I had a feeling he was just avoiding me. Dell was a member of the Volunteer Fire Department. Maybe they swore him to secrecy. It probably wouldn't be good publicity for Mystikos if it got out that there was some kind of hell beast running free in the school basement. I wondered if the hodag could be what had attacked Maybelle? Did it follow us into Mystikos to finish the job? I also couldn't help thinking that if Dell had been out in the street that night, he could have been protecting the hodag, and not me.

The only light in the room was a blue night light plugged into the wall. Watcher and Sentinel were still snoring at my feet. I wanted to think some more, but my brain insisted on sleep.

It was a restless slumber. My tossing and turning caused the dogs to wake and decamp to the living room. Without them, the bedroom felt like a cavern, filled with dark crevices and secret dangers, so I quickly decided to rejoin the pups. I could read myself back to sleep in a chair, so I wouldn't disturb my canine bodyguards.

When I got out of bed, I noticed I was wearing a long, flowing nightgown. I didn't remember changing out of my school clothes. Maybe it belonged to Eteri. As I left the bedroom, the diaphanous folds of fabric swept out behind me and trailed down the hall. When I stepped into the living room, the moonlight shining through the windows reflected off the soft fabric's silvery threads. I felt like a beautiful fairy cloaked in gossamer spider webs. Watcher and Sentinel lifted their heads but didn't make a sound. They weren't impressed by my new glamour. I felt a light breeze in the room. Maybe Eteri had left a fan on somewhere. It should have made me cold, but instead it felt refreshing, like a first drink after a long journey in the sun. I wanted to put my face near the fan and sing into it, to hear my voice broken into a quick vibrato by its blades, but I couldn't see it anywhere.

"Where are you?" I whispered to the fan, as if it could hear.

I reached out my hand and felt a stream of air fold around my wrist and pull me forward, but I wasn't afraid.

"Yes. I'll follow."

I took another step. It felt like I was walking through a curtain. I knew that whatever was on the other side was beautiful and powerful and I desperately wanted to see it. When I moved forward again, I heard Watcher and Sentinel growl, but I couldn't see them, because suddenly, I wasn't inside the apartment anymore.

Trees surrounded me and the ground was damp beneath my feet. I was standing in the spot where we had parked Maybelle to camp. There was no sign of disturbance. The broken branches from the attack were gone, as well as the tracks Maybelle had left in the mud when she was towed to town. Perhaps it had all washed away in the rains. I didn't have a flashlight or a candle to find my way, but I didn't really need one. I only had to follow the moon's glow.

Most people say there's a man in the moon, but I've always seen the silhouette of a woman staring down at me from the sky.

"I just want to see the lady."

I took a few more steps. My dress suddenly began to feel unbearably heavy, but the light was so beautiful. I couldn't stop. I tried to move forward, but the nightgown's long train was caught on something. I turned and pulled, but it would not come free.

The woman in the moon beckoned. I felt like I might die if I didn't touch her face. I looked for anything that could cut the dress away from my body and set me free, but there was nothing within reach. I stretched towards the woman in the moon with all my might. I could almost reach the light that surrounded her, almost, just a little farther... My body jerked back roughly. I heard a growl and tipped forward as something began dragging me backwards.

"No! I want to see the woman!"

As the growling grew more frenzied, along with the force pulling me away, the silver orb of the moon began to shrink.

"No! Not yet!" I begged, but whatever held me wouldn't let go.

The circle of the moon got smaller and smaller until it disappeared with a crack. I screamed into the darkness.

I woke and it was morning. I had been sleepwalking again. I was on the front porch of the apartment about to tumble down the stairs, but Watcher and Sentinel were holding onto the back of my Patsy Cline t-shirt with their teeth and had probably saved my life.

"I'm awake! I'm awake! You can let me go!"

Once they were certain I had my footing, Watcher and Sentinel released the hem of my shirt. There were large rips where their teeth had torn through the fabric, but it was worth a shredded shirt not to be a pile of broken bones at the bottom of the stairs. I sat down on the top step and gave the dogs thankful ear nuzzles.

"We should get inside, it's going to..."

Before I could say, "rain," the sky opened up and began dumping buckets. I squealed at the cold drops and sprinted inside. I looked over my shoulder for Watcher and Sentinel, but they had already run back to the garage to look for Dave and their breakfast. I closed the door and stood dripping on the carpet, trying to make sense of the last 24 hours.

"How on earth did you get so wet?" Eteri was dressed to go to her shift at the café.

"The dogs wanted to go out. I just got caught in the rain walking them back down to Dave."

I made sure to erase any hint of worry or confusion from my face. The last thing I wanted was for Eteri to call out of work and spend the whole day watching me for signs of distress. I had a lot of research to do.

"I guess I don't have to wash this shirt."

I wrung out Patsy Cline's face to keep Eteri from seeing the rips and threw in a laugh to prove I was back to my old self.

"You've got your color back. It's the turmeric tea. Works every time." Eteri kissed me on the cheek and grabbed her raincoat. "I'm running late. I'll just grab some coffee and a croissant at the café. If you need ANYTHING, I'm right across the street."

"Have a good day, Mom. Maybe we can watch a movie tonight?"

"It's like you read my mind." Eteri gave me one more peck and dashed through the rain to the Wistful Willow.

I watched until my mom was safely inside the café. I imagined the perfume of pancake syrup and coffee that now surrounded her, and my stomach growled, but breakfast would have to wait a few minutes. I needed to deal with the small puddle already forming on the carpet beneath my dripping frame. I could also use a hot shower. Maybe it would wash away what was left of last night's dream from my mind. Mystikos made me hear voices and sleepwalk. I wondered what other ways it was changing me.

CHAPTER NINE

My fingers barely hovered over the seam of the library doors before they clicked and slowly swung open. Julie was waiting right inside the entrance with her usual helpful smile. Today's cardigan and skirt was a deep reddish brown, perhaps in honor of the beginning of fall.

"Good morning, Soara. I hope you're feeling better. You had quite a scrape yesterday."

"News travels fast around here I guess."

I stepped inside the library. It had only been a couple of days, but I'd missed the place dearly.

"I've taken the liberty of setting you up in the fireplace room. I hope you don't mind."

Julie didn't wait for an answer before she led me across the foyer and up the stairs.

"How did you know I was coming?"

"That's a very good question."

I waited, but Julie didn't follow her statement with any further explanation.

"I think you'll find these books quite engaging. I've gotten a kick out of inferring your interests. It's a skill I haven't put to use in a long time."

"I still don't understand why everyone wouldn't want to be here all the time."

"I'm here all the time," Julie gestured for me to take a seat on the couch, "And I haven't gotten tired of it yet."

"How long have you been the librarian?"

Julie's head cocked to the side while she mentally calculated time.

"Forever."

I laughed at the joke. The librarian didn't seem the type to play around, so I counted it high praise she'd be sarcastic with me.

"I'll leave you to your reading. We close at sundown."

"Thank you."

"You're more welcome than you know."

With that, Julie's sensible heels clicked across the marble floor and back to wherever it was she performed her librarian duties.

I picked up the first book on the stack. Its cover was leather made shiny by the centuries of hands it must have passed through. A symbol was tooled in leather where the title for a modern book would be-a cross with a rose at its crux, surrounded by two sets of mirrored triangles. As the book fell open on my lap I noticed its pages were made of gold-edged vellum covered in hand lettered, illuminated script. All the s's looked like f's so it was hard to read at first, but once my brain began translating the text into modern English, I allowed myself to settle into the sofa cushions and become engrossed.

The book's scribe was unnamed, but he (or she) was an assistant to a great alchemist by the name of Paracelsus. Paracelsus was a medical doctor, philosopher, and mystic in addition to his quest to unlock the secrets of creating gold from common metals. According to the scribe, his master was a deeply religious man, convicted that all things seen and unseen in nature were created by God and therefore sacred. Paracelsus had begun a series of experiments that would allow him to cross the breach between the natural and supernatural, thereby revealing the secrets of time and existence. These experiments put both the scientist and scribe in great danger. Mortal men weren't meant to unravel these mysteries, but Paracelsus felt that curiosity was God given and therefore a call to action.

The scribe wrote of doorways to a place he called the Ether, where monsters and spirits resided. The doorways had been seen, but no man had crossed their thresholds, for according to Paracelsus, no mortal could survive in such a place. The creatures could move freely between the realms, but the spirits were as fixed in the other realm as man was on earth. Paracelsus called the spirits Elementals, because they were the essence of all things, but they considered their realm a prison, and were forever seeking a foothold in this world. Should man dare to take a place among the Elementals, he would forfeit his individual soul. But should the Elementals remain permanently with man, it would mean chaos, destruction, and the end of times for all living things.

In the last pages of the journal, the scribe wrote of Paracelsus newest discovery. The mystic had learned that the doors to the Ether only opened at night (with the exception of twice each journey the earth made around the sun). On the summer and winter solstices, the longest and shortest days of the year, the doors remained open from sunup until sundown, and the Elementals could walk the earth. This ensured the changing of the seasons, but the Elementals were compelled back to the Ether when the solstice ended. It gave them just a taste of our side of creation, and that was enough to make them incessantly hunger to make it their own. Paracelsus was going to attempt entry into the Ether at the winter solstice. The scribe would follow his master to the breach, a rope tied around both their middles. If Paracelsus met danger, he would yank at the rope and the scribe could pull him back to this side. The solstice was the next day, but that was the last entry in the journal.

I flipped the final pages of the journal back and forth in case a few of them were stuck together. I wanted to know what happened to Paracelsus. Did he cross the breach? Did he survive? Was the scribe able to pull his master back or was he also sucked into the Ether, never to be seen again? There had to be another journal! I was frantically sifting through the rest of the books Julie had left me when a deep voice caused me to jump, knocking the whole stack to the floor.

"It's nearly sundown. I'll walk you home."

It was Dell looking muscled and confident as ever. Apparently, the gas leak didn't do him any damage.

I knelt down to pick up the books. My heart was racing, and I didn't think it was from being startled. I really, REALLY didn't want to be one of those girls who turns into jelly at the sight of a cute boy. This betrayal by my internal organs upset my temper, and per usual, my temper ran a direct line to my mouth. I smacked a book down on the side table and snapped at Dell.

"Did they send you to make sure I don't cause any more trouble?"

"You said you wanted to talk."

"How did you even know I was here? Are you following me or something?"

Dell refused to let me ruffle his feathers, despite my accusatory tone.

"I just asked around. Somebody saw you walking in."

"Is privacy against the law in Mystikos too? Or is it just walking around after dark that gets you assigned a permanent security escort?"

"I can leave if you want."

Dell turned and started towards the stairs.

"No!"

I stood up too quickly and it made me see little black spots, but I'd be damned if I'd faint in front of Dell Percie. I put my hand on the arm of the sofa to steady myself.

"I do want to talk to you."

"O.K."

Dell didn't wait for me to join him before making his way to the exit. I hated traipsing after him like a puppy.

"Shouldn't I tell Julie I'm leaving?"

"Don't worry. She knows."

Dell ran his hands over the library doors, and we stepped outside. I guess he had been to the library before, at least once.

It was already getting dusky. The day had flown by while I was engrossed in the journal. I was beginning to understand how it was so easy for Eteri to lose track of time. I expected Dell to start the conversation, but he seemed totally comfortable walking in silence. I was tempted to play a game of "who can hold out for longest," but that would mess up my chance of getting answers about what we had seen in the school basement.

"It wasn't a gas leak, was it?"

"No. It wasn't a gas leak."

I was surprised Dell told the truth so easily, and I wanted to stay on the roll.

"What's a hodag?"

Dell took a deep breath but didn't avoid the question.

"A demonic, blood thirsty behemoth, born of the ashes of cremated oxen, that feasts on raw flesh."

I laughed because my brain didn't know what else to do.

"Of course, it was a blood thirsty behemoth. Why on earth would I expect you to say anything from the known catalogue of species?"

"They're known. It's just that most people haven't seen one."

"Would it be too much to ask you to elaborate?"

Dell stopped. This was a welcome relief because I had to take three steps for every one of his strides.

"Look, I won't lie to you if you ask me a direct question, but I shouldn't be telling you anything at all. I took an oath."

"An oath to who?"

"To the Volunteers."

Dell started walking again to get away from the words he had just allowed to leave his mouth.

"Who are the Volunteers?"

If Dell needed simple, direct questions, that was what I was going to give him.

"We protect Mystikos and everything inside of its borders."

"Including demonic, flesh-eating oxen?"

"Everything."

Dell was back at pace, and I had to jog to keep up.

"What did the Volunteers do with it?"

"They returned it to its home."

"Will it come back?"

The thought that it might scared me more than I wanted to admit.

"If it does, we'll be ready."

"Dell, is this normal? For here I mean?"

"Not during the day, but there's been an unusual amount of activity since this storm came in."

As if on cue, it started to rain, gently at first, then gradually growing more intense. Dell didn't slow down. I was concurrently attempting to process everything I was hearing and not drown in the downpour. I finally grabbed Dell and pulled him under an overhang.

"I need a second to process."

"It's almost dark."

"What are you afraid of?"

"It's more like who I'm afraid for."

"Dell, my mother and I live in a bus. We've traveled the world, alone, and not always through the nicest places. I'm not a damsel in distress."

"Come on. The garage is right there."

Dell tried to move me towards the street again, but I stood my ground.

"Where did the hodag come from?"

"I can't answer that."

"Did it come from a place called the Ether?"

It was getting darker by the second. Dell looked nervously towards the horizon.

"Let it go, Soara."

Dell accidently pulled me hard enough that I tripped over my own feet. He grabbed me around the waist so I wouldn't fall. His touch sent a lightning bolt through my spine. I jerked myself free.

"I'm not done asking questions."

"Well, it'll have to wait until next time."

We were right in front of the garage fence. Dave was waiting just inside with Watcher and Sentinel.

"Is he a Volunteer too?"

I leaned my head in Dave's direction.

"No, but he's on our side, and that's the last answer you're getting today."

Dell pushed me through the gate.

“Stay out of the dark.”

Dell turned and walked into the shadows just as the last slice of the sun dropped beneath the trees. I wanted to go after him, but Sentinel and Watcher forced their heads under my hands demanding ear nuzzles.

“O.K., O.K. Don’t worry. I made it home in one piece.”

Dave politely waited for me to acknowledge him.

“You didn’t have to watch for me.”

“Your mom was getting worried.”

The creases in Dave’s forehead showed he had been worried too.

“Oh crap. I thought I left her a note.”

I started towards the apartment, then stopped.

“Hey, can the dogs sleep with me again?”

Dave clicked his tongue, and the dogs ran up the stairs and waited outside the apartment door.

“Thank you.”

“Tell Eteri to put the lasagna in the oven at 350 for 20 minutes. I didn’t put any meat in it, so you can eat it too.”

“Can’t wait to try it.”

I joined the dogs on the balcony and opened the apartment door. Dave watched until I was safely inside.

THE CLEARING

Most of the locals don't venture into the forest at the edge of Mystikos. Even the Volunteers keep within the town borders for their patrols. The air feels a little different there, thicker and charged with electricity. It's also very easy to get lost. If a person finds themselves wandering into the woods after dark, they might never wander out. At least this is the scary story little kids trade at Mystikos slumber parties.

In truth, it's a perfectly normal forest. It's the clearing you have to watch out for. Stumbling into that circle during the day, you'll only find dandelions and rocks, but at night, the clearing becomes something other. Few have actually laid eyes on it. Those that do are never quite the same, but the people of Mystikos respect it and would protect it at any cost. It's a promise they made a long time ago. A promise that sometimes proves difficult to keep.

CHAPTER TEN

The rain had gotten bad enough overnight that I didn't think I should venture to the library. I wasn't even sure why my mom went to work. I argued that surely no one was going to be at the café, but Eteri told me that Roselyn and Fred would never let down their regulars. I had laughed at that. Not the idea of loyal breakfasters braving a deluge, but the very idea of something regular in Mystikos.

Watcher and Sentinel were busying themselves with a special treat of lasagna leftovers. I didn't have any dog food and I didn't want to be in the apartment alone, so I had improvised their breakfast. I took out my laptop. If I couldn't get to the library for research, at least I could poke around online.

My first search was for Parcelsus, the name of the alchemist in the journal. Paracelsus was a pretty prolific guy. He had upset the medical establishment of his time with his assertion that all things could be poison, but could also be a cure, with the determining factor between the two depending solely on the amount given to a patient-the precursor to the pharmaceutical idea of measured dosages. He was the first medical chemist, a pioneer in wound care, and was considered the father of toxicology, all of which seemed pretty cut and dry by historical standards. A deeper dive proved more interesting. Just as the scribe had written, Paracelsus was a deeply religious man. He believed everything in existence came from God and was sacred. He also believed all matter in the world was ruled by one or more of the four elements- water, earth, air and fire, and that an understanding of these elements would unlock all great mysteries (and by great mysteries, I discovered he meant the kind of stuff that conspiracy theorists think lizards in people suits sit around discussing while eating the spleens of unicorns). Paracelsus' studies in astrology led to a series of prophecies about the end times. He was convinced it was possible to create life from inorganic matter, and even left a recipe on how to create something called a homunculus, which was apparently a teeny, tiny, but perfectly formed human child. He believed in ghosts, angels, and demons and wrote about their makeup and purpose. He studied fairytale creatures and spirits, and also considered them part of creation, asserting that not to believe in them was not to believe in God. As such, Paracelsus thought the church was wrong in linking the supernatural with evil. The multi-layered scientist also practiced astral projection and thought his spirit, separate from his physical body, could manipulate solid objects.

A couple of hours down this rabbit hole convinced me that Paracelsus was a weirdo, possibly mentally ill, and probably a liar. All the same, I would have loved him to pop into my living room so I could ask him his view on things like giant screaming monster birds and hodags. I wondered if Paracelsus wrote anything about spirit guides. Maybe he could shed some light on the voice in my head (which, by the way, I hadn't heard since the school basement incident). Eteri talked to her spirit guide about all kinds of boring stuff like whether or not to invest in a bamboo toilet paper company, so why did I only get to talk to mine when I was in danger?

A knock at the door sent Sentinel and Watcher into protection mode. I figured their barking would scare off anyone with nefarious plans, but I still put them between me and the door before opening it. Much to my delighted surprise, Sierra and August, basically dressed in scuba gear, stood on the little porch. They'd braved the storm to check on me, since I had gone incommunicado over the past couple of days. They both stomped through the door without waiting to be invited in. Sierra was the first to attack.

"Don't you ever answer your texts? Hi, puppies!"

I was thrilled to discover that Watcher and Sentinel were the perfect warm and fuzzy distraction from questions about myself, but while Sierra was focused on scratching their bellies, August took a turn.

"My mom's totally gone off the rails again, so I'm gonna need photographic proof you're alive to calm her down."

August snapped a photo of me on her phone, then stepped around to get another one of my back, as if one side of me could exist without the other.

"What's your mom so upset about?"

I batted August's phone away when she tried to take a close-up picture of my face.

"She says the rain is a bad portent and evil is coming, and that they'll take away Mystikos just like they took my hand."

"Who's "they" and why does everyone steal your hand? Maybe you should lock it up in a drawer or something."

August ignored my suggestion and kept going.

"To be fair, my mom also says that there's a tiny person living in our T.V. who makes the garbage disposal go off all by itself. She's nuts."

Sierra had a gentler explanation.

"August's mom sometimes has a difficult time staying grounded in reality. When she's not on her meds, it gets worse."

"She's on her meds. I've even been checking to make sure she doesn't hide the pills under her tongue. This is next level."

"But what do I have to do with that?" I asked.

"The storm started when you and your mom got here and it hasn't stopped." August plopped down on the sofa. Obviously, this information didn't freak her out too much to hang out. "And then there was the fire drill."

Sierra looked uncomfortable passing on the next piece of information, but she clearly felt it had to be done.

"We haven't had any "fires" in a long time."

She didn't say anything about the hodag, but even if Sierra didn't know specifically what had been in the basement of the school, she seemed to know it wasn't just a routine safety drill. Sensing a window of opportunity, I went for it.

"Are "fires" the reason no one can be out at night in Mystikos?"

"I don't know," Sierra mumbled while avoiding eye contact by going back to petting the dogs. Maybe August would be an easier well to pump information from.

"What about you, August? You got any ideas about the strange "fires" of Mystikos?"

"We're not dumb, and we're not going to tell you what you want to know," said August giving Sierra a look that meant she better not crack under the pressure.

"Are you all in a blood cult or something? Is someone gonna kidnap you from your beds and cut you into little pieces if you tell the truth?"

"There's no cult," Sierra promised.

"We just have a lot of really old traditions," August added.

"O.K., tell me this, Sierra, can your grandparents get a license from the state Fish & Wildlife Department to hunt the things they like to shoot at around here?

"Some yes and some no. But my grandparents are different. Most people here don't believe in hunting," Sierra touched Soara's arm gently. "We believe in protecting, and we want to protect you too."

"How can I be safe when no one will tell me what's after me?"

"Nothing is after you," Sierra grimaced, "At least we don't think so, but when August's mom gets like this, it usually means something is about to happen, so we just want to make sure you follow the rules and stay inside when it's dark, Ok?"

I wanted to feel angry that Sierra and August were playing mommy with me, but I could see the real concern in their eyes.

"Fine. I'll follow the rules."

"But we didn't say you have to stay inside *here*," August told me with a wink.

Sierra's smile suddenly returned.

"My grandparents said we can have a sleepover! But they probably only said yes so they can make sure you're the kind of nice young woman I should be associating with, so don't cuss."

"I won't cuss."

August bumped my shoulder with her own. Her smile had turned mischievous.

"Just because we don't go out at night in Mystikos, doesn't mean we don't have any fun."

I had no idea what fun might look like to a group of teenagers who grew up in the weirdest, most secretive town on earth. I briefly considered the possibility I was being invited to a party where someone would take pictures of my feet while I slept and sell them on the internet for beer money, but at this point, anything was better than staying home and waiting for another nightmare.

***

I had never been to a slumber party, much less a Mystikos one, so I had no idea what to pack. It wasn't that I hadn't made a few buddies over the years, I just didn't usually stick around long enough to get to the sleepover stage. My longest friendships were all of the pen pal variety.

Eteri was extremely excited and insisted on me taking a variety of fancy nightgowns with matching satin robes and whatever make up she had laying around. She hadn't really slumber partied either growing up and her entire idea of sleepovers was informed by watching 1960's teeny bopper movies where all the girls wore frilly pj's and did makeovers. I shoved my favorite sweatshirt and sweatpants into my bag when Eteri wasn't looking.

Dave and Eteri drove me over to the Claybourne's house. Actually, it was more like a compound, fully fenced with security cameras and you had to be buzzed into the front gate. I spotted wildlife cameras and feeders all over the wooded property as we drove up the gravel path to the main house. I wondered if the feeders were set up to lure in unsuspecting creatures for front porch target practice.

"Yvonne and Dean can be a little bit intimidating, but they're good people," Dave said as he put the truck in park.

"So, they're Sierra and Zion's grandparents? What happened to their mom and dad?"

"They passed away when the girls were little, but I should probably let them tell you the story when they're ready."

I tried not to sigh. More mysteries.

"Have the best time and text me if anything juicy happens." Eteri gave me a kiss on the cheek and waved me out of the car.

"What are you gonna do while I'm gone?" I sort of knew the answer, but I wanted verbal confirmation.

"Dave's making me chicken and dumplings, then we're gonna play Egyptian Rat Screw."

"What?"

I nearly choked on my own spit.

"It's a card game," Dave was quick to interject.

"Oh. Right. Cool. Well, have fun and be safe and stuff."

I slid out of the truck, grabbing my bag from the floorboard. When I turned around to give Eteri and Dave a last wave goodbye, she was still sitting in the middle spot of the truck's bench seat, so that she and Dave's knees were touching. It looked like there was nothing I would be able to do to stop a romance from blossoming. Honestly, it seemed like it was already in full bloom.

The house's big oak door opened. Sierra and Zion were waiting with gigantic smiles. Once they knew I was safely inside, Dave and Eteri pulled away, with Patsy Cline blaring on the old pick up's tape deck.

"August and Matthew are already here. Our grandparents let Matthew sleep over because they know he's not into vaginas," Zion offered without so much as a blush.

"They're waiting to meet you. Everyone calls them Nana and Pops, by the way. They like to adopt all the kids in town."

Sierra took my bag and set it down in the hallway.

"So they can indoctrinate you," Zion said with an eye roll.

I noticed that a menagerie of taxidermied animals made up the majority of Nana and Pops' décor. We passed one room with a large set of opaque glass double doors. I could see the shadows of stuffed prizes behind the glass, but it blocked any details. I felt Sierra push me past the room quickly, as if she didn't want me to spend any time guessing what was in there. After winding through a hallway and down a couple of stairs, we finally made it to the house's massive great room. It held a blazing fireplace, big leather couches and more feathered and furry "friends." Nana and Pops were already waiting for me. They both wore crisp, dark denim jeans that had probably been ironed and starched, and near matching button down shirts with the sleeves rolled up. I noticed they each had on a pair of cowboy boots and wondered if a few beasts had gone to the cobbler instead of the taxidermist.

"Come in. Don't be shy!"

Nana stood and gave me the firmest hug I had ever received. She swatted at her husband lightly.

"Pops, you should stand when a lady enters the room."

"Would you give me half a second before you start beating me up?" Pops chuckled. Then he gave me a hug as well. So, the Claybournes were huggers. Duly noted.

"First things first,"

Nana wagged a finger in my face. Maybe this was the intimidating part. "We only have two rules here."

Zion couldn't stifle her guffaw, "More like two thousand."

"We only have two rules for our GUESTS," Nana said, shooting Zion a dirty look, which she ignored, "No leaving the house after dark."

"And no going in my solarium," said Pops and he obviously meant business.

"Is that the room with the double doors?"

"We got a smart one here!" Pops smacked me on the back. I took a step forward from the force, "Now that that's all figured out, time for lockdown."

Nana grabbed something from in between the side table and the couch. It was a well-oiled rifle with a heavy-duty scope and a leather strap so she could hang it over one shoulder. Pops had a matching weapon on the side of his chair too. I looked at Sierra, then Zion. Neither one of them seemed fazed by this display of fire power.

"We'll be back once we've walked the perimeter."

The Claybournes disappeared down an adjoining hall.

"What are they looking for?" I asked.

"Things that go bump in the night."

Zion pulled me down yet a different hall and into a game room. Matthew and August were already playing one of those dance video games where you get points for accuracy and rhythm. I prepared herself to lose big (both in points and dignity). Dancing has never been my strong suit.

"How much dancing will be involved in this sleepover?"

I wondered if I should be warming up or stretching. Blessedly Sierra saved the day.

"Oh, I can't. There's no way. That's Matthew and August's thing. I'm more of a Monopoly girl when it comes to games."

"We also have Uno, but I cheat."

Zion climbed over the back of the couch and reached for a bowl of popcorn just before August and Matthew finished up their round with a flourish and pose. Matthew won by ten points.

"Give me the card."

Matthew reached out his hand, palm open, and waited.

"Fine. I'll just get it back next time."

August dug in her pocket and pulled out a laminated card that had "Most Awesome Dancer in the World" written on it in marker.

"They've been doing this since fourth grade. Sometimes it gets bloody."

Sierra pushed Soara over to the couch too.

"That was one time, and it was an accident!" August argued.

"It was sabotage pure and simple. And my profile will NEVER be the same."

Matthew turned to the side to try and highlight his horribly crooked nose, but as far as I could tell, any damage had only contributed to the perfect symmetry of his face. August sat down on the floor.

"Are Nana and Pops gone?" Zion consulted her watch, "We should have 15 minutes."

August dug back into her pockets and lay a couple of smooth stones and a small stick on the coffee table.

"Guys, I really don't think we should do this tonight," Sierra said looking super nervous and glancing towards me.

"What exactly should we not do?" I asked, reaching out to pick up one of the stones, but August swatted my hand away.

"No one can touch the stones except the guide. That's me."

"Is this some kind of Ouija board thing?"

If that was the case, I was out. I had seen too many teen horror movies where the bloodbath began with a casual Ouija board session.

"That's for dumb asses who want to conjure up a Victorian ghost and drink absinthe. We don't mess with the dark stuff. This is earth magic." August retorted as she spread out the two stones on the coffee table and put the twig between them.

"It's more like how people find water with sticks. There's nothing ooky spooky about it. It uses the earth's magnetic pull."

Sierra slid off the sofa onto the floor. She'd given up on trying to stop the process. Zion joined her and Matthew was already sitting down. He puts his hands palms down on the table, and the others copied him, so I did the same.

August closed her eyes and took a deep breath.

"You all know the rules, but this is for Soara. You each only get one question, and it has to have a yes or no answer. The white stone is yes. The black stone is no. Everyone must keep their palms on the table and only the person asking the question can open their eyes. We'll start with Matthew and go clockwise."

Everyone closed their eyes. The order August had chosen put me last. I decided to use the extra time to search my mind for the perfect question. I currently had about 500 of them, but it had to be a yes or no question and something I wasn't embarrassed to ask in front of my new friends. August (at least I assumed it was August since my eyes were closed), hit the table with her palms, playing out a specific rhythm. As soon as she stopped, Matthew asked his question.

"Am I going to fail my biology test on Monday?"

I was pleased that it seemed like we weren't going too high stakes with our queries. No truth or dare style sexy stuff. I heard a light scraping sound and guessed it was the twig choosing yes or no. When it moved, it felt like a compass dial was moving in my stomach. I knew which stone the twig had chosen as if I'd been staring at it the whole time. I wondered if everyone else could feel it too. After Matthew had time to read his answer, August beat out the rhythm once more and it was her own turn.

"Is my mom going to come back this time?"

I wasn't sure what this meant. I had gotten the impression that August's mom barely left the house. There was another scraping. I felt the same pull in my stomach. The twig had said yes. I heard August's deep sigh of relief, then she beat out the rhythm again.

Zion's question was equally intriguing, but far less emotional.

"Does Pop hide his gold in that tree with the weird knot that looks like Benjamin Franklin?"

My stomach told me the answer was no.

"Damn it!"

Maybe Zion was checking off hiding places one by one.

Sierra took a little time before asking her question. When she finally spoke, she said each word slowly and clearly, to make sure she didn't make any mistakes.

"Did IT come back with the other things?"

That time the pull in my stomach was different. It felt like the twig was struggling against some outside force that didn't want it to answer, so it just vibrated in the center of the stones. I could feel the heaviness of the outside force. The strain made my intestines cramp. I grit my teeth against it, but still let out a grunt of pain.

"It isn't answering."

Sierra sounded a bit panicked.

"Just ask it again," August said calmly.

"Did IT come back with the other things?"

The pain in my stomach instantly doubled and the shock of it caused me to open my eyes. The stones and the stick were floating in the air. I could see an unidentifiable darkness moving around them. I wanted to scream, but all that came out of my throat was the curling snake of air I had seen in my dreams. It reached out from my mouth, meeting the darkness and the darkness noticed. It had no face, but I knew it recognized me and was happy, or maybe the feeling was victorious. I let my breath reach a little closer to the darkness. I was almost touching it.

"Soara, Stop!" Sierra yelled.

I looked around for the first time since I had gone into the trance. The darkness was gone. The stones and twig were back on the coffee table and everyone was looking at me. August grabbed the pieces off the table and threw them into the burning fireplace.

"I told you not to open your eyes unless you're asking a question!"

"I'm sorry. I couldn't help it."

"Fuck. Pops and Nana are coming. Just be cool."

Zion put the dance game back on the T.V. and pulled Matthew up to join her.

"Everything's clear. We're locked down and safe for the night," Pops announced proudly.

"You all need any more snacks?"

Nana's look of grandmotherly concern that any child might starve under her watch was offset by the giant rifle she still had at her side.

"If we need anything, we can get it. Don't worry about us." Sierra trilled as she jumped up and gave her grandparents each a hug and kiss.

"Don't drink too much soda. It rots your brain."

With that dire warning, Nana and Pops left us alone. As soon as the coast was clear, Zion turned off the game again and interrogated August.

"All right, what the hell was that?"

"I don't know. I'll have to ask my mom."

"But you said she's "isn't here" right now."

Matthew's attempt at coding whatever "isn't here" meant, only emphasized the fact he was hiding something from me.

"Did your mom go out of town or something?" I asked.

Before August could answer, Sierra interrupted, "Why don't we make cookies?"

Everyone, including me, turned to look at Sierra like she was insane.

"We should really do something else. Like NOW."

Sierra was doing the nervous glance thing towards me again. Matthew, Zion, and August noticed and nodded obediently.

"But you can't put any frickin oatmeal in them this time. That's a breakfast food," Zion barked, then started for the kitchen and Matthew followed her out.

August checked the fireplace one more time. The stick had burned away, and the stones were beginning to glow from the heat.

"I think it's ok. I'll just let it burn until it goes out on its own," she said as she walked out too.

Sierra couldn't stop shaking. I wasn't sure if I was supposed to try and help or just leave her alone.

"I'm sorry you didn't get an answer to your question," I offered nervously.

I watched Sierra flip some kind of internal switch from this new vulnerability back to her bubbly, "everything's great" self.

"It's just a game. We better get in the kitchen before Zion burns it down."

I knew there'd be no use in trying to get Sierra to tell me what she had asked the game about. I was learning fast that the only way to get answers in Mystikos was to find them yourself. I made the conscious decision to flip my own worry switch, so I could at least try and enjoy my first sleepover.

"Oatmeal really is a travesty in a chocolate chip cookie," I teased.

"Sheesh! It's not like I put raisins in them!"

Sierra seemed relieved that I was willing to play along with forgetting. She gave me a playful punch in the arm and then pushed me into the kitchen.

***

The baking was fun, and the cookies were delicious, followed by an epic, multi-round Uno tournament (where as promised, Zion cheated), and a viewing of some black and white movie with a lot of singing and dancing. At this point, everyone had found a sofa, chair, or pile of blankets to collapse on in various stages of R.E.M. I was the only one not sleeping and I was making up a song in my head to go along with the subtle rhythm of Matthew's snores.

I stared at the glowing remains of the fire in the fireplace. The stones were still there, nestled in the ashes. The white one had cracked from the heat but was still intact. The black one had broken into several pieces already. I guessed whatever magic may have been in the rocks was now gone. I thought about the weird, swirly darkness I had seen during the game. Why had it seemed happy? I wasn't even sure how I could have known darkness had any feelings at all. Maybe it was my spirit guide trying to show itself. On the other hand, whatever it was had caused me physical pain and I didn't think my spirit guide would do that to me.

As I looked around the room at my sleeping friends (taking particular comfort in the fact that I suddenly had friends to watch doing anything), it struck me that almost nothing seemed to shock the people who lived in this town. They brushed weirdness under the rug and kept on truckin. If I thought hard enough, I had to admit that Eteri and me kind of did the same thing. We just tended to put a physical distance between ourselves and anything uncomfortable. Maybelle was home, but she was also an easy way to escape relationships, responsibility, boredom and the dreaded thought of being normal. Maybe Mystikos was the perfect place for us to settle down. We found a home where we could leave things behind without going anywhere.

I closed my eyes and breathed in the vanilla and brown sugar scent that still wafted from the kitchen. It mixed with the slight smokiness of the dying fire, and I found myself thinking that combination would make the perfect cologne. I decided to come up with a whole marketing campaign for my fragrance. I named it, Soul Fire, and decided to use sexy firemen (like the ones who pose for charity calendars) in my ads. But when I flipped through the imaginary calendar I was using to audition potential spokesmodels, every month was Dell...Shirtless Dell chopping through a door with a hatchet; shirtless Dell saving a kitten stuck in a tree; shirtless Dell hosing down a bonfire; shirtless Dell being sprayed by a fire hydrant. I pinched myself to stop the endless loop of shirtless Dells, but it didn't work very well. I'd have to find another distraction.

I slid off the couch with the blanket still around my shoulders and nearly tripped over a snoring Matthew but recovered just in time and crossed the room to part the heavy, brocade curtains. The stars were so beautiful in Mystikos. It was terrible that no one was ever outside at night to enjoy them. Not that anyone would want to be out in the rain, but it couldn't rain forever, could it? What would it be like to live in a world of perpetual rain? Would the earth flood? Would everyone be forced to live onboard submarines? Then no one would ever see the stars again anywhere. A cataclysmic event emanating out of Mystikos and drowning everything on the planet... such a thought was pretty dark, even for a teenage girl. I was scolding my brain for its new tendency toward negativity when I noticed something glowing in the trees, two somethings, like a pair of shining, red eyes. I didn't think a deer or a bear had eyes like that. I turned to tell the others, but decided maybe I shouldn't wake them after the trouble I had caused earlier.

When I turned back to the window, the eyes were closer, and I realized they were set into the same dark, hulking shape that watched my house the night Dell and me were attacked by the flying mystery creature. But this time, instead of being terrified, I felt warm and comforted. I took a chance reaching out with my mind.

"Are you my spirit guide?"

Almost immediately, my head was flooded with words.

"No, but I won't hurt you."

"Why are you here?"

"I've always been here, but you never needed me."

"What changed?"

"You must defeat her."

"Defeat who?"

"For now, stay with your friends. You'll be safe until you are ready."

"I don't understand."

"She wants you, but you aren't strong enough yet."

"Who wants me? Can you come closer and let me see you?"

There was no answer. The two glowing orbs blinked out and the warm feeling inside

my head vanished. Whatever it was was gone. I desperately wanted to run outside and find that feeling again, but the thing had told me I was safe if I stayed with my friends, and I didn't think it told lies. It was frustrating, but I had learned my lesson. I wouldn't go against it again. I dragged my blanket back to the sofa and snuggled into the cushions. I thought I'd be staring at the darkness all night trying to figure out who I'd eventually have to defeat, but almost immediately, I fell into a peaceful sleep.

***

Nana made a huge breakfast- biscuits and gravy, bacon, eggs, and fruit. When she asked us if we had fun last night, everyone exchanged a look, but no one mentioned anything weird happening. Luckily Pops came in and changed the subject. He wanted everyone to eat quickly and pack up. He and Nana planned to make a trip to the ammo store three towns over and they were going to drop everyone home on their way out.

Zion didn't bother to say goodbye. She went right back to bed after breakfast, but Sierra gave me a big hug at the front door.

"Thanks for coming over."

"I really had fun."

I hugged Sierra back shyly then hopped into Nana and Pops' SUV with August and Matthew.

The first stop was Matthew's. He lived with his parents in what qualified as the White House of Mystikos. Matthew's dad was the mayor, and his grandad was the mayor before him, and before that it was his great grandad, etc. So many generations of the Lovells had inhabited the house that even though it was owned by the city, folks called it the Lovell Mansion. Matthew hopped out of the Claybourne's SUV and turned to offer one of his perfect smiles.

"Thanks for letting me sleep over, Mr. and Mrs. Claybourne."

"Anytime, Matthew," Pops returned. "And tell your dad that he better extend that city curfew sooner rather than later. He wouldn't want to end up with the same legacy as his father."

"Yes sir."

Matthew nodded and ran through the front gate that swung open as he approached.

"Those Lovells have always been soft. I like Matthew, but he's not any different," sighed Nana.

"You mean because he's gay?" I shot off, causing August to nearly choke on the piece of gum she was chewing. I wasn't going to give Nana and Pops a pass on being small minded just because they were giving me a ride.

"I couldn't give two farts who anyone wants to kiss," said Nana, "But Zion and Sierra's parents would still be here if Donald Lovell had listened to us fourteen years ago. Matthew and his daddy are cut from the same cloth. All the Lovells ever want to do is keep the promise and keep the peace."

"Calm down, honey. We shouldn't talk like this in front of the kids."

Pops gave Nana's knee a squeeze and she clamped her mouth shut, realizing how comfortable she had let herself get.

As we pulled down the road towards August's house, I looked over to August and whispered, "What promise?"

August just shook her head and darted a glance towards the front seat.

The rest of the ride was taken in silence. I stared out the car window at the lawns passing by. So many houses had big front gates. A little white picket fence in the front yard is a pretty normal thing, and a good backyard fence keeps in wandering toddlers and pets, but in Mystikos, the fences are tall, imposing and have a regional style I can only describe as "pointy." That day I decided my favorites were the ones coiled with ivy or climbing blooms. I imagined standing against one of those fences and waiting for the vines to pull me in. I morbidly decided a death by photosynthesis didn't sound bad at all.

August's house was the kind with the vines. They grew wild, reaching tendrils into the yard and onto the driveway. There were windchimes, ribbons and tiny talismans hung everywhere amongst the branches and I gasped at the sight. August rolled her eyes.

"They're charms. My mom makes them all the time. She says you can't take them down. You have to let nature have them back."

I was mesmerized.

"I think it's beautiful."

"Yeah. Well, they don't work. They've never helped my mother."

August got out, grabbed her bag, and quickly disappeared behind the vines.

"Can you tell me what's wrong with August's mom?" I asked Nana and Pops as they backed out of the driveway.

Nana turned. Her eyes were serious and sad.

"She went to the other side, and part of her stayed there."

Nana didn't offer any further explanation. Not that I expected a straight answer. Out of the corner of my eye I noticed we were passing the fire station and without thinking I yelled, "STOP!"

Pops slammed the brakes, and we all lunged forward.

"What did you see?"

"I'm sorry. I didn't mean to scare you. It's just you can let me out here. I was planning to go to the library anyway and I can walk," I said, blushing and hoping they believed my excuse.

"Alright, but straight there and straight home before dark. *Way* before dark," said Nana as she handed me my bag from the front seat.

I waved until the Claybournes were out of sight, then walked towards the firehouse. Dell met me halfway down the drive.

"How did you know I was here?" I asked, genuinely surprised.

"We have these things called windows," Dell smirked, "What's up?"

I didn't answer right away. My brain had already gone back to flipping through my imaginary shirtless Dell the fireman calendar. I blinked to try and erase the pictures.

"I want some more answers and I'm not leaving until I get them."

CHAPTER ELEVEN

Dell and I sat on a bench in the courtyard of the firehouse which was surprisingly lovely. Beds filled with rosemary, mint and thyme lined the perimeter and snaked their way into a canopy knit so tightly that it kept out the rain. The rest of the space was paved with marble tile. At the center, a large bowl-like structure was set into the ground, a monument to the four Elements. The bowl was separated into quadrants, one filled with dark soil, one filled with fire which burned from an unseen source, one bubbled with water that never overflowed, and one quadrant appeared empty, but was carved with delicate, curving lines that emulated swirling air. I wondered about the other firefighters. It seemed like Dell and me were the only two people in the whole place. I hoped the others weren't off battling another beast. I shivered even thinking about it and stood to move closer to the monument's flame.

"Did the original settlers build this too?" I asked in a whisper.

"Yes."

Dell gave his usual short answer.

"Why were they so obsessed with the four Elements?"

I hoped my question was succinct enough to get a real answer this time.

"The original settlers of Mystikos came here to find religious freedom."

"I know that already," I said, fighting down the urge to throw something at Dell. "Let me try again. What did the original settlers believe?"

"They believed everything seen and unseen is God's creation and therefore has a purpose."

I shrugged my shoulders. "That just sounds like regular church stuff to me."

"For the seen stuff, yes. It's the unseen stuff that got people in trouble," Dell said and rose to join me in front of the fire.

"What's the unseen stuff?" I asked, but I felt like I might already have an inkling.

Dell took a deep breath.

"That's why we have the Volunteers."

"Why can't you give me a normal answer?"

I could feel the angry heat rising up my spine as Dell opened his mouth to speak, but before he could start, several Volunteers entered the courtyard. They all looked exhausted, their clothing scorched and one or two had gashes on their arms or faces. When they saw me standing with Dell, their eyebrows went up, but no comments were made.

"I should go help. I'll see you later."

Dell moved around me and followed his fellow Volunteers into the firehouse.

I bit my cheek to keep from letting out a frustrated scream. I considered staying and waiting for Dell, he couldn't hide in the firehouse forever, but when I glanced up, one of the other Volunteers was watching me from an upstairs window, and his look was not welcoming.

***

Julie, on the other hand, was all smiles and cardigan when the library doors slowly swung open for me. She was holding her usual stack of books and today was decked out in a symphony of greens.

"I think this may help you to understand August's mother a little better," Julie said handing me the books.

"But how did you know I wanted to ask about August's mother?"

Julie was practically psychic in terms of her book recommendations, but was she literally reading my thoughts?

"Isn't the world filled with funny coincidences? Settle in wherever you like and pull the bell if you need me."

Julie smiled and spun on her kitten heels. They clicked across the marble as she disappeared around an intricately carved pillar.

I sought out the fluffy pink chair I had promised to return to on my first day at the library. It didn't disappoint. Even the tattered upholstery had worn to a softness that made resting a cheek against it more comfortable than the highest threadcount sheets.

On top of Julie's most recently curated reading collection was a cookbook with dried leaves sticking out from its pages and a wooden spoon for a bookmark. Most of the ingredient lists were easy enough to come by. A lot of herbs and edible flowers, although I saw the occasional surprise ingredient like spiderweb. On closer inspection, the book was filled with recipes for charms and spells. No school for wizards stuff- these charms helped the user connect with the energy of the earth and better predict against chaos. There were drawings of the different wards. Someone passing by, might just see a bit of feather and string hanging from a branch, but to the learned eye, it was a marker that a Wise Woman had been nearby. I was pretty sure a lot of people would call these "Wise Women" witches, semantics often being the only difference between burning at the stake and living to a ripe old age in a cottage in the woods. A few of the charms looked familiar to me. I'd seen them on the vines encircling August's gate. Ms. Midwinter either was, or had been a Wise Woman, before she left part of herself on "the other side."

The second book in the pile was filled with marvelously illuminated drawings of fantastical beasts surrounded by golden curlicues and calligraphy. I was particularly drawn to the unicorn. I had lived an unusual life, but that did not mean I had escaped my obligatory "unicorn phase" as a little girl. As I turned the pages, the beasts became more sinister. They grew claws and fangs. I couldn't read the Latin descriptions, but I did recognize "sanguis" had something to do with blood. I shivered remembering the hot, fetid breath of the hodag and closed the book before anymore nightmares imprinted on my brain.

From my spot in the pink chair, I had the perfect view of the library's stained-glass windows. Depending on the time of day and the position of the sun, the pictures seemed to morph. It was a trick of light and shadow, but all the same spectacular. The sun shifted ever so slightly, and something appeared that I had never noticed before on the panel with the beautiful Air Elemental. I realized I had yet to take the time to examine any of the panels thoroughly and put aside my books to get a closer look.

All of the panels were intricately beautiful. If one didn't know they were made of glass, they would think they were looking at a series of oil paintings by some Renaissance master. With outstretched arms, each of the four Elementals stood watch. They were wrapped in robes made of earth, fire, water and air and surrounded by the flora and fauna associated with their individual element. Their faces showed calm indifference, or maybe it was boredom. They didn't seem to care for the world that was entrusted to their control.

I took a step towards the Air Elemental. She was exquisite. Long, copper hair swirled about her, reaching out like fingers of wind. She floated in a clear, blue sky surrounded by birds of every imaginable variety, and the clouds beneath her seemed to wait for her command. The sun had highlighted a piece of script below the Elemental's bare, dangling feet. I couldn't quite read the lettering, so I took a step closer. Everything suddenly went silent. A breeze gently floated over me, slowly picking up strength as it twisted around my body. My eyes darted around the room. This feeling was familiar but still disquieting. Nothing else in the room moved. The mini tornado only seemed to affect me. I felt my feet lift off the floor as my body rose closer to the towering windows. I wasn't frightened or surprised that I could float this way. It somehow seemed perfectly natural. When I was finally level with the Elemental's face, I reached out towards the beautiful colored glass. At my touch, the russet haired Elemental came to life and leaned forward from the pane. The Elemental's eyes were no longer indifferent. Instead, they were filled with a sad longing. I could finally read the letters on the glass panel. I moved my lips and instead of my voice, a breathy wind whispered the name, "Zepherine."

I could feel myself being pulled towards Zepherine, whose longing had swiftly turned into an angry need. I tried to fight against whatever force was holding me off the floor, or to scream for help, but it was impossible. Zepherine's face twisted into a grimace of frustration and the window began to heave and stretch, reaching out towards me. In a moment, I'd be enveloped into the Elemental's cold, crystalline arms and probably disappear forever. I closed my eyes and pictured Eteri. I wanted my last thought to be of love, not fear. As I visualized the tiny details of my mother's perfect smile, I heard the glass begin to crack and a storm of stinging shards suddenly exploded all around me. I dropped to the floor with a violent crash. My hands clutched at my throat, willing my voice to come back, but all I could do was gasp for air.

"Soara, you're bleeding!"

Julie's kind voice pierced my terror.

"It moved! It was alive! She tried to take me!"

I managed to get the words out, but they felt like sandpaper against my throat.

"You are always safe in the library."

Julie pulled an embroidered handkerchief from her pocket and dabbed a bit of blood off my cheek where I'd been cut by a shard of glass.

"Who is Zepherine?" I asked.

Julie's eyes filled with sadness. She shook her head.

"There are rules. I can't tell you. I can only help you along the way."

"Why does she want me?"

I grabbed Julie's hand, pleading for some kind of answer. The unflappable smile returned to her face as she helped me up from the floor.

"I think your date is here."

"I don't have a date," I said, shaking glass from my hair.

"Don't you? Dell is waiting outside."

Julie gently took my arm and led me to the library doors.

"Come back tomorrow."

I wanted to argue with Julie, but I quickly found myself on the library steps with the doors clicking softly closed behind me. On the street in front of the library, Dell sat in the driver's seat of a fully restored, vintage pick up. He looked up at me and smiled.

Despite my surprise, I climbed into the truck without question.

"Seatbelt," Dell said reaching across to help me pull the buckle across my lap.

The gesture made me laugh. How infuriatingly ridiculous was wearing a seatbelt in a town filled with living monsters and windows that came to life and tried to drag you to another dimension?

"What? It's the law." Dell clicked the seatbelt around me and pulled forward.

Neither of us talked for a bit. The only sound was Dell mechanically shifting gears. This was pretty par for the course with Dell and I was thankful because I needed to let my mind reassemble after what had happened in the library. That took most of several blocks, but when I finally spoke, my voice was clear and sure.

"Now is when you tell me the truth."

"I will. I promise. But it's almost dark and I need to get you home. And it's not something I can just tell you anyway. I'll have to show you."

We pulled up to Dave's shop. Watcher and Sentinel were waiting for us outside the gate. As soon as the pickup came to a stop, the dogs started barking and jumping at the window to get to me. The racket was too much. There was no use trying to talk now. No matter how mind-bendingly frustrating this was, I'd have to wait again for answers.

As soon as I stepped out of the car, Watcher and Sentinel calmed down. Dell rolled down his window.

"Take care of her."

I could swear I saw the dogs nod before they began nudging me through the gate. The sun was just setting on the horizon as Dell drove away and I heard the automatic locks click shut for the night.

***

That evening's dinner included a culinary class in tamale making. Dave's cooking knowledge appeared to be international in scale, and I wondered if he had been a chef or a merchant marine before he became a mechanic. There were already tamales (some of them bean and cheese for me) steaming away on the stove. Dave was washing corn husks in the sink and Eteri was at the table spreading masa and filling into the clean husks and wrapping them up into delicious little parcels.

"Come help me. It's fun!"

Eteri scooped some masa out with her hand and pressed it into a corn husk.

"Ok."

I walked to the sink and Dave scooted over, so I could wash my hands, then I sat back down with Eteri and stuck my fingers into the masa.

"It's kind of like Play Doh."

"As if you ever had any of that stuff. We made your modeling clay from scratch and colored it with natural dyes. Oooh, it might be fun to make colored tamales!" Eteri said, scooping out another glob of masa and giggling.

"Don't worry, Mom. No one is going to accuse you of raising me on store bought fun."

We settled into a comfortable silence after that. The only sound other than the rain on the garage's corrugated metal roof was the scrape of masa leaves and the doggies snoring happily in the corner. Dave walked over to check the tamales in the steamer, and I realized that any stranger looking through the window would think we were a normal family making dinner together. Something pulled in my stomach, something that liked this little life, but I knew better than to get attached to any specific future.

"What did you do today?" Eteri asked happily.

"Sierra and Zion's grandparents dropped me off at the library. I spent most of the day there."

"I bet Julie's thrilled to have a new customer."

Dave had now moved on to opening a can of refried beans.

"I think I'm her only customer, but something weird happened today."

I noticed Dave stiffen across the room.

"What's that?" Dave tried to inquire casually.

"You know the big stained-glass windows on the top floor? Well one of them broke. Like it completely shattered. I was standing right in front of it when it happened."

"Are you ok?"

Eteri dropped her tamale and started checking me over.

"Yes. I'm fine. Just a few little scratches. I'm mostly worried about the window. They're so old and beautiful. I'm sure they're priceless."

I gently batted my mom away.

"Maybe you shouldn't go to the library until the storms calm down. What if it had been lightening or a branch blew through the window? You could have really gotten hurt," said Dave, now checking me over too in a way that was perturbingly fatherly.

"Julie said I'm always safe at the library. I trust her."

"Julie can't protect you from everything," Dave said, raising his voice a little. It sounded more like worry than anger, but my temper couldn't tell the difference.

"What should I be afraid of, Dave? Why don't you tell Mom the truth about the safe, lovely little town we've moved to? Why don't you tell her about your friends, The Volunteers? Or you could explain to her why you don't even go home anymore so you can lock us all in here like prisoners every night!" I shot back.

"Soara! What in the world are you talking about? Dave has been nothing but a good friend to both of us."

Eteri stepped between me and Dave.

"Oh stop it, Mom. I know Dave is your latest great love affair. Enjoy it while it lasts, Dave. As soon as she gets a whiff of any real commitment, you won't see anything but Maybelle's taillights."

I had already worked myself up to a defcon 5 fit.

Eteri doesn't get angry often, but when she does, she doesn't blink, and it's really unnerving. I practically saw her eyelids lock into place.

"Leave right now. Walk straight to your room and shut the door because if you stand here one more moment, I will say something mothers should not say to their children."

I knew better than to argue with this version of my mom. I turned and started towards the apartment.

"I'll come and see you when I've recollected myself." Eteri's voice lacked any of the trill it usually carried.

Tears stung my eyes. I was frustrated, scared, and lonely and at the same time I realized I'd never felt more connected to a single place. I was certain that I belonged in Mystikos, but I wasn't sure the thing that wanted to take me would let me stay.

***

I hate being in fights with my mother. We don't always agree, but we usually operate on the principle of yin and yang, complimenting one another with our differences. Being out of sync with Eteri feels like trying to stand on a basketball. And all I could do that night was stay as still as possible, so I didn't fall off and break something.

I texted August. "How is your mom?"

The dots started moving on my phone to show August was typing, but then they stopped, and a response never came through. I tried picking a book from my nightstand. I still hadn't finished the one I was reading the night the mystery monster attacked Maybelle, but no matter how many times I read the same page, I wasn't absorbing a single word. I briefly considered trying to force myself to sleep so the time would pass more quickly, but honestly, I was starting to be afraid of my dreams. Finally, there was a soft knock and Eteri stepped inside.

"Hello. I'm back to myself now. We can talk." Eteri sat down on the bed. She was blinking again. That was a good sign.

"Mom, I'm sorry. I shouldn't have said all that stuff to Dave. Even if you do like him, it's fine. I like him too. He's really nice." I scooted closer, hoping Eteri would acknowledge the imaginary white flag I was waving.

"I do like him very much, but you weren't wrong. I've been known to run away from people, places and situations, and sometimes it's the right thing to do, but sometimes it's just selfish." Eteri put her hand out and I took it. My world started to realign.

"Mom, you are the least selfish person I know. You care about everyone."

"But I don't always listen, and I'm sorry about that. So, I need you to tell me the truth. Do you want to leave Mystikos?"

I knew to think before speaking. This was one of those moments when my words would irrevocably write the future in the book of my life. If I told Eteri I was scared of Mystikos, we'd be gone within an hour, but I also knew if I told Eteri I wanted to stay, my mother would shut all her wanderlust into a box and put it away forever.

"No." The word came out of my mouth without my permission, but I knew I'd made the right choice.

Eteri smiled. "Won't this be a wonderful new adventure? We should do something to commemorate this night. Let's go forage for mushrooms in the moonlight! It's the perfect weather. All the rain will have made them sprout in every log!"

The muscles in my body relaxed. It was so easy and fast, but of course that was life with Eteri. Big decisions were not something she dwelled on. "Mom we can't go out after dark." I laughed at the fact my mom had forgotten so easily.

"What no one knows won't hurt them. We'll stay up late and sneak out after Dave goes to bed. He gave me the secret code to unlock the gates, remember?" Eteri's eyes sparkled with mischief.

"But all the rain, and it's dangerous. What about the bears?" I wasn't sure I should mention any other kind of monster to her yet.

"I've made up my mind, little Sparrow. Tonight, we fly!" Eteri patted my leg then skipped out of the room.

I knew I wouldn't change her mind. As with the choice to stay in Mystikos, once Eteri decided to make something happen, it did.

***

Eteri kept running to the window and pulling aside the curtains to see if Dave had turned out the lights in the garage. She loved being sneaky, especially if it meant she got to frolic under the stars. The longer it took for Dave to go to bed, the more nervous I got about going out. What if the wind tried to take me again, or we met a bloodthirsty goblin in the streets, not to mention if one of the Volunteers caught us? Dell had been relatively easy on me for my curfew infraction, but one of the senior Volunteers might not be so kind.

"Lights out! Give it 15 minutes and we're on our way!" Eteri ran to find some baskets and a couple of flashlights.

The butterflies in my stomach turned into pterodactyls. "We could probably find them easier during the day."

"But that's not an ADVENTURE." Eteri grabbed my hand and pulled me to the door.

I held my breath until we were at the bottom of the stairs. Good news! We didn't burst into flames immediately. Eteri pointed to the security keypad just outside of the garage office door. I was tiptoeing behind my mom when I noticed she once again wasn't wearing any shoes.

"Mom, are you crazy? You'll get pneumonia!" I yell whispered.

"You can't hunt mushrooms with shoes on. It makes them tough" Eteri whispered back.

The logic was sketchy, but I couldn't prove it, so I kept following Eteri to make sure she didn't wake up Watcher and Sentinel in her excitement.

Eteri flipped open the keypad lid and punched in the secret code. I was certain that a thousand alarms were going to go off and helicopters would start circling the yard, but once again, nothing happened. We were safe.

Eteri waved me towards the back gate. I had never been on this side of the yard. Apparently, the space behind the garage was an empty, overgrown lot. There weren't any lights, so the flashlights made excellent shadows, but didn't do much to light our way. "Mom, how are we going to find anything out here? It's pitch black." We were probably out of earshot of the garage, but I still made sure to whisper.

"Don't look with your eyes. Feel with your soul," Eteri sang back. "And take off your shoes before the mushrooms see them."

I could not believe I was listening to my mom, but I dutifully took my shoes off and let my toes squelch in a week's worth of mud. "Stay where I can see you," I said as I flicked my flashlight in Eteri's direction and listened for anything alive in the vicinity besides the two of us.

Eteri let out a squeal and I immediately panicked. "Mom!" I flew towards the sound of her voice, swinging my flashlight and accidentally tossing it into the darkness. It hit the ground with a sucking sound and went out, leaving me stranded in a velvet darkness. "No! Mom, can you hear me? Are you ok? Answer me, please!" One second of silence felt like a million years. I couldn't see even an inch in front of my face.

"Found some! A whole mountain of them!" the tinkling of Eteri's voice sent sparks of joy through my body.

I ran towards the magical sound and found my mother happily plucking wavy eared mushrooms from inside a spongey log. The drizzle clung in droplets to Eteri's curls and threatened to drip off the end of her nose. She bent over to reach into the log for one last mushroom and started to tip forward, but I caught her by the foot before she planted face first in a bed of moss. "I forgot about this." I said, still holding onto Eteri's foot.

"Forgot about what? Eteri managed to regain her balance and turn herself on one leg. She accidentally flashed me in the eyes with her flashlight and I involuntarily let go of her foot to cover my face, which caused us both to fall backward again.

"The birthmarks." I steadied myself by sitting on the log and pulled Eteri down beside me. The wood was so wet it was more like a bean bag than chair at this point.

"Let me see." Eteri pulled her flashlight from the log. She put her foot out and I mirrored it with my own, lining up the matching brown marks we each have on the bottom of our left feet. "Our little scorch marks."

"Proof we belong to each other." I said, then paused touching my "scorch mark" to hers. My stomach fluttered. "If I ask you something, will you tell me the truth?"

"I always tell you the truth."

I didn't very often call out my mother's whimsical memories. But with everything suddenly feeling so upside down in my life, I needed a few touch points to prove that we were both real. "Tell me the story of when you were born but tell me the real story this time. Not the fairytale."

Eteri traced a rain drop down my arm and guided it off the end of her finger. "The fairytale is the only thing I know. I think I knew the real story a long time ago, but my spirit guide told me to forget."

"Mom, please don't." I pleaded.

"That's the truth. The spirit guide said I should forget that story forever and I did." Eteri stood and started hunting for mushrooms under another fallen limb.

I followed her. I wasn't going to just let this go this time. "Didn't you ever ask the Sparrows? Weren't you even curious?"

"I trusted the Sparrows and I trusted my spirit guide. There was no reason to worry about it."

"We could have a family somewhere out in the world. You could have brothers and sisters and cousins. Why wouldn't you want to know them? And what if there's some scary diseases hidden in our DNA and knowing ahead of time is the only thing that could save us? Or what if one of us needs a kidney someday?" I was trying not to get upset. At least the darkness and the raindrops would hide any wayward tears.

"We've always had what we needed. I don't worry about the past or the future. All I care about is right here and now." Eteri handed me her full basket and took my empty one.

"Have you ever heard the name Zepherine?" As soon as I uttered the word, Eteri stopped in her tracks and dropped the basket. I reached out to turn Eteri around and she crumpled to the ground.

"Are you kidding me? Stop being dramatic!" I grabbed Eteri's arms to pull her up, but her body began to jerk. "Mom, what's wrong?" I kneeled beside her trying to steady her head. "Mom, I'm here."

A thousand bits of first aid knowledge burst into my brain. Should I put something in my mother's mouth so she wouldn't bite her tongue? No, that was outdated. Should she be on her side or her back? Maybe she tried a bad mushroom. My mom was a pretty expert forager, but it was so dark. I wondered if I screamed for help if anyone would hear me. My mind flew to Dell. Suddenly, a cold blanket of air wrap around me. My fingertips and toes went numb. I thought it was the adrenaline and willed myself not to pass out. It felt like someone had wrapped their arms around my center and were pulling me backwards, but no one was there. I started to slide in the mud. I tried to dig my knees into the ground, but the mud was just too slippery. Eteri was my only anchor, and she was fighting her own battle against the convulsions that sent her entire body rigid every few seconds. I heard thunder and a clap of lightening lit up the sky. I took a deep breath of the cool, night air. Petrichor mixed with the scent of something half dead. The monster bird was coming!

Another burst of adrenaline rushed through my body giving me just enough strength to pull up onto my knees. There was no use in trying to pick up my mother. We were nearly the same size and at that moment, she was dead weight. I grabbed Eteri by the ankles and pulled her towards the only shelter I could see, the giant log where we had just harvested mushrooms. The slippery mud finally worked in my favor making it easier to slide Eteri closer to safety. I got to the log and shoved Eteri inside, then crawled in after her and pulled some loose brush over the opening to hide us.

I thought the night was impossibly dark, but this was like sitting in tar. I reached out to touch my mother and said a silent thank you that the convulsions seemed to be slowing a little. All I could do now was wait.

The wind and rain began to whip into a frenzy. I wondered if the ground might flood and the log could float us to safety, but lately we didn't seem have that kind of luck on our side. Another flap of wings and lightening lit up hundreds of tiny cracks in the makeshift shelter. I could hear the bird approach. The log tipped to one side as giant talons scraped against its bark. At any moment, the water-soaked wood could easily shred to bits. I wrapped myself around Eteri again, prepared to be a shield.

A great guttural roar shook the ground. I screamed. The bird gave an angry shriek and let the log go. I braced for the wood to crack open, revealing us like the soft inside of a boiled egg, but somehow the log held together. I could hear the tearing sounds of a battle going on beside us, but I didn't dare to look. Lightening flared, the ground rumbled, and the fight continued to rage on. I lay my cheek against Eteri's chest, part for comfort, part to make sure she was breathing.

The giant flying monster gave a last blood curdling cry then the sound of its wings flapping into the night grew fainter and fainter. The wind died down and the rain began to slow. The battle was over. I waited, and waited some more, then finally pulled the branches away from the mouth of the log and crawled out looking for a sliver of moon. Instead, I found two red, glowing eyes staring into my own. I started to back into the log again, but a familiar and comforting voice filled my mind once more.

"It will not come back tonight. Take her home."

I answered back softly, "Thank you."

The red eyes disappeared. I turned back to Eteri, now sleeping peacefully, and wondered what I had unleashed with that single word, Zepherine.

CHAPTER TWELVE

Eteri woke up with a headache and zero memory of what had happened the night before, other than being disappointed that we didn't make it back with any mushrooms. Despite several thorough check-ups, I couldn't find a single thing wrong with her. Eteri knew what day it was, who was president, and could list every album in Fleetwood Mac's discography as proof her brain hadn't turned to mush. I had to use my *really* bossy voice to keep her from going into work. Ultimately, the only thing that convinced Eteri to stay in bed was me promising I would go over to the Wistful Willow and offer a hand if they needed it.

I slipped on my raincoat and galoshes and made my way out of the work yard. The city drainage systems couldn't keep up with the rain and the roads were finally starting to flood. Luckily most folks in Mystikos drove big trucks and SUV's, but I imagined pretty soon we'd all be commuting via boat ala gondoliers in Venice. I looked across the street. Fred should have been at the café hours ago patting out biscuits and frying doughnuts, but the lights weren't shining in the restaurant's big painted windows. This wasn't right. The Wistful Willow never shut down. I took a step closer and realized the café's front door had been pulled off its hinges and was laying on the sidewalk. I ran across the street, trying to tamp down the panic that was jolting through my brain.

Inside the Wistful Willow several of the regulars stood silently taking in the damage that had been wrought upon their beloved café. A few folks were picking up chairs and tables and righting them. One regular was gathering the singed remains of the little train whose tracks had been ripped off the wall and rerouted into a now smoldering pile of dishrags on the floor. Fred had a large push broom and was sweeping broken dishes and coffee grounds into a pile. He looked at me and shook his head, then went straight back to sweeping. A couple of gloved up Volunteers were using tongs to put what appeared to be a small, makeshift arrow with a fiercely jagged point into an evidence bag. I finally spotted Roselyn. She was sitting on the floor picking up pieces of broken mug and gently placing them inside a cardboard box. Only a few coffee cups remained intact on the regulars' wall. This was perhaps the most devastating loss of all.

"What happened?" I kneeled beside Roselyn and picked up a piece of pottery that said, "Addicted to Pot" with a picture of a coffee pot under it.

"Puckwudgie." Roslyn sighed. "They usually stick to the forest, but I guess the rains have driven them out."

This was the most straightforward answer anyone had given me since I moved to Mystikos and whether Roselyn was in shock or just feeling like sharing, I wasn't going to miss the opportunity to ask a few more questions. "What's a puckwudgie?"

"They can be a lot of things. Mostly they try to figure out what will scare you most. They're shape shifters." Roselyn found a mug handle and tried to match it to one of the pieces in the box.

"Why would they tear up the Wistful Willow?"

"Mischief, anger, boredom. Who knows? I'm just glad nobody was here when it showed up. Those arrows are poisonous." Roselyn nodded her head towards the Volunteers who had found a second arrow.

"Do all the monsters come from the forest?" I tried to make my voice calm, so Roselyn would keep talking.

Roselyn stopped trying to match the handle and tossed it into the box. "Soara, you have to earn the answers to your questions, just like the regulars earned their mugs on the wall. It's how we protect Mystikos."

"But how do I earn it? Is it a test or something? I'll do whatever I have to do."

"It takes time." Roselyn shifted onto her knees, bringing the box up with her as she stood. "That's all I can say." She slowly made her way to the kitchen.

I poked at the remains of the mug wall with the toe of my galoshes. " But I don't know how much time I have left."

***

There was nothing I could do to help at the Wistful Willow. I pulled my rain hood down low, ducked my head to step back into the deluge and ran smack into Dell and his washboard abs. He put his arms around me to stop from knocking me over.

For a flicker of a second, I wanted to lay my head on Dell's chest and let him hold me, but A- that was silly and B- he hadn't offered. "Sorry. I didn't see you." I forced myself to take a step back.

"I was looking for you. Your mom said you were here." Dell seemed tired. I wondered if he had gotten any sleep over the past few days.

"Did you hear what happened?" I asked.

"Yeah."

"You promised to show me some stuff, remember?" I gave Dell one of my most bossy stares. He grabbed my arm and gently pulled me out of the middle of the road.

"I can't right now. I'm on duty." Dell pushed me under an awning to avoid the rain.

"You're ALWAYS on duty." my temper was picking up again.

"That's sort of the point. When you volunteer, it's forever."

"You're not like a Jedi or something. You didn't take a blood oath. Wait. Did you have to take a blood oath?" I was grossed out thinking about legions of Volunteers dripping blood from their wrists onto a sticky, crimson soaked alter.

"No! And I don't think Jedi's have to take a blood oath either. Look, it's not always like this. I promise. When things calm down again, we'll be able to talk." Dell's eyes kept darting over to the café. A couple more Volunteers had arrived.

"But I'm starting to think it won't ever calm down. Not as long as I'm here." I looked up at Dell. I had been considering this since yesterday, but now that I said it out loud, I was pretty certain it was true.

"Soara, this has been a part of Mystikos since the beginning of time. Maybe before that even. None of us have any real control over it and neither do you." Dell put his hand on my shoulder. I could feel the warmth all the way through my raincoat and sweater.

"I think something brought us here. Something powerful. And I think it wants me to come to the other side." I looked up at Dell. His eyes flickered with fear at the mention of the "other side."

"Dell, we need you. Now." One of the Volunteers called out to Dell from the doorway of the Wistful Willow.

Dell waved to acknowledge his elder. "Soara, I want you to go home and stay safe. Please." He gave my shoulder a squeeze that sent an electric shock through my entire body. My skin was still prickling when he disappeared inside the café.

***

Whatever Dell said, I had no intention of going home. I knew Eteri would be safe with Dave and the dogs nearby and besides, I wasn't up for an afternoon of girl talk. My biggest concern was figuring out a way to protect myself and Eteri when we were outside the padlocked gates of the garage, and I had an idea of how to do it.

Finding my way back to August's house was just a best guess scenario. The tinkling of bells told me I had taken the right path before I ever saw the cottage surrounded by tangled vines. I walked around to what I thought was the front of the house but couldn't figure out a way in. I went up and down the sidewalk and still didn't see any opening or gate. I tried jumping to see over the vines, but they reached too high. I could stick my hand into the dark, oily leaves to try and feel my way to the entrance, but honestly that sounded terrifying. I had read far too many fantasies where the vines secretly had teeth. After 15 minutes of pacing around the cottage, it finally occurred to me to text August and see if she could come outside.

"Hey." August walked up behind me and nearly scared me out of my skin.

"Hi." I squeaked to squelch a scream. "I couldn't figure out your gate."

"Oh yeah, you can't get in unless my mom says its ok and she has to meet you first." August motioned for me to follow her around to what might or might not be the back of the house. "But she'll like you. It's no big deal. Hang on."

"Wait. Is your mom a Witch?...I mean, not a Witch. I know for some people that can be a pejorative term, even though it's not. That's just like a stupid patriarchal construct that witches are something bad. Sorry I'm rambling. I'm nervous."

August suddenly looked annoyed. "I don't really know what she calls herself. But she's not going to put a spell on you or anything if that's what you're afraid of. That's not how it works."

I was mortified I had offended my new friend. That's exactly what I hadn't wanted to do. "No! I know that. It's just...August, I need her help. I need a protection charm. Would she do it?"

August squinted at me, appraising the seriousness and safety of this request. I was aware that everybody knew that Ellie Midwinter cast charms. But most people also thought she'd left whatever real power she had in the same place she left her mind all those years ago.

"You know my mom's not really here right now, right?"

"I don't know what else to do." I shrugged and waited.

After what seemed like an agonizingly long pause, August shrugged back and disappeared into the vines.

I felt oddly exposed standing on the sidewalk outside of August's house. I'd been out in the rain for long enough that the damp space between my raincoat and my galoshes was starting to branch out to other areas of my outfit. Cold, wet, and nervous was not my favorite combination. I wondered how the charm thing worked. Did you pay for it with money? Did you have to promise a future child or give away a couple of days of your life? I'd read some things about teeth being powerful, but I didn't really want to give August's mom any of mine.

August and Ellie weren't on the sidewalk. And then they suddenly were, but I didn't almost scream this time, so that was a good start. I didn't know what I had expected Ellie to look like, but this wasn't it. She didn't seem a bit sick. She was beautiful, with long, shiny black hair and blue eyes. She wasn't dressed like a witch. She was wearing an oversized cardigan and jeans with a pair of faded navy sneakers. And she looked young. If I had met her at school, I would have thought she was another student. It felt somehow disrespectful to keep my rain hood up, so I pulled it back like a cowboy doffing his hat for a lady.

The instant my face was in full view, Ellie's eyes flashed with terror, and she started yelling, "She wants you! I can feel her anger. She was tricked once, but She won't be so foolish again!"

"It's ok. Soara's nice." August tried to calm Ellie.

"She wants to use you, because you have the power to stand on both sides and not get burned! You are the beginning of the end!" Ellie started to pull at her hair, so August gently held her hands.

"You just don't feel good, Mom. Come on, let's go." August pushed her mother through the vines. "I'm sorry. Maybe we can try again when she comes back." Then she followed Ellie into the leaves.

I was left on the sidewalk stunned and shaking. Who was "She?" What was this power Ellie talked about? And what was going to end? My life? Was I going to die? My feet felt like they were sinking into the pavement. Maybe the end was me lying down on this sidewalk and waiting for the rain to wash me away. At this point, it seemed as good an option as anything else, so I tried it. A loud honk pulled me out of my tailspin. It was Nana and Pops with Sierra and Zion in the back seat.

Nana rolled down the passenger window. "What in the heck are you doing passed out on the pavement like a vagabond? You shouldn't be out here all by yourself. Get in. We'll give you a ride home."

I was more than willing to follow orders at this point, so I picked myself up off the sidewalk. Sierra threw open the back seat door and I climbed right inside. I had to crawl over a few boxes to get to the middle seat and sit cross legged because the floorboard was full. Upon closer inspection, I realized the SUV was filled to the brim with boxes of ammo and explosives and I wondered if the FBI was keeping tabs on the Claybourne's munitions supply.

"Try not to sneeze, you could blow us all to kingdom come." Zion joked in her usual sarcastic manner.

"Nana and Pops just wanted to do one last pick up in case the roads close." Sierra shot her sister a look.

The car pulled past the Lovell Mansion. As the government headquarters of Mystikos it was hopping. Two Volunteers stood outside the front gate checking various citizens in and out. It struck me that the town didn't seem to have a police department. "What about the police?" I asked.

"Don't need 'em. The townies use the Volunteers and Pops and I serve our own brand of justice," Nana shot back.

"But who makes the laws?" I was genuinely curious.

"Police don't make the laws. They enforce them. Mystikos' laws were written a very long time ago. Nana and I don't agree with all of them, but for the most part they keep people in line," said Pops, dodging a pothole.

"But what happens if someone breaks the laws?" As soon as I said it, Sierra gave me a look that warned I was entering dangerous territory.

"That's why our house is built just outside of town. We moved when the girls' parents were killed. Decided we were done protecting anyone or anything but ourselves. The Volunteers have tried to stop us a few times, but they don't have any power outside of the city limits." Pops chuckled. He clearly loved their little loophole.

"I thought your parents died in a car accident." I gave Sierra a puzzled look.

"They did." Said Sierra nervously.

"Uh-oh cat's out of the bag now," said Zion.

"Which one is it?" I looked at Zion this time. She didn't seem to be too tied to the Mystikos oath of silence.

"A big, fat, wendigo bit my parents while they were on a camping trip and turned them into bloodsucking cannibals that harvest souls," Zion spit out in a way that dared me to be shocked.

"Zion, stop," Sierra begged.

"Pops had to help the Volunteers hunt them down, kill them, and burn them to ashes so they couldn't infect anyone else." Sierra was now reaching past me to pinch Zion's leg, but she knocked her hand away. "But they couldn't bury them because it might curse the ground, so we keep them in a jar in that room you can't go into in the house. Along with whatever other gremlins and ghouls Nana and Pops have shot and stuffed for "educational purposes."

"That's enough, young lady." Nana warned.

"What, are you gonna do, ground me? Locking me up in your compound 24 hours a day, except for ammo excursions isn't enough?" Zion spit back.

"Zion, Nana and Pops just want to protect us." Sierra was the peacekeeper.

"Whatever. Here's your house." Zion nodded towards the window as the SUV pulled up outside the garage gates.

Dave was once again waiting with Watcher and Sentinel. He stepped forward to help me out of the car and spied the boxes on the floorboard.

"You know that isn't how we do things." Dave gave Nana and Pops a disapproving look.

"See how you feel when one of those things comes after your kid." Pops revved the engine and pulled away before I could say goodbye to my friends.

"I told your mom you were still at the café because I didn't want her to worry. You have to be careful, Soara. This weather is getting out of hand. Anything could happen," Dave gently admonished.

"Right. It's the *weather* I need to be scared of. Thanks for the warning. I'm going to the library." I started to walk away but Dave grabbed my arm.

"At least take Watcher and Sentinel with you and make sure you're home before dark," Dave said shoving the dogs' leashes into my hand. His face registered fatherly concern, something I wasn't used to. On the one hand it felt safe and on the other, I wasn't interested in new authority figures. I accepted the leashes but didn't respond as I let the dogs lead me down the street.

I liked belonging to Watcher and Sentinel. Though they were indisputably graceful and lithe, which made them seem more like precious lap dogs than vicious protectors, I certainly wouldn't want to make them angry. I had a feeling they could do some serious damage if they wanted to. Eteri and I had taken several self-defense classes over the years, and I was more than aware of all the tender spots on a human being (particularly of the male variety) but there was something much more confidence inducing about walking with your very own set of matching bodyguards. I was lost in this thought when the leashes jerked me suddenly to the side, almost causing me to slip on the wet sidewalk. "No, we're going to the library." I tried to right the dogs, but they had picked up an interesting scent and wanted a closer look.

It struck me that Watcher and Sentinel were greyhounds with the power of super speed. If they really tried to take off, my choices were let go or be dragged across the pavement like a human cheese grater. "Ok, compromise? We can take a quick look, but then we gotta go." I relaxed my grip on the leashes and let the dogs lead me where they wanted to go which was across the street and over some grass with a very clearly posted "Do not walk on the grass" sign. "Ok, rule breakers. Let's stick to the approved paths." I teased. The pups pulled me up a set of steps, through a gravel planter and into a gutter that had been dammed up with fallen leaves. "Seriously, where are you going?" They were getting farther and farther from the library.

Watcher and Sentinel tugged me around a corner, down a narrow alley and sat down directly in front of a dumpster. "All this for some trash? They have trash at the library, you know." I shook my head and tried to pull the dogs back to the sidewalk, but they wouldn't budge.

"What? I get it. There's probably some delicious, rotted leftovers in there or something, but I'm not going in to get it for you, so can we just move on?" I pulled again, but the dogs remained fixated by the dumpster. "So, what do we do here? Do I leave you at the dumpster and tell Dave to come get his very bad doggies? Do you want me to call your dad? I'll do it. I have a cell phone." Watcher and Sentinel weren't one bit phased by my threats. "Fine. Let me see what's in here."

I slowly stepped forward and put my hand out to lift up the dumpster lid. I had just gotten my thumb under the lip when there was a huge bang and the whole dumpster lurched out of my reach. "Oh, hell no!" I started pulling on Watcher and Sentinel's leashes with all my might. Whatever was in the dumpster had woken up and now it was angry. It continued slamming itself into the insides of the bin.

Watcher and Sentinel started barking and pulling. "This is not how bodyguarding works. You don't take me TO the danger."

I suddenly thought I heard someone call for help. It could have been my own mind, since I was hearing thoughts that were not my own lately, but I was pretty sure it was coming from inside the dumpster. It could also be a trick. I didn't think there was any honor amongst monsters, but when I heard the voice again, I knew I couldn't leave without making sure there wasn't an innocent person trapped inside.

"I'm opening the lid and I have two very bitey dogs out here with a questionable vaccination record." I let go of the leashes and shoved at the lid, flipping it all the way back. Nothing ate my face off, so I dared to look inside.

I imagined a million different nightmares waiting for me in that dumpster, but instead I found Dell, with his wrists and ankles tied together and his whole body covered in some kind of disgusting goo. I didn't scream, I didn't faint. I laughed. I laughed so hard I couldn't breathe. Watcher and Sentinel became concerned for my mental health and started licking my face to stop the fit.

"Can you help me out, please." Dell was understandably annoyed. It looked like he'd been stuck for a while.

Somehow, I managed to pull myself together, but peering into the dumpster, it became undeniable that the only way to help Dell get out, was if I got IN. "Give me a second. I need something to stand on." I looked around for something to give me a leg up, but my only option was Watcher and Sentinel. "You guys, I need your help. Can you give me a push?" As if the dogs understood perfect English, they scooted towards me and I was able to nudge myself up onto the lip of the dumpster and let the dogs gently tip me in.

"Ow." I went in headfirst which was neither graceful nor painless. Luckily there didn't seem to be anything in the dumpster but Dell; however, whatever he was drenched in smelled like rotting regret.

"Can you untie me?" Dell scooted himself closer and I tried not to audibly gag from the scent.

"Yeah. Just a second." I fumbled with the slimy fabric holding Dell's wrists together. "What is this stuff?"

"I don't know if there's a name for it." Dell mumbled, trying not to get any of it in his mouth. "Frog man got me."

I finally managed to get Dell undone but he stayed curled up in a ball.

"My arms and legs are asleep. Can you straighten me out?" Dell was clearly embarrassed about his predicament, but there was nothing he could do about it.

I helped Dell stretch out his stiff arms and legs and sit up. I now had about as much of the frog man goo on me as he did on him, but at least I was starting to get used to the stench. "Do you think you can climb out?" I asked.

"I'll try." Dell slowly tried to stand while I climbed back out of the dumpster. Once I was on the ground, I reached my hands back in to help pull him out.

"Ok, on three I'm gonna pull and you jump out." I steadied myself to take best advantage of leverage. "One, two, three."

I heaved, and in Dell's mind, he jumped, but his legs weren't listening. He ended up hanging over the side of the trash bin and I could swear I saw the dogs laughing at him. "Let's try one more time. One, two, three!" I pulled again and this time the goo worked in our favor, making Dell just slippery enough to slide out of the dumpster and right on top of me. The dogs ran over to check on us and started licking at the goo. "Ew. Don't. You're gonna have frog man breath." I swatted at the dogs and then realized Dell was still on top of me. "Um. Are you stuck?"

"I think I can roll off." Dell swayed himself left and right and rolled onto his back beside me. Frog Man goo was apparently water soluble because the rain was starting to wash it away. We silently agreed we might as well let the weather do the dirty work and stayed on our backs on the pavement, with Watcher and Sentinel trying to sneak licks in when they could.

Dell started his story. "They sent me from the café to follow up on a call that someone had seen a large, amphibious creature walking on two legs, skulking around the downtown area."

"Sounds super normal," I added sarcastically. Dell ignored me and kept going.

"I spotted the Frog Man ducking into this alley and followed him, hoping to take him into custody without any issue. Frog Men aren't generally considered dangerous, so I didn't think I needed to call for back up."

"Ah, twas hubris that got you." Dell shot me a dirty look. "Sorry, I won't interrupt again."

"When I got into the alley, it turns out there were two Frog Men and they jumped me, tied me up, and threw me in the dumpster. I don't think they wanted to hurt me, but they definitely weren't interested in going home. I figured someone would find me eventually and you did, so, thanks." Dell was starting to get the feeling back in his body. He sat up and stretched his arms.

"Where is home for a Frog Man?"

"The other side. That's where all of them are from."

"What is the other side?" I held my breath, hoping Dell would keep giving me answers.

"I think we should go see Julie." Dell stood up and offered me a hand.

I let him pull me up. For a moment we were so close I could feel Dell's breath on my cheek, and under any other circumstances, standing face to face in the rain would be the moment when the two lovers share their first kiss. I did want to kiss him. I had absolutely thought of kissing him, way more than I wanted to admit. I had an ongoing theory his lips tasted like a mixture of chapstick and maple syrup. But instead of kissing Dell, I took a step back and whistled for Watcher and Sentinel.

***

Julie was waiting inside the library with a couple of towels and a bottle of vinegar. "Rub it on your skin. It's strong, but it'll cut through the frog smell." She handed everything over. "I'll take the dogs to get rinsed off and bring you back some clean clothes. Why don't you go to the fireplace room?" Her smart heels click clacked across the marble and she vanished into the stacks.

Dell and I made our way to the fireplace room. We were afraid to touch anything, so we stood on either side of the hearth and started peeling out of our raincoats and galoshes.

Julie came back in with a pair of pants, a sweatshirt, and a clean pair of socks over either arm. "I'll just leave these on the couch. Ring the bell when you're ready." Then off she went again.

We eyed the clothing and then each other. Were we just supposed to change right here in the middle of the library, together?

"I can turn my back and then you can turn your back." Dell shyly suggested. "If you're ok with that."

"Sure. Ok." I motioned for Dell to turn, and he did so dutifully. Once I was certain there wasn't anything reflective he could sneak a peek with in front of him, I started to pull off my wet, stinky clothes.

"If I didn't say thank you before, then thank you." Dell said, keeping his back turned.

"You thanked me. Besides, it's not like you've never saved me. Guess now we're even." I poured some vinegar on my towel and rubbed it all over myself as quickly as I could. I smelled like a freshly dyed Easter egg now, but it was better than frog stink. "The vinegar actually works." I slid the bottle across the floor to Dell.

"Does it?" Without thinking, Dell started to turn around to grab the bottle.

"Don't turn around! I don't have anything on!" I ducked behind a chair until Dell's eyes were back to the front.

"Sorry. I didn't mean to." Dell apologized.

"It's ok." I pulled on the clean clothes as quickly as I could and put my back to Dell. "I'm turned around now. You can go."

Dell performed the same routine of removing his clothes and wiping off the last traces of frog goo with vinegar. "Where do you think Julie got these clothes from?" he asked.

"I don't know. She always has everything. Maybe she's a secret hoarder and her lair is under the building." I laughed at the thought of neat as a pin Julie hoarding anything.

"I've known her forever, but she still always makes me feel a little bit weird. I'm done." Dell kicked his pile of clothes away and waited for me to turn around.

"What should we do with these" I asked, pointing to the piles of clothes.

"Burn them." Dell answered and kicked his pile into the fire.

I followed suit. Maybe we shouldn't have both done it at the same time. Frog goo was apparently highly flammable. The fire jumped in the fireplace and spit a confetti of smoking orange coals onto the probably extremely expensive rug.

"Stomp it. Quick!" I jumped onto the rug and started clomping around in my stockinged feet.

It took a minute or so, and I'm sure we looked like we were doing an improvisational version of Riverdance, but we got all the embers stomped out before there was any major damage to the rug, then both of us collapsed onto the sofa in a fit of laughter. "My stomach hurts." I gasped in between giggles.

"I thought we were going to burn down the library. So much for my new socks." Dell held up his foot and wiggled his big toe through a burn hole.

"My mother would tell you to just go barefoot. I can hardly ever get her to wear shoes." I pulled my singed socks off and held my naked foot out towards Dell. "She says it helps her connect her energy chakras."

"Did you burn your foot?" Dell leaned in to get a closer look. He ran his finger over the bottom of my foot and it felt strangely intimate. I pulled it back.

"No. It's a birthmark. My mom has the exact same one," I said, still buzzing from his touch.

"May I see it?" Julie entered the room with Watcher and Sentinel. She let go of their leashes and they ran to lay in front of the fire.

Dell and I broke apart as if we'd been doing something far more fun and interesting than what was actually occurring. Julie sat in the middle of us and reached out for my foot.

I hadn't spent a whole lot of my life thinking about my birthmark. I rarely even saw it- it was underneath my foot after all, but for some reason in the past couple of days it was becoming a hot topic. "Is there something wrong with my foot?"

"No. It's exactly as I suspected." Julie put my foot down and set her hands in her lap.

It was silent for a moment. Julie stared into the fire and smiled. If weird was something palpable, this was it.

"How did you know about my birthmark?" I scooted in closer. I wasn't going to just let Julie disappear this time.

"It's a commonality among your kind. The mark of your creation."

I looked at Dell, but he just shrugged.

"What is my kind?" I had always assumed my "kind" was human, but figuring out the right questions to ask Julie was almost as much of a mystery as the answers you were looking for.

Julie cocked her head to one side. "That's very complex," but she offered nothing else.

"My mother has the same birthmark. Is she like me too?"

"Yes, that is why both of you have the mark. Another kind has the mark for a different reason." Julie smoothed her skirt and stood. I stood with her. I wasn't done asking questions yet.

"Ok. What *other* kind has the mark?"

Julie's eyes looked up towards the stained-glass windows. There were only three Elementals left. Of course, there was no way to recreate the one that had shattered. That windowpane was now filled with clear glass. "They do."

I felt like a sword had stabbed through the top of my head and pinned me to the floor. I couldn't speak. I couldn't move, but I was suddenly hyper aware of everything in the room. Dell kept opening and closing his mouth, but no sound came out.

"It's nearly dark. I'm afraid I have to send you home now." Julie gently took Dell and me by the elbows. She clicked her tongue and

Watcher and Sentinel followed as we walked to the doors. "Good night." Julie handed us each an umbrella, and with that, we found ourselves standing outside the library doors with Watcher and Sentinel by our sides.

***

Dell and I didn't speak on the way home. We each held a dog leash and let ourselves be led back to the garage while our thoughts jumped forward and backwards through time trying to make some sense of what was happening. Watcher and Sentinel sat down in front of the garage gates and waited patiently. I finally turned to Dell and whispered, "Tell me about the other side."

Dell took a deep breath. It was obviously a lot for him to try and put together all at once.

"The people who built Mystikos believed that there were places in the world where the curtain between dimensions is open, allowing beings from the other side in. People on this side call those beings monsters and demons. Legends and folklore are full of stories of mythical creatures people swear they've seen but humans can't find any proof of. Some of them have powers, some of them are destructive, but to the Volunteers this was part of the push and pull of existence, the natural order. No one thing could exist without all things, so, they didn't attach evil to what they didn't understand. They wanted to learn more about the other side, but in their own country, they were considered witches or devil worshipers in communion with the wicked. It wasn't safe, so they came to the new world to search for a doorway here. And they found Mystikos. The first Volunteers took a vow to protect the creatures from the other side because destroying them would mean destruction of our own world. The doorway only opens at night and most times the creatures that come here are gone by the morning. They're just curious or bored, maybe they're hungry, but they aren't really after humans. If we stay out of their way, they go back home and nothing happens, but something has upset the balance. It's like a traffic jam, and we can't get the monsters back in as fast as the doorway is spitting them out. It started happening the day you and your mother got here."

I had to will my mind not to split into a million pieces. Monsters were real, Mystikos was a portal to another dimension, and me and my mom had somehow hung the "welcome one and all" sign on the door. "Then we have to leave Mystikos. We can't stay here if we're the reason all this is happening."

"You leaving won't stop it."

"How do you know?"

"Because if that's all it took, the Volunteers would have made sure you left a long time ago. And also, Julie wouldn't help you if you were something bad." Dell reached out to touch my arm and I found myself crumpling into him.

"Why didn't anyone tell us? We could have made a choice."

"Because if we told everyone who passes through town what Mystikos really is, every Big Foot cryptid conspiracy theorist in the world would descend. Part of protecting Mystikos is keeping its secrets.

"Something from the other side wants me. It's been coming for me in my dreams. It's hasn't been able to take me yet, but I think it's getting stronger."

"I won't let anyone hurt you. I promise." Dell bent down and kissed the top of my head.

I don't think he even realized what he was doing, but I reacted to the gesture with equal lack of thought. I lifted my chin and devoured Dell with the kind of kiss that leaves an imprint on your soul. I didn't consider who could be watching or whether or not this was an intelligent move. Every molecule of my body was either made of fear or need in that moment and one of those things could be fixed by kissing Dell.

"Sun's setting. Dell, are you staying here tonight?" Dave had unlocked the gate and who knows how much he had seen, but he asked the question without a hint of judgement.

"Yeah. I'm staying."

Dave nodded and allowed us inside. Watcher and Sentinel trotted behind us, then the gates closed and locked with a metallic click.

CHAPTER THIRTEEN

The thing about having a mom like Eteri is they go with the flow. It was no big deal that my new friend Dell was spending the night, and although Eteri adored listening to me tell her all about my day, she didn't double down on the details if they weren't given.

Our new little "family" ate dinner together down in the garage. Afterwards, Eteri stayed to talk to Dave and me and Dell went up to my room to get some privacy. We definitely needed to talk about some things. And now kissing was on the table, which was very, very nice, and incredibly hard to stop thinking about, but definitely not going to help me figure out how to keep us all safe.

"This is so... blue." Dell started by stating the obvious.

"Yeah. I didn't decorate it, but I like it. It's kind of like being in the sky, or underwater, whichever place you prefer to float." I sat on the bed and then stood right back up because I didn't want Dell to think I was making some kind of suggestion. Instead, I plopped onto the blue vinyl bean bag chair on the floor and motioned that Dell could take the end of the bed for himself.

"Do you want to talk about it?" Dell asked.

"Which part?"

"Let's start with you and me."

"Ok. Me first. I think you are very attractive and that was a spectacular kiss, and I would like to do more of that."

Dell sat down on the bed. "Same."

"But let's not put any kind of label on this until we figure out if I'm gonna be sucked into a portal to another dimension. Very one day at a time."

Dell seemed to run this scenario through his mind. "I mean any of us could be sucked into another dimension at any moment. Life is unpredictable."

"True. I have a lot of questions about that. But let's kiss first and talk later."

And so, we did.

I had kissed other boys and several girls as well, but I'd never felt so melty about it. I wanted to walk through Dell. I wanted to trace a map of the universe on his body with my fingers. There was no part of him I didn't want to touch. I could kiss him forever, but I knew that Eteri would be coming upstairs soon and even though my mom wouldn't care if I was kissing a boy in my room, it still felt like an "ew" scenario.

I pulled back and placed two blue flowered bed pillows in between myself and Dell to try and weaken the magnets that seemed to be pulling our bodies together. "When did you become a Volunteer?"

"Technically, you can't be one until you are 18, but because my whole family has been doing it forever, I'm kind of allowed to be an apprentice I guess."

"Is everyone in Mystikos a Volunteer? I mean is the whole town like some kind of cult or something?"

Dell laughed softly. "It's not a cult. I mean, it's kind of a way of believing I guess, but you don't have to believe in anything if you live here. You choose if you want to live here, and you choose if you want to become a Volunteer."

"Do you get like secret tattoos or take vows or what?"

"No tattoos. You do take an oath, just like people do when they go in the army or become a Supreme Court justice, but that's because it's a big deal and you have to know what you're getting into."

"And you protect the monsters from the other side, even the dangerous ones? What about that wendigo thing that killed Sierra and Zion's parents?"

Dell took a deep breath. "It's like I said. Yes, some of the monsters are dangerous, but they aren't HERE to hurt anyone. It's like if a bear mauls somebody who surprises it in the woods. It's terrible and violent, but we don't say the bear is evil. It was being a bear. It's the same way with the monsters. We are all part of the universe. The other side exists for a reason, and we have to preserve it."

"Well, what's the reason?" I sat up. I wanted my wits about me for this explanation and vertical seemed like a better way to achieve that goal.

Dell sat up with me, so we would still be face to face. "We don't know everything. I don't know if that's even possible, but there have been people over time that have come up with theories about the other side."

"Like that Paracelsus guy? Julie gave me a book about him."

"Yes. So, the Elementals. Do you know what I'm talking about? The things in the windows."

I nodded at Dell then my stomach flipped over. Julie had said the Elementals are the only other beings with the mark me and Eteri share, so there must be some connection.

"They are sort of "in charge" of nature. They each have a thing, earth, air, fire, and water. And they control that part of our world, but they have rules too. They can only come into our world during the two solstices each year, and even then, only from sundown until sunrise."

"What do they do when they're here?"

"We aren't sure, but something about them being here is important for nature to keep going. Like the changing of the seasons and weather and all kinds of stuff we probably don't even know about yet."

"Why can't they be here the rest of the time if the monsters can come whenever they want? I've seen the monsters during the day too. Is that just because the portal won't close?"

"The monsters can only enter and leave our dimension when the portal is open, but they can exist here all the time. I mean I'm sure you've heard stories of people seeing lake monsters or yetis during the day. Sometimes they just decide to live here for a while. They can basically go back and forth, but the Elementals can't. They don't have a soul and without a soul, they can't stay here. Well, technically there have been times when they did. They tried to push the rules, but it causes chaos in our world. That's when you get things like ice ages. It's apocalypse stuff."

"Can we go to where they live?" I knew that something wanted to take me to the other side, but would that mean I'd burst into flames or disintegrate immediately upon entry?

"No. Humans can't exist in their world either. A few have tried to enter, but they don't come back, and if they do, they aren't the same."

"Is that what happened to August's mom?"

"Yeah. When Ellie was pregnant with August, she went into the woods at night. She had had a hard time getting pregnant. She thought that the portal's magic helped give her August and she wanted to offer it a thank you. So, she made a charm and she planned to wait for the portal to open and put the charm in, as a gift. She didn't go alone. She took August's father. The portal opened and Ellie thought that because she didn't want anything from it, that it would accept her. She only got as far in as her wrist, and something started happening. We'll never know what for sure. August's dad tried to save her. It killed him on the spot. Ellie lived, but her brain came back scrambled and even though the portal didn't take the part of her that she put inside, it took August's hand while she was still in her mother's belly."

"So, if whatever wants me succeeds, I can look forward to either death or going crazy. Great choices." I had nervously picked a tiny hole in my bedspread. I had the urge to start ripping the whole thing to shreds. My nose burned with tears that were trying to race up to my eyes, but I gritted my teeth to keep them at bay.

"There has to be a way to figure out your connection to the portal. We'll find it." Dell reached out and took my hand.

"Hey you two. There're extra blankets in the hall closet if you need them." Eteri had come back into the apartment without us noticing. We weren't doing anything, and she was only talking through the closed door, but it still made both of us sit up straighter and stop holding hands.

"Thanks, Mom. Goodnight."

"Goodnight my little Sparrow. You too, Dell." Eteri trilled through the door and then we heard her bare feet pad down the hallway and close the door to her own room.

"We should sleep too. We'll go back to see Julie tomorrow." Dell pushed my hair behind my ear and gave me another gentle kiss.

"Your parents won't worry about you?" I asked quietly.

"They'll just assume I'm out on patrol."

I nodded, and without any more words, me and Dell scooted under the covers and wrapped ourselves into the perfect spoon where I almost instantly fell into a deep sleep.

***

I was back in the woods in the clearing full of dandelions. Every step I took sent millions of white fluffy fairies floating all around me. I held out a finger, waiting for one to light there, but soon realized that none of the feathery seeds were coming down. Once I began to pay attention, I noticed that the fluffs were coming together into a shape. Long, thin fingers reached out from a hand that hung above my head. The dandelion hand reached down and gently cupped my chin, then led me across the clearing. On the other side, a Trompe l'oeil forest was painted on a curtain. The dandelion hand pulled the curtain aside and I found myself staring into a reflection of the clearing, but in that reflection, the colors were brighter. Everything vibrated with a glimmer and even though it was silent, it felt like the sky was singing to me. With every fiber of my being, I wished to go to this other clearing and hear the rest of the song. I stepped inside. Instantly, I felt electricity pulse through my body. It didn't hurt, it felt glorious, powerful, strong. The song was so beautiful. I wanted to know who was singing in the sky and I wanted to join them. The only thing that could make it more perfect was if I could share this moment with my friends. I looked across the boundary of the curtain. Dell, Sierra, Zion, Matthew, Noah, and August were in the clearing searching for me. They were frantic and sad. I called out to them, but they couldn't hear me, so I asked the Dandelion hand to show them the way.

Dell was the first to step into the portal. He smiled and ran to me while the others made their way inside. I had never felt so happy or fulfilled. I reached out for Dell's hand, but as soon as we touched, his face morphed from happiness to intense pain. Tiny flames licked his fingers, but I couldn't let him go. The sparks spread over his body, consuming Dell in fire. The rest of my friends came to help Dell, but as soon as they touched him, they also caught fire. I screamed for it to stop. I tried to let go and save everyone, but it was too late. All around me the clearing burned red hot. When my friends were burned to nothing but bones, the dandelion hand scooped up the inferno and took it to the other side of the curtain, where it turned my own world into a fiery hell.

I woke up screaming. Dell was wrapped around me, trying to calm me down. "Soara, it's just a dream. I'm here."

Soon there was a frantic knock at the door. Eteri's usually calm voice was shaking. "Soara, let me in. What's happening?"

"She had a nightmare." Dell called from the bed.

I was finally starting to come back to myself. I could still taste the smoke from the dream in my throat, but I managed to crackle out an answer to my frightened mother. "I'm ok, Mom. I'm ok now."

"Are you sure?" Eteri was not convinced.

"Yeah, Mom. Just give me a minute." I balled myself into Dell's arms.

Dell held me gently and waited until I was ready to tell him about my dream.

#

Zion, Noah, Matthew, Sierra, and August sat on the floor in my living room. Dave was at work and Eteri was helping at the café. Roselyn and Fred had convinced Eteri the storm caused all the damage at the restaurant, and luckily, she was more than happy to pitch in for the cleanup, so we all had a place to talk where no one would overhear. Every time I blinked I thought I could

Still see flames dancing around the silhouettes of my friends, and it caused me to shiver. Dell grabbed a knitted throw from the end of the couch and placed it around my shoulders.

"So, in the dream, you could go into the portal, but we couldn't?" Sierra asked, holding a spiral that she was taking notes in.

"Yes. Actually, no. I mean you could go into the portal, but if you did, you caught on fire." I answered.

Zion was much more, well Zion, in terms of her participation in the conversation. "So we would basically turn into roasted people kabobs."

"Yes." In spite of the terrible imagery, I couldn't help laughing a little.

"Was there anybody else there but us?" Matthew asked.

"Just the dandelion hand."

"But it was just a hand, right? You never saw a face or heard a voice or anything?" Noah was sitting knee to knee with Zion, but they were putting on their usual show of just being friends.

"Well, I heard the singing, but that was more like a choir. And I don't even know if there were really words to the song. I wish I could at least remember how the tune went." I tried to squeeze any other tiny bits of info out of my brain, but there was nothing.

"What about your mom? Have you told her about these dreams?" Sierra was flipping back through her spiral and making notes on her notes.

"My mom is not a worrier. She'd make it out to be the manifestation of birth canal trauma or something equally weird. I love her, but she's not the best about being grounded." I tried not to sound as exasperated as I felt about this.

"Where's your mom's room? Let's snoop." Zion stood up and did a stretch to ready herself for espionage.

"It's down the hall, but really, you're probably just gonna find some crystals and half-drunk glasses of barley tea in there." I stood up from the couch, letting the blanket fall around my ankles and followed Zion to Eteri's room. Everyone else was right behind me.

Zion opened the door to my mother's room and put her hands on her hips. The bed was unmade, and some incense was still burning in the corner. Per my premonition, there were many mismatched tea mugs scattered around the room and a little cloth laid across the dresser with Eteri's collection of crystals on top placed in a semi-circle. The closet door was open and revealed a few feathery, lacy, gypsy dresses and a couple of shawls on the hangers, alongside several bunches of wildflowers and herbs tied to the closet pole to dry for making smudging bundles.

"Everyone has a habitual hiding place." Zion walked into the room and sat on the bed to better scope things out.

"I don't think my mom's hiding anything." I returned.

"Not from you, but maybe from herself. Or maybe in her mind, she calls it a "collection." But everyone has a stash of interesting crap. Humans are essentially packrats with phones." Zion bounced on the bed a few times, then leaned over the side and reached her hand between the mattress and the box spring. "Well, well, well, what's this?" She pulled out a knife about as long as her forearm, with a delicately carved pearl handle.

"There's this superstition that if you sleep with a knife under your mattress, it'll stop a backache. Mom swears it fixes her lumbar issues." I had seen that knife many times.

Zion shrugged and tucked the knife back into its spot, then she stood up and pulled a nightstand away from the wall. "You guys look behind the other one."

There was nothing behind the nightstands, nothing in the drawers that was terribly interesting (although we did find a jar with a dead, dried out frog in it and an envelope filled with a bunch of sugar packets). There was also nothing on the top shelf of the closet. To be fair, Zion knew these were all rookie places to start, but she saw no reason to leave off the obvious in a thorough search.

"Ok. What does your mom love the most?" Zion asked.

"Me, I guess." I answered.

"You'd probably know if she hid something IN you. Ok, what does your mother hate the most?"

"Eteri doesn't hate anything." I thought for a moment. "Ok. She hates television. She says they were made to steal time.

"Noah, give me a hand." Zion walked over to the little black and white T.V. sitting on a wooden crate filled with John Phillips Souza records. Eteri had thrown an embroidered pillowcase over it, to pretend the machine wasn't there. It wasn't even plugged in.

Noah picked up the T.V. and set it on the bed. "Do you have a screwdriver?"

"Um. Maybe." I answered. I tried to think of where to start looking, but Matthew pulled a camping knife out of his pocket instead.

"There's nail clippers and a level on it too." Matthew handed over the knife and Noah set to work.

"This seems weird. I can't really see my mom engaging in appliance tampering." I was starting to really feel uncomfortable going through Eteri's things.

"Maybe it's like how people sometimes hide their money in a soup can." Dell offered.

"Our Pops hides money everywhere. He doesn't believe in banks." Sierra interjected.

"Ah Ha!" Got it!" There was a little click as Noah pulled the back of the T.V. away and Zion stuck her hand inside. "It's hollow."

Everyone piled on the bed. Zion lifted a pink box from the console. The kind with a removeable lid that you might get at a fancy department store. She held it out to me. “Here. You should open this. She’s your mom.”

I took the box and looked at Dell. He nodded. I slowly removed the lid and set it aside. There was yellowed tissue paper covering the contents of the box, so I put it on the bed to get to what was underneath. Inside was a tattered blanket and a small piece of paper upon which someone had written the name “Eteri” in scratchy print.

“This is like my mom’s story. This is how she said they found her when she was a baby.”

“Something fell out of the blanket.” Sierra pointed near my leg.

I picked up the small memento. It was a triangle of twisted twigs with another bit woven into a line across the top. “She never said anything about this. It was always just the blanket and her name.”

“I think I’ve seen that before.” Matthew gently took the piece from Soara.

“Yeah. We’ve all seen a triangle genius.” Zion thumped Matthew in the forehead for emphasis.

“No. It’s not just a regular triangle.” Matthew held it up to show the extra line across the top quarter of the shape. “I think it’s a symbol.”

Watcher and Sentinel started barking at something in the yard and everyone jumped.

“Is there anything else in there?” Dell asked.

Zion looked around and declared the TV otherwise all clear.

“Put everything back.” I refilled the box and started to put the lid back on when the voice in my head suddenly spoke again.

“Keep it.” Although the voice didn’t specify what I was supposed to keep, I took the twig triangle back out of the box before replacing the lid and shoving it back into the T.V.

Noah hurried to screw the set back together, then stuck it back on top of the crate and everyone scooted out of the room, landing back on the sofa just in time for Eteri to throw the door open holding two paper bags out in front of her.

"Fred sent over lunch!"

Eteri had barely tossed the bags onto the table before everyone attacked them. Espionage clearly whipped up the appetite. I wrapped my fingers around the twig triangle and slipped it behind my back.

***

After everyone had gone home, Dell and I walked into town. He had a shift with the Volunteers and I was going to the library to quiz Julie.

"Why didn't you tell everyone else about the voice?" Dell whispered as if the voice might be spying on him too.

"Because it makes me feel like I'm one of them and not one of us."

"One of who?"

"The monsters." I walked a little bit faster, so I didn't have to look Dell in the eye.

"You are not a monster, Soara." Dell reached out to slow me down.

"You don't know that. You said they can live here or on the other side. Maybe I'm a monster and I just don't remember, and I look like everybody else, but I'm different on the inside. I've never broken a bone; did you know that? So I've never even had an x-ray. There could be anything in here." I pointed to my chest and Dell grabbed my finger and pulled it away.

"Stop it."

"What if you found me that night because you're supposed to take me back to where I belong?"

"This is where you belong." Dell pulled me into a kiss.

I wanted a million more kisses. I wanted to breathe in every molecule of Dell. I could happily be lost in Dell's arms forever, but the voice in my head brought me back.

"You need to show her." The Voice was cryptic as ever, but I knew I needed to show Julie my mother's memento.

"You're gonna be late." I forced myself to take a step backwards.

"I'll call you tonight." Dell snuck in one more kiss before walking towards the fire station.

I waited in case the Voice had any more instructions, but it was silent, so I turned towards the library.

Julie joined me at the fireplace for tea and cookies that day. She was wearing gray, but it didn't suit her. I thought Julie looked drained, as if her outfit used to be a brighter color that had been leached away. I was distracted by a tiny pull on the cuff of Julie's cardigan. On her, even an insignificant flaw seemed horribly out of place. I noticed that Julie hadn't taken a single sip of her tea. "It's gonna get cold."

"I really don't drink tea, but it seems lonely to only put out one cup." Julie answered, recrossing her hands in her lap to cover her imperfect cuff.

"I want to show you something." I dug in the pocket of my jacket and plucked out the small triangle.

Julie gently took the little handwoven piece and held it in the palm of her hand. "Each of the Elements has its own symbol. This is the one for air."

"My mother was abandoned as a baby. All she had when they found her was a blanket, her name, and this." I was hopeful Julie would have some explanation.

"She doesn't know who she is." Julie held up the triangle and let the firelight shine through it.

"Can you tell me who my mother is?"

Julie looked back at me. There was the briefest flicker of sympathy in her eyes, and then her usual neutrality returned. "You know the rules."

"But nobody asked me if I wanted to play the game."

"I have a book for you." Julie lifted the teapot from the tray. It was sitting on top of a tiny, blood red manuscript, tied closed with a velvet ribbon.

"I never thought I'd say that I'm sick of reading." I took the book. It felt much heavier than its size indicated, and I wondered if the weight was some kind of magic, or if I was just that tired.

"I have to go. There's so much to do. Thank you for showing this to me. It's a treasure." Julie stood and smoothed her skirt. She handed the talisman back to me and within a blink, she had disappeared around a bookcase.

I untied the ribbon on the little book. The leaves of paper-thin vellum within were fragile and nearly transparent. It had to be extremely old. The ink on the first few pages had faded or been scratched away, the words lost forever. For a moment, I panicked that the answers I needed were on those pages, but then I remembered that Julie did not make mistakes. I flipped forward and discovered what looked like a jumble of random pictographic symbols. But on closer inspection, I realized it was text written in an alphabet I had never seen before. My stomach once again lurched at the thought the answers could be here, but still out of reach. I closed the book and took a deep breath to center myself, then I gently flipped back to where I had been before and set the little triangle of twigs on the page to hold my place. The instant the Air talisman touched the page, the words within the triangle became clear to me. I bent closer to the book. Outside of the triangle the letters were still foreign, but inside, it wasn't that the letters were different, but that I was somehow able to understand what I was reading.

The book told the tale of a creation split into three separate worlds, the realm of the humans, the realm of the spirits and the realm of chaos. Within the human realm, the sun and moon shared rule over time and all beings were born with a soul which anchored them in this world until death. The spirit realm was filled with great beings who controlled nature and fate. Their power was so strong that it created beings of its own, which populated their world. Some of these beings were terrible and violent, some of them were benevolent and given the power of protection, but not being wholly spirit or soul bound, the creatures could travel amongst all the realms. The great ones had no soul, but were anchored by their magic, only allowed to pass into the human realm twice yearly to continue the cycle of nature. They were jealous beings and wanted to possess all creation, so they were forever seeking ways to escape the spirit realm and take over the world of souls. The third realm was chaos. It was locked until the end of all times. Only a great upset in the balance of the realms could open the world of chaos, but if it was unleashed, this creation would end, and chaos would form another.

There was one other set of beings called Natsiliani. Conceived in the human world and born of the spirits, they also could cross realms, and had power in both worlds. The Natsiliani were few, and were taken from the great spirits, for they were keys that unlocked the doors between the realms who could either defend this creation or unleash chaos upon the earth. The Natsiliani had souls and walked the earth with humans but were set apart by a mark of divinity they all shared.

I felt my birthmark sting. Was the mark I shared with Eteri and the Elementals a sign of divinity? I gathered the book and the triangle into my raincoat. I wasn't sure I was allowed to take it from the library, but I wanted to show it to Eteri and see if it jogged anything in her memory. When I approached the library doors, of course Julie was waiting. She looked even more tired without the glow of the fire to give color to her cheeks. I felt uncomfortable hiding the book. I crossed my arms in front of my chest guiltily.

"You may take it. It is yours." Julie waved her hand and the library doors opened.

I wanted to explain myself, and to apologize for the almost deception, but before I got a word out, I was all alone on the library steps again. The rain had picked up and the sky was filled with menacing clouds. I realized I held an umbrella in my hand. Julie must have given it to me without me noticing, and the kindness made me tingle with guilt once more. I opened the umbrella and headed back to the garage, filled with more questions than answers, but certain I had found my path.

Watcher and Sentinel met me at the garage gate, happily wagging their tails. Watcher kept nudging at my raincoat pocket, until finally I reached inside and found two treats (must have been another gift from Julie). Once they had their presents, the doggies trotted off to enjoy them in private. Dave was in the garage, with Maybelle's old manual spread out on the table. He was studying the inner workings of her guts.

"You in a rush to get Miss Maybelle fixed and get me and my mom out of here?" I teased. There was also a little bit of fear in my voice. Now that I knew me and Eteri might be the reason Mystikos was in danger, I was worried Dave might actually *want* us to leave.

"No, not hardly. Eteri keeps talking about turning her into a yoga studio and I was thinking there might be a way to run a radiant heat system under the floor and hook it up to the existing solar panels, but I'd have to find the best way to get in without tearing out all the walls."

"You're very good to her." I smiled at Dave. I had had reservations at first, but now I knew that Dave was just the right person for my mother. He was kind and patient, and he wasn't jealous or looking to tame Eteri. He just liked to be in her orbit.

"She makes me happy." Dave blushed.

"Where is mom?" I asked.

"Oh, she's still helping Roselyn. They're re-opening the Wistful Willow for dinner tonight and she wants us to eat over there so she can wait on us and show off how good she's gotten at it."

"I have something to show her. I think I'll go over now. Meet you there later?" I really wanted to ask Eteri about the talisman without Dave. I tried to sound welcoming, secretly hoping he wouldn't offer to come with me.

"Sure. Got a few more things to figure out." Dave went back to studying the manual and I let myself out quietly.

***

With the assistance of a lot of hungry helpers, Roselyn and Fred had gotten the Wistful Willow back to some semblance of its old self. All the tables and chairs were where they were supposed to be. A large piece of plywood had been fitted as a makeshift door until it could be properly replaced. The inside of the café was clean and sparkly again, but the mug wall had not recovered. Most of the little cubbies were empty. A few badly chipped mugs had survived, and there were a couple without handles, but the regular's wall was the heart of the café, and the energy seemed a bit off without it.

Roselyn smiled at me from behind the counter and motioned for me to come take a seat. She had a big, steaming cup of coffee and a pumpkin walnut turnover already waiting by the time I crossed the room and climbed up on a stool. "What are you up to this dim and dreary day?" Roselyn gave the already pristine countertop a swift wipe down with a dish cloth.

"I went to the library. Want to show my mom a book Julie gave me." I took a sip of the coffee. I wondered if Fred was one of the magical creatures from the other side and his power was that everything he touched turned delicious.

"She's in the salon hunting up some extra mugs for me. We've got to do something till we can fill up the wall again. I'll be serving coffee in soup ladles if we don't figure it out."

"I bet we have a bunch of coffee mugs at the apartment. There's at least one collection of everything on earth over there." I chuckled but I wasn't kidding.

"I appreciate the offer and I'll take you up on it." One of the regulars walked in the front door hopeful that the Wistful Willow was already open ahead of the dinner shift. Roselyn gave the regular a wave and stepped from the behind the counter. "It's a couple more hours till we're officially open." She leaned back towards me and whispered, "I'll give him a turnover as a consolation prize. Finish up your snack and your mom will probably be back by then."

While I waited for Eteri to get back, I slipped the little book out of my jacket, then put it right back in, because I really wanted to eat the turnover and was afraid I'd get pumpkin fingerprints on the pages. Fred peeked his head out of the kitchen and waved his spatula in salute. My mouth was full of turnover, so I pointed to it and gave him a big "thumbs up." I looked around the café. Of course, I had seen hundreds of roadside restaurants, truck stops and diners over the years, but the Wistful Willow had become my instant favorite. It felt like an extension of the apartment, an extra dining room where all my friends were always playing dominoes and eating the daily special. I didn't know how Fred and Roselyn felt, but in my mind, they had quickly earned aunt and uncle status. This place was very precious to me, and I felt a strong need to protect it.

Before I knew it, I had finished my turnover and had nearly polished off a second cup of coffee, but Eteri still hadn't returned to the café. "Hey Roselyn, do you care if I go over to the salon to look for my mom? Maybe I can help her find the mugs."

"Sure. And while you're over there, bring back a couple of boxes of straws. I need to refill the dispensers," Roselyn hollered from a booth in the corner.

"Will do."

The salon was just as the last time I had seen it. It looked like the Puckwudgie had not been interested in vintage beauty paraphernalia or bulk restaurant supplies. "Mom, where are you?" I called out.

There was no answer. Eteri was probably off in another room up to her ears in boxes, but I didn't mind the opportunity to discover. I picked my way past the dryer chairs and shampoo sinks, then peeked into a box or two, but my mom wasn't there. Maybe she was in the old supply room.

I flipped the light switch on and off a couple of times, but the bulb wouldn't turn on, maybe it was burnt out. "Mom?" I had to feel my way around the boxes and shelves. The room couldn't be that big, but there was no knowing in the darkness. "Eteri?" I tried again. Still no answer. Now I was starting to worry.

I tripped over a pile of old beauty smocks and fell to my knees, hitting my face on a shelf on the way down. I reached out with my tongue to feel my already swelling upper lip and tasted a salty bit of blood. My first thought was that if Mystikos' list of surprise guests included vampires, I could potentially be inciting a frenzy. My second thought was annoyance that I was forever having to hunt down my free-spirited mother, who had probably found a moth wing in a dusty corner and become mesmerized with its intricate pattern. "MOM!" I yelled angrily.

Something creaked at the back of the room. I jumped up and whipped around defensively just in case the vampire thing had been a reliable premonition. A gust of wind howled through the darkness and the humongous metal storeroom door slammed open against the building's outside wall. I raced towards the light and out into the rain. "Mom. Please answer me!"

A single sandal lay in a puddle just outside of the doorway. Eteri conceded to wearing shoes if society required it, but insisted that her toes be free, even when it was cold. My heart stopped for a moment. I desperately wanted to believe that my mother had just wandered off again by herself on another adventure, but the trail of large, heavy footprints I found pressed into the mud and along the sidewalk could not have been made by human feet or any animal native to Mystikos. I fought against logic, but there was only one conclusion. Eteri had been taken by a monster.

CHAPTER FOURTEEN

The sun was setting, but curfew would be set aside for the night. The Volunteers had gathered at the Wistful Willow, along with a few deputized regulars, Roselyn, and Fred. Dave held Watcher and Sentinel on leashes. His skin was pale with worry, but his eyes spoke volumes on the violence he would inflict on anyone or anything that hurt Eteri.

I paced the floor. I wanted to leave now. All this preparation felt like wasted time we did not have the luxury for. Dell touched my shoulder. "WHAT?" I whipped around and snapped at him, then immediately regretted it.

Dell didn't take it personally. I assume he could only imagine how terrified I must be. "We're leaving in five minutes. They've decided to split into three groups. One is going to search in town, one is going to concentrate on the back roads, and one is going to the portal."

"I'm going with the portal group." A flare of panic hit me at the thought of my mother being taken to the other side.

I was sure Dell would argue and tell me it was dangerous in that absolutely gross way men like to think women are too delicate for war, but instead he nodded and said, "I'm going with them too."

It felt a little bit like Frankenstein, all the villagers saddling up with torches and pitch forks to hunt down the monster, but the torches were hunting lights mounted on top of souped-up trucks and the villagers wouldn't destroy the monster if they found it, they'd escort it safely back home. I just prayed that they found it soon.

***

"Do they have any idea what took her?" I asked as the truck rushed down the rain slicked county road. I was wedged between Dave and Dell. Watcher and Sentinel were both in the bed of the pick up. They didn't mind the rain.

"The storm washed away the trail and the few prints we had weren't clear. There wasn't any other evidence left behind," Dave said calmly, never taking his eyes from the road.

"Weren't there fingerprints on the door or something?" I asked.

"Magical creatures don't leave fingerprints." Dell said gently.

"We should have told her about everything sooner. She didn't know to be careful. She didn't know anything bad could happen to her." I grasped the dashboard in a desperate attempt to speed up the truck with the force of my will.

"You know your mother. She wouldn't have cared. To her, everyone is a friend. For all we know she went willingly." Dave glanced in the rearview mirror. There were several other trucks behind us.

Dave pulled off the road. It was dark, but the spot looked familiar. I realized that this was the place we had camped with Maybelle when we first came to town.

"The portal is here?" I looked at Dell.

"It's close." Dell scanned the landscape, looking for any signs of movement.

Dave's truck came to a stop right outside the stand of trees where Eteri disappeared on our first night in Mystikos. Watcher and Sentinel immediately started barking. This was a fun, exciting night for them and they couldn't wait to be let loose.

I had my seatbelt undone before Dave turned the car off and was pushing myself against Dell to get out of the truck. The rain was coming down harder here and stung my cheek. With all the search lights, the area was lit up like day, but the blanket of trees stopped any light from entering the forest.

"It's the clearing. The one with the dandelions, isn't it?" I looked up at Dell.

"I've only been there once. The portal is dangerous and it's tricky where it starts and ends. A single step in the wrong direction and you'll disappear forever."

"Then we have to hurry." I started to run towards the trees, but Dell pulled me back.

"You aren't listening, Soara. There are ways to do this safely. We're not losing you too."

Dave flipped down the gate of the truck and Watcher and Sentinel jumped to the ground. "Seek!" As soon as he uttered the command, Watcher and Sentinel went flying into the forest and the Volunteers quickly followed.

The search party stayed behind Watcher and Sentinel, scanning their flashlights through the trees for any sign of Eteri or the creature who might have taken her. No one spoke, being careful not to startle any other "friends" who could be hiding in the trees. I thought I saw a large, black shadow slither past my feet and had to bite my tongue not to scream. I'd never been afraid of snakes, but it seemed like everything that came out of the portal had been sent through a machine that tacked on extra eyes and teeth.

"Just remember, most of them aren't interested in you." Dell whispered.

I nodded and tried to keep my eyes focused directly in front of me.

It seemed like the trees had no end. I wondered if the dogs were leading us in circles and then a puff of white went up around me.

"STOP!" Dell yelled and grabbed my arm.

When I looked up, the Volunteers had surrounded the clearing, shining their flashlights towards the center. There was no rain inside the circle, but the dandelions swayed softly in a gentle breeze. Watcher and Sentinel bound into the field, but no one followed them. They sniffed at the dandelions, sending more puffs of white flying up, as if they were just playing a game. Then suddenly, the dogs froze. Their ears lifted and they set into a fit of barking.

"Do you see anything?" I asked Dell.

Watcher and Sentinel shot across the field and suddenly disappeared into thin air.

"Nooo!" I screamed and started to run after them.

"Let them do their job, Soara. This is why they're here." Dave's hand on my shoulder was firm.

I was frantic. I couldn't stand to lose anything else I loved. It seemed like hours passed and no one was concerned for the dogs, least of all Dave. Then suddenly, Watcher and Sentinel were back. Both dogs were perfect and happy, as if they'd never been gone. They walked up and down an invisible line, then each of them sat down at one end and remained at attention. One of the Volunteers whistled, and the group moved into the field to start their search. I looked at Dave, trying to understand.

"Watcher and Sentinel aren't normal dogs. We don't really know what they are, but they came from the other side. We found them when they were babies, either abandoned or lost, but they were too weak and small to be left on their own. I raised them myself, so they choose to live on this side, but they can move in and out whenever they want to. We taught them to find the doorway and mark it, to keep anyone from accidentally stepping through."

"Oh." Was all I could source from my brain. Everything in Mystikos made sense, but not the kind of sense that worked anywhere else in the world.

The clearing was not that large, but The Volunteers were going to search every last inch of it. The entire space was considered magical, and therefore could easily trick the eye. I wanted to be helpful, but I also didn't want to make the Volunteers' job harder, so I stayed at the outskirts of the circle, praying that someone was going to yell, "I found her!" at any moment.

I stared into the darkness cut with shafts of flashlight beams and the pattern started to swim before my eyes. I blinked and shook my head. I needed to stay alert, but every part of my body was heavy. Suddenly, it was as though a cloth began wiping away reality and I could see what lay past it peeking through. Shapes that could not possibly exist formed and then turned themselves inside out. My senses were awakened in strange ways. I could smell colors and feel sound. I had no idea what I was looking into, but I desperately did not want to go into that place. I wanted to run in the opposite direction and get as far away as I possibly could, but when I tried to move, my ankles were tied together.

No one seemed to notice what was happening to me. I tried to scream, but no sound came out. As coils of air enveloped my chest, I could feel the breath being pressed out of my body. I could barely gasp, but each time I breathed in, the coils wrapped more tightly. There wasn't even space for panic. The coils slithered around my neck, then slowly began to cover my face. Everything grew dark. I could feel myself start to turn inside out like the odd shapes. It didn't hurt, but it was uncomfortable, something that I wanted to be over as soon as possible. I considered that time probably had no meaning anymore, and I wondered if this process was happening for the rest of forever, or in the space of a blink.

And then my eyes opened. I stood in the field of dandelions alone. The trees were gone, and the dandelions stretched as far as my eyes could see. Above me, the sky was clear and full of stars. The moon hung enormous, so close I felt I could reach out and touch it. I had never seen the night sparkle so beautifully and I wanted to look at it forever, but a shadow soon covered the sky. I heard the sound of great wings flapping and a terrifying screech that was all too familiar. Thunder and lightning filled the heavens and then I saw it. Its feathers were an oily black that reflected iridescent green and purple in the moonlight. Wings spread out on either side blocking out the stars. The head came to a peak of feathers, which gave it the appearance of an arrow taking aim. The beak of the beast was also black, but sparkled, as if it was made of crystal and came to a sharp point, which split into two when it opened to shriek. I couldn't see teeth inside the mouth, but the dark nothingness was equally frightening. As the great bird flew over me, its scaly, bluish claws contracted, and I imagined how easily they could rip apart human flesh. The feeling that moved through my veins was not fear, but pride, and the little part of my brain that was still completely myself could not imagine why I'd be proud of such an awful thing. The bird landed without disturbing a single dandelion. As it's talons touched the ground, it bent to me, laying its cheek upon the ground.

I knew I could touch the bird, and I knew that it loved me. Suddenly, the fact I had ever feared this magnificent creature felt utterly ridiculous. It was a part of me, and I was part of it. The dandelions divided to make me a path. I crossed the field with my arms already outstretched, burying my fingers in the blanket of obsidian on the great bird's head, then leaning down to kiss its silky feathers. It was glorious. I felt powerful and adored. I wanted to climb onto the bird's back and fly away into the night, never to feel fear or worry again, but as I dug my fingers further into the bird's feathers, I was also certain that if I let myself go completely, I would never feel love or empathy again either.

A bolt of lightning entered my mind. I thought the bird had cracked the sky with fire once more, but instead a familiar voice broke through shouting, "NO!" I held tighter to the feathers; I wanted to stay with this creature. Another, more piecing shout clanged through my brain, "NO, SOARA!" Suddenly the feathers no longer felt soft, they became millions of microscopic shards of glass, cutting my face and hands. I tried to let go, but the feathers hooked into my skin. "YOU MUST TRY!" The words felt like fire.

I screamed.

All at once, I was back in the trees. I couldn't see the dandelion field anymore, but I could hear the Volunteers calling my name. I looked at my hands. Blood was just beginning to blossom in thousands of tiny cuts. I tried to sit up. The world felt upside down. I turned over and wretched into the grass. I could hear something moving closer, but was barely strong enough to hold myself up, let alone fight off another monster. I looked around for anything that could be a weapon, but all I found was an oily, black feather. The creature had been real. Another wave of nausea came over me and I felt myself slipping into the blackness of a faint, when something wet and cold licked my face.

It was Watcher, followed closely by Sentinel. They kept licking at me, one pushing up against each side of my body to hold me up. The dogs started barking. It hurt my head, but I realized they were trying to help the Volunteers find me and I didn't have the strength to make them stop anyway.

"Soara!" It was Dell's voice. He must have heard Watcher and Sentinel's howls.

I could hear him running in my direction. It was so difficult to keep my eyes open and I couldn't see through the darkness anyway. All I wanted to do was lie down in the soft grass and sleep forever.

When Dell lifted me from the ground, he cradled me against his chest. "I've got you. It's ok. You're back."

I took a deep breath of him. He smelled like sweat and a strong mixture of herbs. I had started to catalogue which ones in my mind, rosemary, mint, rose...

Dell carried me back to the dandelion circle.

"Take her to Julie." Dave told him, barely hiding the worry in his voice. "We'll keep looking for Eteri."

Dell gently put me in Dave's truck and pulled back onto the blacktop road passing the "Welcome to Mystikos" sign.

CHAPTER FIFTEEN

I woke up in a part of the library I had never been in before. There was no marble or grand windows, but it was wonderfully cozy. The books here had dusty, cracked spines, and were stacked happenstance in the shelves. I could tell this was the lair of a reader, the kind who starts and stops, reading multiple books at once, bouncing back and forth as interest and need arises. Candles lit the space. I wasn't sure if there was no electricity in the room or if the storm had knocked out the power all over Mystikos. I didn't remember coming to the library, and to be honest, the fact I was in the building at all was an assumption based on the walls lined with bookshelves and the smell of Julie's special hot cocoa brewing nearby.

Sitting up proved more difficult than I expected. My whole body was sore and heavy, like I'd been in a terrible car accident. I tried to push past the thick curtains that cloaked my memory, but they wouldn't move.

"Just rest. And drink this. I put something extra in it." Julie touched the mug to my lips and tipped it up. The drink was as delicious and warm as ever, but there was an earthy aftertaste to the cocoa and milk. "It will help you heal."

I took another sip. I could feel the velvety beverage moving down my throat and the heat begin to radiate through my body. As the warmth made its way towards my brain, I started to receive flashes from earlier that night, the dandelions, the darkness, something soft and black...and then I saw my mother's face. I tried to jump off the couch, but my feet tangled in the afghan that had been lain across my lap. Julie gently pushed me back down.

"My mom! I have to find her!" I was frantic.

"They are searching for Eteri, but you must stay here with me. We came so close to losing you and that cannot happen." Julie's hands were gentle but surprisingly strong.

"It doesn't matter what happens to me! She doesn't know about the monsters! She doesn't know about any of this!" I tried to get up again, but I clearly wasn't going anywhere without Julie's permission. "Please. You have to at least let me help!"

"That's what they want, Soara. I fear that Eteri has been taken as bait. Drink another sip."

I dutifully drank, feeling stronger with every swallow. "Who is THEY? Please don't give me anymore riddles." I grabbed at Julie's hand and pulled her face close to my own. "Please."

Julie stood up and smoothed her skirt. That's when I noticed how old Julie suddenly looked. There were wrinkles at the corners of her mouth and bags beneath her eyes. Her usually glowing skin had turned dull and grayish and she seemed thinner. Julie made her way to one of the many bookshelves in the room. She had to move several tomes to get to what she was looking for. It wasn't a book really, more a sheaf of papers tied with cord. If there had ever been a cover, it was long gone. Julie carried the papers carefully, making sure not to lose a single page, then laid them gently in my lap.

"Julie, what's happening to you?" I was genuinely worried about my new but dear friend.

Julie patted my knee. "I've been through worse. My job is not always easy. But I chose it."

"Will this tell me how to find My mom?" I held the stack of papers. They felt strangely warm, like I was touching skin, and I pulled back sharply.

"You'll get used to that." Julie lit an oil lamp on a nearby side table, it's glow immediately filled the room. "I don't know if this will help us find Eteri, but I think it's time for you to see it."

"Do you live in this room?" I was equal parts curious and afraid to find out what the pages might say, so I was stalling, but truthfully, I had wondered for a while now if Julie ever left the library.

"Strictly speaking, I don't live anywhere, but this is my favorite place to exist. I need to take care of something, but I'll be back to check on you soon. Promise me you won't leave this room without me." Julie raised an eyebrow. It was the closest I had ever seen her come to being stern.

"I promise." I pulled the afghan up over my shoulders for effect and began to untie the cord that wrapped the papers.

It was no longer surprising to me that Julie was already gone when I looked up again. I took one more sip of the special cocoa and bolstered by its benefits, began to explore the pages in my lap.

The first sheet of paper was yellowed and burnt at the corners. It almost looked like a fake craft project someone had aged to look like an ancient treasure map. There didn't seem to be an author listed, and the ink on the page was fading, but I was able to make out that it was a kind of description of the collection.

PAGES FROM THE MYTIKOS LIBRARY

Over time I have gathered several lores surrounding the existence of the Natsiliani. While folklore by its very nature is made up of collections of stories with differing details, in my own research, I tend to take the opinion that the truth is available if one knows what to pick from each tale. While the existence of living Natsiliani has never been confirmed, and perhaps it is impossible to do so, several of the stories focus on the trope of "the foundling," raised by outsiders who are unaware of its power and provenance. I have collected many of those stories here.

Found in a book of Gorale Highlander fairytales purchased from a used bookstore in Chocholow, Poland. Translated into English.

The great Elementals could enter this world on the longest and shortest days of the year. They spread themselves out across the earth, seldom visiting the same doorway twice over many hundreds of years. The presence of pure Air, Fire, Water and Earth in our world fed the seasons and formed the path of days. Man created great festivals to welcome the Elementals. They danced, feasted, drank, and burned fires in their honor, celebrating the Earth's great turning, and in those brief times when the Elementals walked among us, they sometimes lay with humans and conceived. No infant grown in a female of this world was known to survive. The magic was too great and would kill the mother, stifling the baby's life with her own. Air and Water, being of feminine essence, were said to be able to hold a child inside of them on the other side, but once born, the half human babies never survived longer than a few breaths. Soul children did not have enough magic to survive infanthood on that side of existence. And thus, the world kept turning, until one day a baby was born of the Air, and her soulless mother, who placed no value in the living, left her behind to die. She was found by a creature the mountain people call Almas, a species of great furry beasts, walking on two feet, with the power to communicate through telepathy. Finding breath still in the child, the Alma spirited her across the bridge between worlds, so that she might live. The creature gave the baby a name and hid her in a garden, where she was found by human parents and raised as their own. But the creature forever watched over the child, knowing if her true mother ever learned she was alive, she would use the child to gain power over all of existence.

Creole Oral folktale, told to me by 68-year-old Sandrine Durafont, passed down as a bedtime story from her mother and grandmothers.

The Elemental of Air conceived, grew and gave birth to a female child during the 24 hours of a Winter Solstice. Thinking the baby did not live, the Elemental tossed her baby into the bayou and re-entered the portal to her own world. A great storm came and a magical creature from the swamps, a monstre marais, sought shelter under a cypress tree. She found the tiny baby, with only one breath left in her body. The magical creature was kind and decided to give the infant some of her own breath, so that it would survive. Once the storm had passed the monstre marais left the shelter of the tree and found a small cabin with a lonely couple inside who had prayed for a child. The couple raised the baby, under the watchful eye of the monstre marais, who's breath now connected them forever.

Found in a book of myths written in German. The book has no date or author and was purchased at a flea market in New London, New Hampshire. The vendor had no recollection of acquiring the book, assuming it may have been part of a bulk purchase from an estate.

The Air Elemental gave birth and lay sleeping with the infant. But the creatures of her world knew this tiny baby held great power. The Elemental treasured the child but not out of maternal love. To her, this baby was the key to great power, for she could exist on either side of the veil and do the bidding of the Elementals. The creatures from the other side made a pact to steal the child and hide her amongst the humans. When the great Elemental awoke and realized the baby was gone, she screamed, creating a great storm of wind and water that destroyed many crops and homes, but the Other Side called the Elemental back and she was forced to leave the child behind. The baby was well loved by her human parents and went on to live a happy life, but The Elemental never stopped searching for her lost child, the key to unleashing her furious power upon the Earth.

Note: November 7, 1954

My ongoing research has led me to believe that the "Other Side" is real. I've found some kind of gate to this other dimension, which I've watched these past several nights. I'm not ready to write down what I've seen leaving and entering that place. My mind can't form the words yet, but now I know the beasts of fairytales, cryptozoological theories, and my own worst nightmares exist and move among us. Tonight, I am going to the gate again and this time I want to try and communicate with one of the creatures. I'm leaving my papers behind. I believe these pages have been affected by the energy of the gateway and are no longer entirely mine. And if I don't make it back, I hope someone finds these stories, so the truth doesn't die with me.

CHAPTER SIXTEEN

On the back of the last page was a drawing. When I held it closer to the oil lamp, I realized it was a map of Mystikos. There was the cafe, the Library, the Firehouse and outside of town, down a winding road, a circle of trees surrounding a clearing. A folded piece of paper slid from between the last few pages, inside was a perfectly pressed and preserved dandelion.

I set down the papers and let my cheek touch the cool leather of the sofa. As per everything in Mystikos, this journal or book or whatever it used to be was super weird and decoding the best way to apply the information to my life, much less figure out if it could help me find my mother, was making my brain feel like a packet of pudding.

Something vibrated in my pocket, and I nearly fell off the sofa. I had forgotten I still had my phone in my jacket. There was a text from Sierra to the whole friend group, plus Dell. I had never technically said anything about my "situationship" with Dell, but I figured the only secret in Mystikos was the big one. Everything else was up for public consumption.

SIERRA: "Nana and Pops have locked down the compound. Is everyone OK?"

ZION: "Nana said a war is coming and we should be thankful our deep freeze is full of meat. I'm not sure what that means, but now I'm hungry."

NOAH: "The Volunteers shut down access in and out of town. They're telling any travelers the road is washed out."

AUGUST: "Mom won't stop pouring salt in all the corners of the house."

MATTHEW: "Is she back yet? Do you need me to come over?"

AUGUST: "She's not back, but I don't think she'd let you in the house. She said we have to set up a barrier charm."

SIERRA: "Soara, are you there?"

I still wasn't used to having friends. It sounded absolutely tragic when I said it in my head, but it wasn't. It was the most amazing feeling ever. Eteri was an incredible mother and I wouldn't trade her for the world, but she didn't really ever worry. Eteri had an unshakeable belief in "happily ever after." This was one of her most beautiful traits, but all the same, it was lovely to have someone wondering if I was safe and sound. The warm fuzzies were followed very closely by an icy chill of fear, as the reality of the current situation crept back into my consciousness.

"Yes."

That's all I typed. I wanted to text, "Yes, but I feel like I'm going to throw up, and I'm scared, and my mother is missing, and I think monsters have her in another dimension, and I might be related to someone trying to destroy the world, but the librarian has assigned me a research project I have to complete before I can confirm this, and if it's true, I might be ¼ pure soulless evil, so maybe you shouldn't be friends with me anyway. Also, I think I maybe almost died tonight, and I just realized I have no idea where Dell is, and he might be risking his life which is all my fault because my mom and I stuck a wedge in the door to monster town and now it will never close."

AUGUST: "Where are you?"

"At the library. Julie said I have to stay here. Guys, what the hell IS Julie?"

There were dots next to every single person's name, so I knew they were all typing the answer...and then my phone died.

"ARE YOU KIDDING ME?!!!"

I tossed the phone down on the sofa and kicked the afghan across the room. I was now completely out of contact with everyone I knew and entirely dependent on Julie's next reading assignment to get any further information. The little angry spot at the base of my spine started to heat up. It sent a couple of shocks to my brain and that's all it took to set off a nuclear fit of anger.

"I'm sick of this! I'm going to get my mother!" I looked up. If this were a movie, there would have been a row of windows near the ceiling of the room, and after I stacked up a couple of chairs and climbed a bookcase, then shimmied out the window (just barely getting my hips through) I would escape into the night. But this was reality, and I was in an underground, stone room, somewhere in the belly of a behemoth historic building.

I growled and shoved a bookcase. I hit it way harder than I meant to and knocked it completely over. It smacked into the wall, kicking up a ton of dust, and forcing me to wipe a powdery film from my eyes to be able to see again. Re-inspection proved that I had just made a righteous mess, but with the bonus of finding the door. I carefully picked my way through the wreckage, placed my hand on the doorknob and turned. There was a pleasing click and the door swung open easily. The heat of my anger was replaced by a deep blush that it had never once crossed my mind to just try walking out of the room like a normal person.

Now the only problem was that I had to sneak out of the library, and I wasn't entirely sure exactly where I was inside of it. I had explored quite a bit of the building in my short time in Mystikos, but I was fairly certain there was far more than meets the eye behind the library walls. I took a careful step into the hall, looking both ways for anything big (or small) and scary, but the coast was clear. I eeny, meeny, miney, moed right or left and left won.

I snaked through a hallway lined with closed doors. Everything in me wanted to explore what might be hidden in those rooms, but it would have to wait for another day. When the hallway finally forked, I eeny, meeny, miney, moed again. My first choice circled me right back around to where I started, but the second hallway proved successful, and I found a narrow iron staircase spiraling up into a vertical tunnel. It was spooky as crap, but it wasn't a dead end. Inside the staircase was pitch black, which forced me to feel my way up, one step at a time. The good news was there was no chance of me falling off the side of the staircase, because it was completely encased in stone, the bad news was I could still fall back down the stairs, and that didn't sound any more appealing. With every step, I had to shove down the panic that was creeping up my spine. I had never been particularly claustrophobic, but I kept reaching out to touch the walls to see if they were getting any closer together. Other than the slow scrape of my shoes on the stairs, it was silent. I realized that I had come to take the sound of pattering rain in the background as a comforting friend. It was gone in this silo of stone and it added to my sense of loneliness.

A sliver of light finally peeked between the stairs above my head. I wanted to take the steps faster but couldn't risk falling now that I was so close to escape. One at a time, one at a time, my thighs were aching and even going slowly I was starting to lose my breath from the long climb. I heard a noise. Maybe someone was searching for me. I called out, "Julie!"

There was no answer. I was smart enough to know there could be anything waiting ahead of me, but there was no way for me to prepare or anticipate. The light was getting brighter, but it had taken on an unnatural hue. It hurt my eyes to look up, so I closed them. I was now moving entirely by feel, my fingers snaking along the stones, and then finally one hand slid forward and found nothing. I had reached the top. I could sense the strange light pulsing against my eyelids. It felt like a headache that lived outside of my skull. I forced myself to open my eyes.

I had been climbing for such a long time, I thought I must be in the library's clock tower or close to the roof, but I was on the ground floor of the library in the main entrance. The marble floors reflected the strange light around the room and folded it back on itself, intensifying the painful brightness. It took a moment for my eyes to adjust, but when they did, I saw Julie's silhouette standing in the middle of the floor. She was surrounded by orbs of a blueish light which floated all around her. It could have been beautiful, but along with the light came an intense, pulsing energy that felt like anger mixed with a deep, hungry jealousy. Looking at it made me feel like I was turning inside out.

More and more orbs floated into the room and as they touched, they melted together, becoming larger, bluer, brighter. Julie stood at their center with her arms held out in front of her. The orbs would move in towards her but if they touched her skin, they would curl back and fly away, as if she caused them pain.

"Julie, I'm here." I wanted to help her if I could. At the very least, I wanted Julie to know that she wasn't alone.

"Don't come any closer, Soara." Julie shouted over her shoulder and even that brief moment with her attention split was enough for one of the orbs to get past her. "Soara close your eyes. It has no power if you can't see it!"

I quickly squeezed my eyes shut. I could feel the energy of the orb getting closer and couldn't help but take on some of its anger. I wanted to fight and scream.

"Soara, just try to stay calm. What you're feeling isn't real. And whatever you do, don't open your eyes."

I turned towards the wall and tried to ease some of my rage into the cool marble, but it seemed to only reflect it back into me. I could feel the light touch me. I knew exactly how badly whatever it was wanted to tear me apart, and I wanted to rip right back. The fury in my brain exploded and I turned, opening my eyes.

What I saw forced my mouth open in a scream that told of thousands of years of longing and pain, and once I let the light speak through me, I couldn't stop it.

"Will-o-the-whisp. Go back to your wood. You do not belong here. Return as you should. Will-o-the-whisp. Go back to your wood. You do not belong here. Return as you should." Julie's chants grew louder, but my screaming continued.

I saw Julie put her arms down, undoing any barrier between her and the wisps. She ran to me, pushing me onto the floor and covering my screaming body with her own. The whole time she kept chanting, "Will-o-the-whisp. Go back to your wood. You do not belong here. Return as you should."

No longer held back, the orbs rocketed towards Julie. I could feel them entering her body with tremendous force. She shook with every hit, but the orbs didn't pass through her into me. They kept coming and coming, faster and faster, and then all at once, everything was quiet.

My scream faded to a hoarse groan. I was slowly coming back to myself and releasing the fury and terror that had filled my brain. "Julie, is it over?"

There was no answer. I heaved with all of my might and pushed out from underneath my protector, quickly pulling Julie's limp head into my lap. "What can I do?"

Julie was still for what felt like a very long time, but finally, her eyes fluttered. It seemed to take all that was left of her strength "I have to rest now." Julie tried to smile, but it didn't make its way past the corners of her lips.

"I'll take you to the fireplace room. You can lie down. And I'll get you some of that cocoa you gave me. You just have to tell me where it is." I started to push Julie up gently.

"That won't help me." Julie's eyes closed again and I panicked.

"No. No. No. No. No. Please, Julie. Open your eyes."

Julie's eyelids didn't move this time, but she was able to whisper. "I have to go back to what I am. Just for a little while. Maybe a few thousand years will do."

"Please, Julie. Stay here. I'm so sorry."

Julie's chest swelled with a deep breath and as she let it out her body warmed. I took it as a good sign. "Yes, Julie. Like that."

And then it seemed like Julie went fuzzy, just around the edges at first. I blinked my eyes, but I was right, Julie was slowly going out of focus. I looked around the room. Everything else was solid and crisp in the moonlight that shone through the library windows. Even the shadows had hard edges. It didn't make sense. When I looked back down, Julie was gone. In her place lay a small, delicate wooden carving. I lifted the figure into the moonlight. It was a gnomelike creature, wearing a hat and boots, the kind of thing a person might place in their garden to keep the snails and flowers company, but instead of jolly and bearded, the carving was hauntingly beautiful and clearly feminine. The wood felt warm and alive against my chest, and my heartbeat calmed. Wherever Julie had gone, she had left this bit of herself behind and I would protect it, just like Julie had protected me.

I wasn't sure if there were more Will-o-the-wisps coming, but either way, I didn't think it was a good idea for me to be in the library alone. I made my way to the front doors and waited for them to open, but nothing happened. I tried running my hands over the seam as I'd done to get into the library, but still there was no movement. It suddenly occurred to me that I had never left the library without Julie or Dell opening the doors and I wondered if I was able to do it on my own. I ran my hands over the rest of the brass panels, looking for any kind of secret button or knob, but didn't find anything. I'd have to escape another way and the only thing I could think of was going out a window. It seemed criminal to be responsible for the destruction of yet another window in the library, but there was nothing to be done.

I looked around for my best option. The main hall didn't have windows, they were mostly on the upper floors. That would mean jumping, but I could look for the lowest spot and pray the ground had softened from all the rain. I took a deep breath. The storm was getting worse. I could smell hail. I held a little bit of hope that I might not have to break a window if the icy rain got to one first.

The Elemental windows rose up before me as I mounted the staircase. With the cloudy moonlight shining through them, the remaining three faces looked dour and cold, yet I was still drawn to them. They were undeniably beautiful. Instead of continuing to hunt for a means of escape, I found myself mesmerized by three sets of soulless eyes. Rain streaked the clear glass of the panel that had been destroyed. It gave the effect the glass was weeping for what was gone. Yet a small piece of the Air Elemental panel had survived. A chunk of colored glass lay on a table beneath the windows. I could just make out the beautiful scrolling letters. I took another step forward and slowly reached out my hand. I opened my lips and released a whisper of wind, just as I had done before, "Zepherine."

From every corner of the room, the blackness snaked out towards me. Wind filled the library and books flew from the shelves. I was lifted from the floor. The blackness wrapped around me as it always did in my dreams, but this time it hung itself around my frame, creating a magnificent gown that puddled at my feet. I held my hands out and let the soft blackness curl around my arms. I felt beautiful and powerful. My hair trailed out all around me in a crown of tendrils.

The blackness began to take the shape of the monsters I'd seen since entering Mystikos (and a multitude of beasts I'd never even imagined). Some were large and hairy, some small and fast. Many of them flew. There were too many of them, and they started to fight. The creatures were nothing but ebony air and shadow, but they could still rip each other apart. With every battle, the loser gave a blood curdling scream of defeat and I wished the blackness could wrap around my head and block out the sound.

"Soara." My name whispered through the cacophony. "Soara." It was Eteri's voice, and it was getting louder.

"Mom, I can hear you! Where are you?" I wanted to come down now, but the blackness wouldn't let me go.

"Soara. Save me." Suddenly all the shadow creatures converged into one, creating Eteri's face. It hung in front of my own and continued to cry, "Soara. Save me!"

"Let me go!" I dropped to the floor and reached out towards the face of my mother, but it began to float away. "No!"

I chased Eteri's face across the room and up to the third floor. It cried out again. "Help me, please."

"I'm trying! Tell me what to do!" I continued to run after the smoky apparition, tripping over books and furniture that had spilled across the floor in the interior storm. I found myself on another staircase. I had never gone up higher than the third floor before, but at this point even Julie couldn't stop me if it was a mistake. At the top of the stairs was a door and Eteri's face disappeared through it. My heart felt like it was being ripped out of my chest. I couldn't lose my mom again. I pressed myself forward and shot through the door, exploding onto the roof of the library.

Wind and freezing rain pelted my face and body, and lightening electrified the sky. It was difficult to see, and I didn't know where the edge of the roof was, but my mother's face was moving farther away from me, and I had to follow it.

"Please help me." Eteri's face called to me once more, then the mouth twisted in pain and started to wail.

"Mom!" I tore across the roof, trudging through the puddled water and ice, every footfall reverberating painfully through my tired body, and then suddenly, my feet hit nothingness and I started to fall. I reached out towards the face of my mother. "Mom, help me!" But there was nothing to grab onto, the face disappeared, and I saw the ground coming towards me. I braced against the oncoming pain.

But it never came.

Before I hit the ground there was a crack of thunder and I found myself face first in a pile of feathers, attached to the great black bird I had met in my dreams. I was flying. The bird rose higher and higher. The only way off was down and jumping now would turn me into a bowl of human oatmeal with a side of certain death. I was still cold and wet, but there was absolutely nothing I could do about it, and it was a strange comfort to be out of choices. I dug my hands into the bird's black quills and held on for dear life.

I was so emotionally and physically worn out that I almost fell asleep on the great bird's back, but as I started to slip sideways, my eyes flew open. I expected to see the kind of miniature landscape one views out an airplane window, but there was nothing but blackness and clouds below me. Even the stars were blocked out by the storm. I was fairly certain I knew where the bird was taking me, to the other side. Whoever or whatever wanted me was finally going to get their way. All I could hope for at this point, was that I could trade myself for my mom's safety. Soaked to the bone and starting to shiver from the icy elevation, I tried to burrow my arms beneath the feathers, but there was no warmth to be found. The bird's skin was cool and hard like glass.

I was scared to let go with even one hand to wipe my soggy bangs out of my eyes. I cursed my impulsive decision to cut them on a particularly boring day on the road before we moved to Mystikos. I could still clearly see that day in my mind. Eteri was up front driving, playing some hippity dippity 70's band and singing every word at the top of her lungs. I was in the back of Maybelle in my bedroom. I had just finished my latest book and didn't have another, and I wasn't in the mood to read any of my few treasured favorites over again. At first, I had tried stretching, then I tried to see how high I could count in French (I got to 378 before giving up). Finally, I decided I would go sit with my mom, but Eteri was so darn happy and content all the time, and when I was in a mood like this, I was jealous of her ability to be amused by almost anything. Sometimes I just wanted my mother to be normal and go to a regular job and make me tv dinners and be nosy and read my non-existent diary. After Eteri kept insisting I sing harmony with her, I got annoyed and went back to the bedroom, where I took out a mirror and scissors and lopped off my bangs, just for the mere 30 second dopamine hit of having done it. And 30 seconds was about all I had before the regret started creeping in. My misplaced frustration all pointed towards this being my mom's fault. I was super angry and stuck on a bus with Eteri for who knew how many more hours. In that moment, I wished more than anything that I could make my mother disappear, so I could steal Maybelle, drive her to the nearest used bookstore, and live forever in the classics section. Now I would do anything to wrap my arms around my mother's neck and smell the patchouli and lavender scent of her skin.

I was lost in this thought when suddenly the great bird gave another shriek and started to drop. I let out my own terrified scream as I slipped to one side and felt nothing but miles of air beneath me. Tearing at the bird's oily feathers, I barely managed to pull myself back onto its back. The velocity of the nosedive was so fierce I thought I'd faint. I felt as though I could be torn off the bird at any moment, but I needed the monster to get me to my mother, so I held on tighter and dug my heels into the bird's sides. I had just begun to recover my balance when something caused the bird to jerk to the side, and I heard the crack of bone splintering. We began to fall faster. I screamed once more, awaiting the pain of impact, but at the very last moment, the bird managed to gain enough strength to land, skidding across the ground and sending dandelions flying in every direction. We were back in the clearing, and standing across from us was the pair of red, glowing eyes I had seen so many times since my arrival in Mystikos. The now familiar voice filled my head.

"Let go."

I uncurled my hands from the feathers and immediately slipped off the bird's back and onto the ground. Crawling away as quickly as I could, I got a mouthful of dandelion fluff and started coughing. When

I sat back up, a battle was taking place before me. The red eyes were set within the face of a great hairy beast. If someone asked me what I was looking at, I would have instantly said, "Big Foot," but now I knew the great monsters people had sighted in forests all over the world for hundreds of years were something other and magical, and the reason no one had ever been able to find physical evidence for their existence was that they could disappear to the other side, whenever they wished. My protector was an Alma, just like in the folklore story Julie gave me in the library. Those red eyes that watched so closely had never meant any harm. And right now, it looked as though the Alma would die to protect me. This wasn't what I wanted. No one else should have to sacrifice themselves for me. I stood up and screamed. "No!"

The inky black sky was starting to break with streaks of greyish dawn. Night was almost over, and the portal would close. The Alma looked towards me, and I heard the words "For you." Without warning, the great bird's talons tore through the Alma's fur, and it immediately went limp. The fierce beast began to drag the Alma's lifeless body across the clearing. I ran towards them. There had to be some way I could save my protector, but just as the sun rose overhead, the bird and the Alma suddenly disappeared. There was a great crack and a hiss, and I was once again alone.

The two monsters must have gone into the portal, but I didn't know how or exactly where. Either way, the portal would be closed now. If Eteri was on the other side, I wouldn't find her until the next nightfall. I gathered every ounce of energy I had left and forced myself to start walking towards Mystikos.

***

When I finally limped back onto Mainstreet the sun had cast a blueish grey canopy over everything, and tiny tendrils of steam were snaking up from the pavement in the swampy heat. It looked as if a devastating tornado had swept through all the buildings the night before. Regular citizens and Volunteers were out on the sidewalks trying to salvage or protect anything that wasn't already irreparably broken. They were all too busy to notice me, but I decided that was for the best.

I snuck past the Wistful Willow. Any windows the puckwudgie forgot during his visit had now been busted by the storm. Roselyn and Fred were inside sweeping up glass. Roselyn stopped for a moment and put her head in her hands. Fred stepped up and put his arms around her, kissing the top of her hair.

Across the street, there was an enormous hole in the chain link fence of the garage lot. Our little apartment was still standing, but quite a few shingles were missing from the roof. The car I'd hidden behind the first time I snuck out after curfew was tipped into a sinkhole. Everything was dark in the garage and Dave's truck was still gone, a sure sign that Eteri was not back.

I didn't consciously know where I was going when I started walking, but I was headed back towards the library. I never should have left the tiny basement room there last night. If I'd listened, if I hadn't been so impulsive and hot headed, maybe Julie and the Alma would still be here to help us. Maybe I'd have my mother back by now. I stuck to the shadows. I was done being selfish and reckless. I didn't want anyone else risking themselves for me. If I could just get to the library, then it would be safe to stop for a moment.

The library doors were open. When I walked inside, I noticed the brass panels were puckered inward, as if a battering ram had been used to force them apart. Mud streaked the beautiful marble floor, accented by the occasional broken branch. I didn't know how to get back to the basement, so I made my way to the fireplace room. There was no fire in the hearth and most of the artwork had been ripped off the walls by the wind, but the couch was still there. I let myself collapse onto the slightly damp upholstery. It smelled of dried roses and old books, which reminded me of Julie, and I began to sob. As sleep finally pulled me into its grasp, I thought I heard someone yelling my name. I wasn't sure if it was friend or foe. And at that point, I didn't care.

CHAPTER SEVENTEEN

I woke up back in my blue bedroom with Watcher and Sentinel curled up one at my head and the other at my feet. I hoped all the madness from the night before had just been another dream. Maybe Eteri was asleep in her own bedroom, snuggled under a flowered quilt. I sat up quickly, ready to run down the hall, but I noticed my bedroom door was shut and Dell was sitting on the floor, leaned up against it with a rifle across his lap and his head lolling against his shoulder.

"Dell!" I yelled, scrambling out of the bed and rushing to him. "Don't be dead."

Dell's eyes slowly blinked awake. "I'm not dead. I'm guarding you."

I carefully pulled the rifle out of Dell's lap, then climbed into its place and put my arms around his neck. "The bird monster tried to take me through the portal, but then daylight came, and it got trapped on the other side when the portal closed. It's gonna come back, Dell. I shouldn't stay here. You'll get hurt but I'm what it wants."

"We're not going to let that bird or anything else take you. I promise." Dell kissed my cheeks and forehead.

"No, you have to. If I go with them, they'll leave Mystikos alone."

“That’s not an option.” Dell pulled me closer, but I wiggled out of his lap and started digging through one of the piles of clothes on the floor.

“I have to get dressed. How long is it until nightfall?” I asked as I pulled a “Virginia is for lovers” sweatshirt over my head.

The door opened, knocking into Dell and he was forced to scoot out of the way to let Roselyn inside. “Fred made you some breakfast. You have to keep your strength up, and a good, hot cup of coffee will set you right.” Roselyn set a tray down on the dresser and noticed me trying to push my foot into a pair of boots. “Just where do you think you’re going, young lady?”

“Back to the portal. They have my mom, but I think they’ll trade her for me.”

“Bargains don’t work the same way on that side. You have to be real careful. They might say they’ll trade you for your mother, then send us back a bag of her bones.”

I felt the bile rise in my throat and sunk to the floor.

Roselyn immediately regretted her words and came forward to comfort me. “No, no. That’s not going to happen. Not if you stay safe and listen to us.”

I looked up at Roselyn. She was the closest thing I currently had to a mother, and I wanted to crumple into her arms and cry. “It’s all my fault.”

“No, it isn’t, sweet girl. It’s ours.” Roselyn said, pushing the hair out of my eyes. “We shouldn’t have kept you and your mama in the dark about what goes on here. All this silly secret keeping is just dumb and dangerous.”

Roselyn and Dell moved me back to the bed. I refused to get under the covers but was willing to accept the cup of coffee. I took a sip, then a memory caught me by surprise and my breath hitched "Julie..." I began to shiver.

Roselyn carefully took the coffee cup from my hand so I wouldn't spill the hot liquid into my lap. "Julie understood what she was doing. And I know it's hard for you to believe, but I promise she didn't feel any pain."

Dell scooted onto the bed and wrapped his arms around me. "She warned us that the scales of chaos were tipping. We've been watching for a breach, but we didn't expect it to come like this."

"I should leave Mystikos, but I can't until I know my mom is safe. I wish Maybelle was fixed."

"Mystikos isn't the only portal. They exist all over the world. Now that the Elementals know about you, there's nowhere they can't find you," said Roselyn.

"So, the only choice is to fight." Dell squeezed my hand.

"How come they never found me before now?" I asked.

"We don't know." Dell answered, then his phone went off. "It's the Volunteers. I have to go." Dell stood up and pulled on his raincoat, but it was clear he didn't want to leave. "You have to promise me that you will not leave this house without me."

"I promise."

"And I'll be here watching her." Roselyn said, raising her eyebrow to let me know she meant business.

Dell brushed his lips across the top of my head and walked out of the room. I desperately hoped it wouldn't be for the last time.

***

I felt raindrops pelting against my skin. I opened my eyes to find myself standing in the middle of a storm. Lightning continuously struck the ground around me but never hit me directly. I reached out a hand and tugged at one of the bolts of fire. It cracked like a whip and electricity purred through my body. It felt good. It felt powerful. I cracked the lightening once again and ripped open the sky. Beasts of air, fire, earth and water poured from the tear. As soon as they hit the ground the monsters began eating. They consumed everything, the trees, the dirt, the light. Sierra, Zion, and the rest of my new friends tried to run away, but the monsters dragged them back into their gaping maws. Dell managed to hold off one of the monsters a little longer. He called to me. I stared back at him, aware that he was someone I should care about, but also amused by his human weakness. I considered calling off the monster and saving Dell, maybe this man could be my special pet, but suddenly his eyes went wide with pain and shock. Dell was sliced in half by the giant claws of a bat like creature and carried off into the night. I reached inside of myself looking for some shred of sadness, but I felt nothing at all.

"Soara, you have to stop it." Eteri suddenly stood before me. I tried to take her outstretched hand, but when our skin met, Eteri instantly burst into flames. I screamed. All that was left of my mother was a pile of ashes. That's when the last of the sky tore away. There was nothing left but fire and monsters and destruction.

Suddenly, I heard laughter, so sweet and pure it sounded like a happy child playing, but no child could have survived this level of chaos. I turned slowly and found myself gazing upon the most beautiful woman I had ever seen. Red tendrils snaked around a porcelain face. Fingers of silk billowed out from the lady's flowing cerulean robe, wrapping themselves gently around my body.

"Why are you laughing?" I asked.

"Because you've made me so proud." Answered Zepherine.

When I woke, I was tangled in my blue bed sheets and shrieking. Roselyn tried to calm me down, but I couldn't stop screaming over and over, "She's coming!"

CHAPTER EIGHTEEN

It was almost sundown. Volunteers stood on every street corner and even regular male and female citizens had been deputized for the cause. Peeking out the window, I noticed that this time the watchmen weren't planning for peace. Many were armed with guns, flame throwers and other makeshift weapons that looked no less capable of inflicting store-bought level damage.

Roselyn sat in a side chair doing a crossword puzzle. She promised me the Volunteers were ready. That we'd be safe. But despite her words, she still got up every 10 minutes or so to look out the window and check on the café.

When Roselyn finally nodded off, I chanced escape. I tiptoed out of my bedroom and through the living room, trying to skulk past any windows. I tried to turn the deadbolt and handle for the front door as quietly as possible, but in the end it didn't matter. Apparently, Dave had employed his automatic locks. I knew from experience that I wouldn't get past them, and even if I did, from this vantage point I could see a couple of Volunteers standing at the bottom of the apartment stairs.

I noticed something light up on the kitchen counter. Someone had had the presence of mind to plug in my phone! There were about a million texts from Sierra, Zion, August, Noah, and Matthew, all of them panicking and wanting me to check in. I perked up my ears. I could hear Roselyn snoring softly, so I snuck past her, grabbed my phone and sat cross legged with it on the sofa.

ME: "I'm alive. And I'm trapped in the apartment."

There was an instant response.

ZION: "That's bullshit!"

NOAH: "It's probably the safest place for you."

MATTHEW: "I heard my dad talking to the Volunteers. They've got guards all around Dave's place. You're number one priority."

ME: "Because they're protecting me from something? Or are they protecting themselves FROM me?" I returned.

AUGUST: "The first thing. You're one of us now."

August added a heart emoji to her text.

Another alert went off on my phone. It was a separate, private text from Zion.

ZION: "I think I can get you out, but I'm not sure you'll like my methods."

I didn't even have to think. I immediately typed back.

ME: "Bring it on."

***

I sat on the sofa trying to look innocent. The plan was laid out and now all I could do was wait.

Roselyn was now awake and in the kitchen heating up some soup that Fred sent over. "Fred just threw this together from pantry stuff, but his surprises are usually his greatest triumphs." she said and smacked the spoon on the side of the bowl for effect.

"Smells good," I called back, but I was only half in that room. Most of my mind was nervously watching my cell phone for Zion's signal.

"I'm gonna sleep over here again tonight. Looks like the two of us are roomies until further notice." Roselyn took out half a loaf of fresh baked bread and set it in the oven to warm.

My phone buzzed in my hand. It startled me, and I dropped it, but quickly scooped it up off the floor and read Zion's text.

ZION: "Now."

"Do I have time to take a shower before dinner?" I asked Roselyn.

"Sure, honey. It'll be ready when you are." she called back from the kitchen.

I tried to walk out of the living room as casually as possible, but it was a struggle to put one foot in front of the other and not hyperventilate from adrenaline overload. I made it down the hallway and into the bathroom, shutting the door and locking it, then turned on the water in the bathtub and the sink (for extra noise), and pulled back the shower curtain. There was a window in the tub wall. It was kind of high up and tiny. I'd be lucky if I could just barely manage to shimmy out of it. I had to stand on the lip of the bathtub and hoist myself up to reach it. The tile was slick and I was still in my stockinged feet. It would have been a lot smarter to put my shoes on at some point, but it was too late for that now.

I poked my head out of the window. Just as Zion promised when she explained the guards' schedule, I caught the back of one of the Volunteers as he circled around to the front of the apartment. As quickly as I could, I squeezed myself through the window and dropped to the ground. My feet squelched into the mud, absorbing most of the impact. I sunk down to my ankles, but in a minor miracle, I didn't pitch backwards. Pulling my feet free, I crouched down and ran towards the back gate. I'd only have moments to get over the fence before the guard came around again. I started to climb, but one of my socks got caught in the chain link. I was frantically trying to release myself when I heard one of the Volunteers call out and I panicked, nearly falling off the fence. I scrambled to regain my balance and looked around. No one had seen me. I was attempting to heave myself over the top of the fence without impaling my middle when I heard a low rumble and looked up.

Nana and Pops' big SUV was barreling towards me across the open lot at the back of Dave's garage. A blacked out, tinted window rolled down and Zion silently motioned for me to hurry. I flung myself over the top of the fence and started to climb down, but I noticed the guards were making their way around the corner of the house again, so I dropped, this time landing on my back. It knocked all the breath out of me, but I wasn't hurt. Zion jumped out of the SUV, helped me up and rushed me into the vehicle which started moving again before we could even get the door shut.

"Did they see us?" Zion asked Nana who was in the front passenger seat. Pops was driving, tearing around corners and taking back alleyways.

"Don't know, but if we make it out of city limits, they can't do anything about it." Nana cocked the gun in her lap and scanned the horizon. "Chupacabra on your right."

Nana's observation was pretty calm considering the hairless demon dog rushing at us from behind a dumpster.

Pops took a sharp turn into another alleyway and the beast only clipped the back bumper of the SUV. I turned around to look. The Chupacabra was unfazed by the blow. It shook its head and took off running the opposite direction. The SUV shot across a street, between two houses and into a stand of trees. I had no idea how Pops was able to drive so fast without smashing into a tree trunk. I pulled my seatbelt around me and tugged to make sure it was secure.

"Where are we going?" I asked.

"Back to the bunker." Pops answered, taking another sharp turn and suddenly shooting us out onto the two-lane highway that led to the Claybourne compound.

"We need to go to the clearing. I want to be there as soon as the portal opens."

"What we need is to rest and get a lot more firepower if we're gonna fight whatever is coming out of that hell hole." Nana rolled down her window and took a shot. There was a screech and something black and scaly fell from the sky.

"What was that?" I asked.

Before Nana could answer, Pops swerved into the driveway to the compound, and my head smacked the car window.

"That used to happen to me all the time. You gotta use your core when Pops is driving." Zion illustrated by planting her feet and sticking her elbows out.

Nana reached up and grabbed a controller from the sun visor. She clicked it and the gates to the compound started to swing inward slowly. I was certain we were going to crash head on before the gates opened wide enough for the SUV. I closed my eyes and employed Zion's bracing maneuver.

"We made it in!" Zion yelled triumphantly.

I dared to open my eyes. We were all in one piece. I turned around to see the gates swing closed behind us. Pops hit the brakes and the SUV skidded across the gravel drive and came to a stop in front of the main house.

"Keep your head down and run straight into the house. Nana and I will cover you." Pops turned off the SUV, opened the door and hopped out all in one motion. Nana was quickly out the other side.

I didn't waste any time. I jumped from the vehicle and ran as fast as I could. Even still, Zion got to the house before me and was already holding the door open. Once we made it safely inside, Nana and Pops were close behind. Pops pressed the door shut and began clicking the multitude of locks then lay a metal bar across the door jamb.

"You know how to use a gun?" Nana asked me.

"I don't want to shoot anything." I shook my head.

"Then you're gonna need something big to swing. Zion, help her find a weapon, preferably one that's non-flammable. Learned that the hard way trying to take out a fire breathing lizard with a wooden baseball bat. Pops and I will be in the ammo vault." Despite her militaristic words, Nana's eyes were filled with grandmotherly concern. She reached out to squeeze my arm before she and Pops headed downstairs to the vault.

"Come on. You need some dry clothes and a pair of boots." Zion pulled me through the house towards her bedroom.

As we passed the solarium, I noticed that the frosted glass doors were slightly ajar. "I wanna go in."

"You sure?" Zion asked.

"I want to see some of what I'm up against." I pushed the solarium doors open and stepped inside the room.

I could only make out hulking shadows until Zion flipped the lights on and even then, it took a moment for my eyes to adjust. All around us on stands, some in glass cases, some posed on branches or rocks, were creatures I had never seen before. Most of them had bits that looked familiar, maybe fur or a tail, perhaps the shape of a snout. Many of the beasts towered over me with arms upraised, bearing claws, but a few were as tiny as kittens.

"I didn't think..." I stammered.

"This isn't the kind of stuff anybody wants to think about. Most people only see these things in their nightmares." Zion turned around a particularly gnarly looking bird so we wouldn't have to look at the multiple rows of razor-sharp teeth that lined the inside and outside of its beak.

"Dell said they aren't all bad. Well, he said none of them are good or bad but some of them don't hurt anyone."

"Nana and Pops don't shoot all of them. They even let me and Sierra try to raise a baby jackalope once, but it grew up and broke out of its cage. You can't tame them." Zion glanced at a stuffed jackalope on a nearby stand. "Don't worry. That's not the same one."

I noticed that the walls of the room were lined with framed photos. Most of them were of Sierra and Zion through the years, but one was of a smiling couple, each holding a little girl. Beneath it sat a solemn black urn on a wooden pedestal. "Is this your parents?"

Zion nodded. I could see the sadness in her eyes.

"Did one of these things kill them?"

You can't really keep a Wendigo. They're kind of already dead and they're pretty much a walking curse so you have to burn them to ash so all their little pieces can't get back together again and rehaunt you.

"I'm sorry." Said Soara.

"It's ok. It was a long time ago. I don't really remember my parents. It's harder for Sierra."

I swallowed the lump in my throat. "What do you think is happening to my mother?"

"Nobody's ever survived the other side before." The words were already out of Zion's mouth before she could stop herself. I looked immediately nauseous. Zion grabbed a trash can and handed it to me. "You can hurl in here. It doesn't mean your mom isn't alive. You guys are supposed to be special, right? That's why all of this is happening."

I took a few slow breaths to fight down the sourness creeping up the back of my throat. I needed to change the subject. "Where's Sierra?"

"She joined the Volunteers." Zion's voice was a little shaky.

"What? Why would Nana and Pops let her do that?"

"She didn't ask. In a very un-Sierra-like series of events she snuck out, met Matthew on the main road and let him drive her into town. By the time Nana and Pops found out and got to her, she had already taken the oath. That's one of those no takesy backsy kind of situations. It's sacred. Even Nana and Pops can't mess with it."

"Is she ok. What is she doing?"

"We don't know. But Nana and Pops have trained both of us well. We know how to take care of ourselves. She's gonna be ok."

A gunshot cracked somewhere outside and both of us jumped. Zion tugged at my hand. "Come on. We don't have a lot of time. You need shoes."

***

The ride back to the portal took place mostly in silence. Sierra's shoes were a little bit big for me and I kept bending down to retie them as tightly as possible. Beside me in the floorboard was the "weapon" I chose, a cast iron fire poker. Not original but I didn't expect to use it anyway. I had other plans in mind.

"So, what are you exactly?" Zion asked in a whisper.

"I read something in the library that called us Natsiliani. I don't know what that means exactly, but basically my mom and I are at least half like them," I answered, looking out the window at a pair of giant, hairy werewolves tearing apart some poor forest creature.

"Are you gonna start eating our faces off?" Zion was trying to tease, but her voice was tinged with fear.

"No. And I know you don't have any reason to believe it, but as long as there's still some of me left in here, I promise I'd never hurt you or anyone in Mystikos." I searched my entire soul to make sure the words were true. "But I can feel it."

"Feel what?" Zion questioned.

"The portal. It's part of me and I'm part of it. It's like a magnet."

"We won't let it have you." Zion promised.

"It's not it. It's *Them*. The Elementals are why all of this is happening. They want me to help them start an apocalypse."

"But you would never do that," Zion insisted.

"I wouldn't have a choice. They're part of me too, and it wouldn't take much for me to forget I was ever human at all. I can feel their thoughts and desires. They want this place so badly. It tears at them, like the worst kind of hunger you can imagine." I took a breath to steady myself. The desire tasted sweet inside my mouth. "But as long as I'm on this side, I'm still me."

Zion couldn't look me in the eye when she asked her next question. "And if you end up on that side?"

"I won't be able to fight them, so I'll have to...end."

"What do you mean?" Zion's voice quivered.

"I'll have to die." I had known this for a while but saying it out loud sealed it as truth.

"Absolutely fucking not. I'm not losing anyone else to the fuckery of this fucking fuck hole portal." Zion punched the roof of the SUV in frustration.

"Watch your mouth, young lady." Nana interjected.

"Who cares about cursing when we're literally driving into hell?" Zion shot back.

As if on cue, the tires of the SUV squealed to a stop. We were back in the woods outside the clearing. Pops parked behind a tangle of vines as camouflage against the Volunteers patrolling the trees. I peeked through the leaves to scan their faces, hoping to confirm that Sierra and Dell were still alive and in one piece, but I couldn't find them.

"This is the meeting spot. Let me sweep the area first. You never know what's hiding." Pops cracked the door open and stepped out of the vehicle.

"Who are we meeting?" I was ready to make a run for it. I couldn't let anyone mess up my plan.

Zion looked out the car window over my shoulder and smiled. "See for yourself."

Pops had his rifle slung over his arm. He was shaking hands with Fred and Roselyn. Standing close by were Matthew, Noah, August, and Ellie. I leapt out of the car without waiting for permission.

"What are you doing here?" I was overwhelmed and confused, and it felt like more secret keeping. Had I been tricked?

"We're here for Mystikos and for you." Roselyn wrapped me in a hug.

My first impulse was to pull away. I didn't want to be babied, but Roselyn still smelled like pancakes and coffee, and I allowed myself to soak in the safety of it a little bit longer. "I'm sorry I lied to you. But I have to help Mom."

"I know. I told everyone you weren't the princess in the tower type, but nobody listens to me."

"But why did I have to sneak out if you all were planning to bring me here anyway?"

"Nana and Pops needed to get you out of town and past the Volunteers. Fred and I were on a need-to-know basis, but as soon as they had you at the compound, we needed to know."

Fred took his turn at a hug. I realized I'd never seen him outside of the Wistful Willow. Apparently, it took the end of the world to get him out of his kitchen. I almost laughed out loud at the thought.

August stepped up. "My mom's here. I mean she's really *here*. She's back."

"Hi Soara. I'm Ellie Midwinter." Ellie took my hand.

The confusion in Ellie's eyes was totally gone, replaced by the most peaceful smile I had ever seen. Ellie's fingers felt warm and prickly, as if electricity were dancing on her skin. I instantly experienced a surge of calm moving through my body at Ellie's touch, but I couldn't allow all this kindness to let me waiver from my plan. I pulled my hand away gently. "Thank you for coming. Thank all of you for coming. And please don't take this the wrong way, but I need you to leave."

"Now you listen here, young lady. It doesn't do any of us a lick of good for you to go lone ranger. We all know what we're up against, probably way better than you, so your bravery is nice, but pretty useless when it comes right down to it." Nana scolded.

"The portal is a part of us too. Maybe not in the same way it is for you, but whatever happens is going affect us all." Matthew added.

Noah joined in. "There's no running from it. Even if we wanted to."

"And we DON'T want to. So, you might as well stop arguing. No one on earth has ever outstubborned me. I'm a professional." Zion planted her feet and cracked her knuckles for effect.

"Face it. You're one of us now." Said Pops giving me a slap on the back.

"And this proves it." Roselyn reached into a backpack at her feet and pulled out something white and shiny which she handed to me. It was a coffee mug. When I turned it towards myself, I noticed that Roselyn had hand painted "The Wistful Willow" on the side just like the sweatshirt she was wearing the day my mother and me first met her. "You're officially a regular."

I fought back the tears stinging behind my eyes. I had never felt more like I belonged with a group of people and now I had to tell them all goodbye. "I love it. It's perfect. But I can't keep it."

"Duh, no one's expecting you to smack an Elemental upside the head with a coffee cup. It's symbolic." Zion tried really hard not to roll her eyes.

"You don't understand. I don't know what's going to happen to me when I get near the portal. I may not be myself anymore. What if I turned on one of you? What if I hurt you or worse?" I couldn't bring myself to say what I knew my Elemental side was capable of, but I could see it very clearly inside my head and it was terrifying.

"Don't be afraid." Ellie stepped forward and laid her hand across my forehead just like Eteri used to do when she was checking me for a fever. The scary pictures in my brain faded away and were replaced by warmth and light.

"How did you do that?" I asked.

"I've placed a ward over you. It should work, as long as I can stay here," Ellie tapped her temple, "It will help to keep you safe and make you brave."

I could feel my thoughts fighting against the ward, but it was stronger than any of my fears. I looked deeply into the eyes of the people standing before me, then slowly took Ellie's hand. Ellie reached out to August and one by one a circle formed. Whatever was coming, we would fight it together.

"Let's kick some monster ass." At Zion's words, the "grown-ups" headed over to the SUV to handle some last-minute details.

I gathered my friends closer around me. This was going to be weird and cheesy and maybe a little bit embarrassing, but I had to say it. "So, I've basically never had best friends before. Which isn't as tragic as it seems. I mean in hindsight it's a little tragic, but mostly I'm just sad I don't have longer to enjoy it."

"Don't say that, Soara." Matthew entreated.

"Let me get through this, please. You guys are the best thing that's ever happened to me. I just wish Sierra and Dell were here too. But I wrote something for them." I pulled two folded pieces of paper out of my pocket and held them out to Zion. "Can you give these to them for me?"

Zion nodded and took the notes.

I reached up and unhooked the golden moon and star earrings from my ears. "These are for Dell. To remember me."

Zion took the earrings too. She was holding her breath to keep from crying. Zion generally didn't give a crap what anyone thought, but she wouldn't allow even the slightest hint to get out to anyone that she had any tender spots.

August put her arms out and pulled everyone into a group hug. Nobody wanted to let go. We were here. We would fight, to the end if necessary. And we were all unified and terrified.

"First thing we're gonna have to do is get past the Volunteers guarding the trees, and that's where these fellas come in." Pops' words broke the sacred silence, we joined him and the rest of the grown-ups at the SUV.

The back door of the vehicle had been popped open and inside sat a beat up, grey metal box pierced with breathing holes. Whatever was trapped in there was clearly angry at its current circumstances. Pops banged his hand on the box and was answered with a cacophony of disturbingly vicious growls.

The Volunteers on duty snapped to attention at the sound and Matthew quickly pulled Noah and Zion behind the tree. "They're gonna hear us!"

"That's what we want." Nana answered. "This will be the distraction we need to get those Volunteers out of the way, so we can get to the portal."

"I don't want anyone else getting hurt." I insisted.

"This kind of creature causes mayhem, not morbidity. Those Volunteers'll be so busy trying to chase these suckers down that they won't even notice us sneaking right by and into the clearing." Nana smiled at the thought of creating problems for the Volunteers.

I was not convinced. Those growls sounded like they came from mouths with lots of extremely pointy teeth. "

Pops snapped open a lock and the front of the box flipped down. "Get after it, fellas."

I braced myself for a scaley beast with red eyes, or a rabid, snarling furball. Instead, the open box was full of nothing. I looked at Nana and Pops but neither seemed surprised. Then I heard the first yelp, and a gunshot went off. I pushed aside the vines and saw five or six Volunteers batting at their heads, tripping over unseen obstacles, losing their weapons and one dude even got pantsed. Whatever was after them was invisible and fast.

Pops smiled. "Lutins. Shapeshifting spirits with telekinetic abilities and a penchant for mischief. That'll keep em busy for a while."

"At the signal, we head into the woods. Once we reach the clearing, we'll hold the perimeter so Soara can get inside and find the portal. Ellie, you just keep that ward on her." Nana was very good at taking charge.

"For as long as I can." Ellie turned to me. "But just know that my magic can't hold if you cross the portal."

"Let's go!" Pops gave a whistle, and everyone hoisted their weapons and tore into the woods.

As predicted, the Volunteers were too busy having their shoes set on fire and being strung upside down in the trees to notice any additional chaos. We all slipped right by into the trees. I kept looking for Dell or Sierra. I wanted so badly to lay eyes on them, just to know that they were safe (at least for now), but maybe they weren't allowing the younger Volunteers to get this close to the danger.

With each step towards the clearing, I felt my body get stronger and my senses grow more precise. I could see the veins on a single blade of grass and hear the footsteps of a beetle. I was consumed by the beauty of everything around me, but also keenly aware of the fragility of this world. I closed my eyes and kept running. Every molecule of the forest was speaking to me. I no longer needed human sight to make my way. Just outside the field of dandelions, I came to a stop. I could feel an invisible hook set in my belly, pulling me towards the source of my newfound power. Whatever wanted me wouldn't wait any longer.

Nana stood nearest to me, taking her place on the perimeter of the clearing. She had her rifle at the ready and was already scanning the tree line for trouble. I touched her shoulder and Nana turned.

"You know what you have to do if they take me. I need you to promise." I couldn't bring myself to make the actual demand.

"I know." Nana nodded solemnly, but the sadness in her eyes quickly turned to steel as she cocked her rifle and steadied herself for the battle ahead.

CHAPTER NINETEEN

Everyone was in place. It was time to get Eteri back. I took a step into the clearing. This time when the dandelions released their feathery parachutes, they moved around me in slow motion. I could see each delicate filament of white and was briefly dazzled, forgetting my purpose. Then all at once, my world went dark. The clearing was no longer a downy field of white. The ground all around me was scorched and thick smoke filled the air. I looked towards my friends at the perimeter, but they didn't seem to notice the change. I felt my lungs fill with black, powdery air and panic began to rise in my chest, but I reminded myself of Eteri and continued forward. There seemed to be nothing but smoky blackness in this place and then suddenly, the portal appeared.

In my mind, when I finally saw the portal, it would be something from a movie, a ringed hole of fire that ripped open in the middle of the sky. The reality was something quite different. There were no edges, no beginning and end, there was just this world and that one, existing side by side, mirrors of one another. But as I drew nearer, the portal began to buzz and crack, reaching inky tendrils towards me. The sky of that other world turned an acidic greenish grey and I felt the earth beneath my feet rumble and churn. I lost my balance and fell to my hands and knees, piercing the skin of my palms on a carpet of burnt dandelion stalks. As I struggled to pull myself up, the portal exploded outward, pushing me back to the ground. In that instant, an endless torrent of inexplicable and terrifying creatures began to spill forth just like in my last dream except this time they were real. I could feel their hunger to tear apart everything of this world to make space for more of the other. My impulse was to chase after the beasts and protect my friends, but I knew I must continue forward.

"Soara. Soara, hurry please." Eteri's voice called out.

"Mom!" with a rush of adrenaline, I jerked myself forward and stumbled to the portal. The creatures continued to stream past me, but they didn't seem to notice me in their frenzy. They were fixated on destruction outside of the clearing and I was going further in. I struggled not to wretch. My sense of smell was overwhelmed with whatever musk the creatures brought with them, coupled with the sickeningly sweet air of the Elementals' world.

Eteri stepped into sight. She had her back to me and her head down. She was wearing a lacy camisole and one of her flowery skirts. Her hair trailed down her back and I could count the freckles on her shoulders. My heart nearly burst with relief. "Mom, I'm here!" But Eteri's back remained to me. Maybe she couldn't hear me over the bedlam. "Eteri!" I called out with every ounce of breath I could muster.

Finally, Eteri's head lifted, and she slowly began to turn around. I was almost at the portal entrance. I reached out a hand, but the figure that twisted towards me was no longer my mother. I found myself staring into the glassy eyes of my grandmother, Zepherine.

Eteri's clothing had burned away from Zepherine's skin, to be replaced by flowing robes like the ones I'd seen in the stained-glass windows of the library. Copper hair lengthened into a glorious train that rippled out behind Zepherine, and she seemed to grow taller, or maybe she was floating, I couldn't tell.

"Soara, come to me." All trace of Eteri's body was gone, but her voice is what spilled from Zepherine's lips.

"Where is my mother?" I spit out angrily, trying to yell above the din of the monsters all around me and the strange hiss of the portal.

"Come to me, my love. I've been waiting for you." Zepherine cooed sweetly.

"You can have me, but only if you release Eteri." On this, I was unwilling to compromise.

Zepherine floated closer to the portal's edge. I could feel her intense desire to take everything from this world and bend it to her will. "We are the same. I know you feel it, little sparrow."

"Don't call me that, and we are not the same." I spit back angrily.

"We could rule together. You would know infinite power. It is your choice, but I don't need you anymore, Soara. I have my Eteri now. My precious daughter. I thought she was too weak, too human. Even you took her strength for granted, but we were mistaken. With Eteri's help, the Elementals shall make a new beginning. Both worlds shall become one."

"She would never help you." I screamed.

"She has already agreed. Now will you join us, granddaughter?"

My stomach lurched. I didn't believe that Eteri would ever accept Zepherine's offer of power willingly, but I had no idea what kind of torture my mother may have been put through to extract the promise. There might be nothing I could do for Eteri at this point, but I could still try to protect my newfound family. "Promise me you'll save my friends and Mystikos."

"It is done." The corners of Zepherine's rose tinted lips turned up in a smile, but I noticed the friendliness didn't quite reach her eyes.

I recalled Roselyn's warning about tricky agreements. I knew I must carefully consider my words. "Promises are easily broken in both of our worlds. How do I know I can trust you?"

Zepherine opened her hands slowly. "Come my brothers and sister." To her right, another feminine face appeared, and to her left, those of two men. Beneath the faces, the bodies of the three remaining Elementals, Earth, Fire and Water, materialized. Just like Zepherine, they each appeared exactly as they were in the library windows, towering yet delicate figures filled with magnificent light. I wanted to detest the Elementals, but no one could hate anything so beautiful. I expected to be afraid, but as I stared into their faces, I was struck by a connection that filled every cell in my body. I knew that I was inextricably linked to their power.

"In the witness of my siblings, we will be bound eternally. Anything we promise here cannot be undone. And so it is." At Zepherine's words, the other Elementals nodded slowly.

I looked back at my friends. At this point, no Volunteers were coming to help or hinder them. The group had pivoted from protecting the clearing, to trying to keep Ellie safe from a never-ending stream of frantic creatures so she could keep her ward on me. They were battling bravely against the onslaught, and I knew they would never give up, no matter the consequences. I knew just as deeply that they wouldn't want me to make a deal to save them at the sacrifice of so many more. I was about to turn around and tell Zepherine to go to hell when I heard Zion screaming angrily. A small, monkeylike creature had climbed her like a tree, and she was furiously trying to bat it away, but it held on, suddenly hurling something towards Ellie. In the next moment, Ellie slumped to the ground, and I instantly felt her protection drop like a heavy curtain.

Without Ellie's ward, my tether to humanity quickly began to slip away. I looked back into the Elementals exquisite faces and suddenly couldn't imagine how I had ever considered anything more important than being a part of their great power. I could clearly see a future when the pettiness of this world was finally burned away, and I had joined my true family in ruling a new earth. Power coursed through my veins. I felt extraordinary and deserving of all my desires. A triumphant smile spread across my face. This was the turning that I'd feared but instead of being consumed, I felt I'd finally shed the prison that had trapped me in a meaningless existence for my entire life.

Across the clearing, I could feel that Nana was no longer part of the circle guarding Ellie. She had moved back into the trees to take cover, and at that moment, her rifle was trained on my exultant face. I turned and took a first step towards the portal. I sensed Nana's rifle lift slightly and cock. With another step, Nana's finger began to squeeze the trigger.

"Soara!"

A familiar voice pulled me back to my self, but this only filled me with rage.

"Soara, no!"

The voice rang out again. I turned, ready to destroy whatever stood in the way of me meeting my destiny.

Dell was running across the clearing with Sierra at this side. "Soara, listen to my voice. Concentrate on me."

Dell pushed through a being made more of slime than substance, splitting it into two angry balls of ooze that Sierra incinerated with the military grade blowtorch she was using to fend off the monsters. As he got closer, Dell's eyes were drawn away from me towards the portal. He had only been a Volunteer for a few months before I came to town and was still technically in training. Dell had never been allowed anywhere near the portal before we came to look for Eteri. It was considered far too dangerous. Of course, Dell knew about the Elementals. Every child of Mystikos grew up on the stories of the powerful ones who turned the seasons. He'd read all the books and passed by the library windows thousands of times, but he was unprepared for the awe of looking directly upon them. The four Elementals were watching me with what could only be described as smug pride, and I knew all five of them together had to be the most beautiful thing Dell had ever seen.

"Dell, watch out!" Sierra yelled, but it was too late.

Dell tripped over one of the tiny monkey creatures that had taken down Ellie. As he hit the ground, his face tore open on a jagged stone. The resulting blood drew the attention of a goat man, a monster over 7 feet tall with the head and horns of the animal, a human torso, and cloven hooved feet. Sierra aimed her blowtorch but when she pulled the trigger, it only spit sparks. She was out of fuel. She struggled to get out of the machine pack strapped to her back so she could get to Dell, but before she could reach him, the goat man tore one of his horns into Dell's calf. He let out a guttural scream of pain.

The sound of Dell's agony ripped me from my trance. "Dell!" I raced to him, throwing the full force of my body into the goat man. This close to the portal, I had gained some of the Elementals' strength. The goat man went flying across the clearing and limped away whimpering. Dell was still alive, but his leg was ripped open in jagged shreds.

"Help me! He's losing too much blood," I screamed.

Sierra rushed to Dell's side and put pressure on the wound. I moved to Dell's face.

"Stay awake, Dell, please." I begged. I tried to wipe the blood off his face, but it just kept coming. I remembered reading something about head wounds bleeding a lot and sometimes looking worse than they were, but I couldn't find the source to confirm if this were the case now.

Inside the portal, the Elementals were no longer smiling. As the rage that I had slipped away from them once more took over, they could no longer hold onto their facades of beauty. The Elementals' mouths opened. Their jaws unhinged. Bones broke, contorting their bodies into hellish shapes and their skin began to twist inside out. As their angry shrieks rang out in a terrifying chorus, Sierra looked towards the portal and tried not to scream.

"Soara, what's happening?"

I took in the Elementals in their true form. I was certain what stood before me had inspired the disturbing biblically accurate descriptions of angels. They were almost too bright to look upon, with multiple claw-like appendages radiating outwards, all covered in eyes and mouths screaming in fury.

"We have to get him out of the clearing!" I yelled over the shrieks. We tried to pick Dell up and move him, but he had passed out by that point and was dead weight. "Take one of his hands."

I moved over and Sierra grabbed Dell's other hand. We were attempting to drag him out of the clearing when all thousands of infuriated eyes focused in on us.

I saw a black tentacle snake out from the portal and screamed. "Hurry!"

Sierra and I doubled down trying to pull Dell across the clearing, but we weren't fast enough. The tentacle wrapped itself around one of Dell's ankles, followed swiftly by others which bound his torso and arms. "Sierra, don't let go!" I begged.

"I won't," Sierra promised, but then another tentacle reached out and wrapped itself around her own neck. Her breath was cut off and she dropped Dell's hand trying to pry it from her windpipe.

Dell's other hand started to slip from my fingers as the tentacles pulled him towards the portal. Even with my newfound strength, I was no match for the combined will of all four Elementals. I looked to my friends outside of the circle in a last bid for help, but they were all fighting their own battles. Even Nana had come out of the trees. She had run out of shells for her rifle and was swinging a large hunting knife.

There was no help and there was no hope...unless I gave the Elementals what they wanted.

"Ok. Just stop, please!" I yelled at the portal. The tentacles relaxed and Sierra was finally able to gasp for a breath, but they did not release her and Dell. I took a step forward. I opened my mouth to pledge myself eternally in exchange for my friends' safety, but before the words could leave my lips, a familiar voice rang through the mayhem.

"Soara, please." Eteri's voice called out.

"You can't trick me again, Zepherine!" I yelled into the wind.

"No, Soara. You mustn't. You'll be bound forever. There's no going back." Eteri begged me.

"I said stop it! I'm doing what you want. Just leave them alone!" I stepped even closer to the portal. The thousands of eyes followed me, blinking eagerly. I desperately wanted to look away, but I had to save my friends. "I promise..."

Before I could utter the rest of my oath, a colossal clap of thunder rang out, shaking the ground and nearly popping my eardrums. I stumbled backwards but was determined to continue. "I promise..."

Another clap of thunder, this time followed by a bolt of lightning which lit up the sky and struck the tree line. A ring of fire encircled the clearing, separating me, Dell and Sierra from our own world and trapping the beasts spilling from the portal inside. I heard a rush of wind. Out of the portal flew the great thunderbird once more. I crumbled to the ground, crawling towards Dell to cover his body with my own. "Sierra, look out!"

With every flap of the thunderbird's wings, the wind whipped higher, causing the flames at the edges of the clearing to rocket into the air. The beast flew in a circle then dove towards me. I braced for the claws to rip into my back.

"Look up, Sparrow." The voice in my head called out and this time I couldn't resist. As my head tilted towards the sky, I saw the great bird moving towards me, but instead of attacking me, its talons slashed the tentacles holding onto Dell and flew towards Sierra. As the thunderbird ripped away the tentacle wrapped around Sierra's neck, I noticed there was a figure upon its back. Another bolt of lightning flashed, and I realized the figure was Eteri!

"Mom!" I called out, but the thunderbird pulled upwards and let out a shriek. More thunder and lightning cracked across the sky, then the clouds released a deluge of rain. I looked back at Dell and Sierra. Sierra had tossed the still slithering tentacle onto the ground and was now removing the rest of them from an unconscious Dell's limbs.

With the sky stirred into a full frenzy, the thunderbird finally started its descent. The beast had helped me save Dell and Sierra, but I still couldn't be sure if it was friend or foe. Either way, it would have to go through me to get to them.

I expected a thunderous rumble when the bird touched the ground, but it landed gracefully. Eteri slipped from the thunderbird's back. I tried to focus in on my mother's face. One look into her eyes would be enough to let me know if I was safe.

"It's ok, Sparrow. I'm here." Eteri reached out and I fell into her arms. "Listen to me. We don't have much time." She lifted my chin so I was looking in her eyes and I instantly felt my fear begin to melt away. "I know what we are now. The Elementals are afraid because we have far more power than they imagined. They can't control us. They can only force us to their will if we swear our allegiance to them."

"I almost promised." I dug my fingers into Eteri's arms.

"But you didn't. And now we have to stop them." Eteri's usual flightiness had been replaced with absolute resolve.

"How?" I screamed through the pelting rain.

"We've had the key all along. Think, Soara." Eteri touched my temple.

Without speaking, I reached into the pocket of my jacket and pulled out the fragile triangle of twigs. Eteri gently took hold of the opposite side, and a beam of light shot towards the sky. The brittle talisman disintegrated, and I could feel my hand meld to my mother's. An instantaneous peace radiated through my body and into my very soul. Eteri's face mirrored the same serenity. We were one in power and spirit. As the beam of light enveloped us, our shapes began to melt away.

Sierra looked up from doctoring Dell and screamed, "Where are you going? Don't leave us here!"

Just before my face faded into the brightness, I smiled at Sierra, "We are more here than we've ever been."

The light began to condense and take shape. From it, Eteri and I emerged, now in the form of a colossal two-headed dragon covered in scales of midnight blue that reflected the stars in the sky. Sierra screamed and began to back away, but when our heads turned, our glittering, faceted eyes radiated assurance.

"Is it you?" Sierra asked.

My mother and I dipped our dragon heads in answer, then turned towards the portal. The many-eyed Elementals began to buzz and shriek, but it was unclear if their reaction was anger or terror. We slowly unfurled a set of wings that nearly spanned the clearing, and digging our claws into the earth, both our mouths opened releasing a torrent of wind which instantly halted the storm and extinguished the fires. All the portal beasts in and outside of the clearing stopped their battle and together went down on bended knee.

August, Matthew, Noah, Zion, Fred, and Roselyn stared in stunned disbelief, but Nana and Pops kept their weapons trained on us, just in case. Unseen by anyone in all the chaos, Ellie had come to. She walked over to Pops and gently pushed his gun towards the ground.

"They're on our side."

The Elementals no longer had any control over their shape. They flowed in and out of a myriad of ever more terrifying forms and began throwing themselves against the boundary of the portal.

Our double necks leaned in, and our foreheads touched. Whatever parts of Eteri and me that remained inside this new form communicated our deep love for one another and the understanding that no matter what came next, we would tackle it together.

The moment we stepped into the portal; the Elementals began their attack. Wind blew us backwards and boulders of hail dropped from the sky, cracking our bones with each hit. The earth fractured beneath our feet and flames shot upwards, licking our scaly belly. We screamed in pain but held our ground which only fueled the Elementals' anger. Lightning struck us and the soil around us quaked violently. A hurricane of wind and rain descended. With every new assault more of our beautiful midnight blue scales dropped to the ground exposing our soft skin underneath. Encouraged by proof we had at least some vulnerability, the Elementals doubled down on their attack.

Outside of the portal, the humans watched helplessly. To them, it seemed we were losing the battle and with it, any hope of stopping the Elementals from taking over their world, but we did not fall.

The Elementals continued their assault, but the more they tore our dragon body apart, the weaker they became. As their powers continued to diminish, they were finally forced back into their recognizable human-like forms. Standing in front of her brothers and sister, Zepherine's eyes blazed with a sudden understanding. "You've stolen our power." she hissed. "It was a trick." Zepherine reached out, but when her fingers grazed one of our midnight blue scales upon the ground, it took on a fiery, iridescent glow and her skin sizzled. She immediately pulled back with a shriek, holding up the shriveled remains of her hand. "How dare you betray your own!"

We opened our dragon mouths once more. To human ears, what came out sounded like the ringing of crystal bowls, but the message was clear to the Elementals.

"You and your siblings are the true betrayers. You tried to bend the natural order to your will, forgetting your gifts were bestowed with a duty."

"But you are mine. I made you." Zepherine screamed.

"We are our own and we will protect our world." At those words, our dragon form rent in two and with a flash of light, Eteri and I appeared in our own Elemental forms. Blinding light spilled forth from our chests and great golden robes trailed out behind us. Each of us wore a diadem set with four stones, representing Air, Fire, Earth and Water.

The Elementals floated backwards, their faces a mixture of confusion and fear. For the first time since their creation, they were beholding an entity more powerful than themselves.

I glided forward. When I spoke, my voice was beautiful and terrible, vibrating the air around me. "You have a choice, surrender or be destroyed."

Zepherine laughed softly, a smug smile turning up the corners of her perfect mouth. "Your world would die without us. The rules of creation cannot be changed."

Eteri joined her hand with mine. We spoke together, our voices blending into one. "But as you say, you have made us. You gave us your powers and our fathers gave us a soul. Surely there are others like us, and we will find our brothers and sisters. You are no less powerful, Zepherine, but your kind are now unnecessary."

The four Elementals once again hissed angrily. They tried to take on their more frightening form, but the most they could muster was shuffling their bodies into ever more ridiculous configurations.

"All the worlds of creation are meant to exist in harmony. Anything outside of that balance brings chaos and destruction. Your aberration will not be tolerated, and the price will be your own demise unless you are willing to accept your true calling and reset the balance yourselves." Our words reverberated as unceasing echoes while the Elementals turned together to consider their fate.

When Zepherine finally stared back into my and Eteri's eyes, there was no need for words. The Elementals would stand down.

The sun was just making its journey across the treetops, and when it hung itself at the top of the sky, the portal would close for the day. Eteri and I called the beasts of this world back to their home. The many lumbered in tired and confused. It had been against their nature to war, and they were ready for the wheel of life to resume its normal turning.

The last to return was the great Thunderbird. It landed in front of us and dipped its head. Zepherine's eyes blazed as her once loyal servant revered its new masters, but she did not make a sound.

When the Thunderbird took flight to its nest, we spoke again as one. "Zepherine, we share much, but we are not the same. We are soul bound and so we feel love. This is why we have shown you mercy, but we are still half Elemental, therefore also bound to protect creation. We release you and your siblings now, but we will return to destroy you if you cannot control your lust for power."

With those words, Eteri and I stepped back through the portal to our own world. The key lay at our feet, nearly hidden amongst the dandelions that were already growing back. We bent to pick it up and upon touching its delicate twigs, returned to our fully human forms. As the sun settled into dawn, the portal closed. Our last sight of that other world was Zepherine's stony stare.

"Mom." I fell into my mother's arms and finally let the tears come. "I thought I'd lost you."

"Never, my Sparrow. Never." Eteri hugged me closer.

"Dell and Sierra!" I let go of Mom and turned to comb the clearing for a sign of Dell, Sierra or any of my friends. At first, I couldn't see anyone. The only things moving in the clearing were the dandelions that continued to sprout up almost magically. "Please, Mom. They have to be ok."

It was just a tiny flash of yellow at first. Some movement in the trees. It could have been an autumn leaf dropping from a branch. But I dared to hope, and slowly that patch of color became Dell's yellow rain slicker emerging from the forest. He was followed by Nana, Pops, Fred, Roselyn, Noah, Matthew, August, Ellie and finally Zion helping Sierra limp forward. They were a haggard bunch, but all very much alive.

I ran across the clearing towards Dell, but when I reached out to touch him, he flinched in fear.

"I promise I'm still just Soara."

"You're like them." Dell stuttered.

"But I'm more like you." I held out my hand again. Tendrils of visible air flowed from my fingertips towards Dell and gently encircled his hands.

"It feels warm." Dell let the air wrap around more of his body and instantly relaxed.

"Do you trust me?" I asked.

"Yes." Dell answered.

I used the tendrils of air to pull Dell towards me and into a deep kiss. It was the most fantastic sensation I had ever experienced. Every molecule in both of our bodies quivered.

"Oh!" I gasped. There were going to be wonderful surprises to discover about my new self.

"Literally, get a room." Zion's voice was tired, but her attitude had clearly not taken any blows in the battle.

I pulled back from Dell with a big smile and ran to hug my friends. The war was over.

EPILOGUE

I'm running late. I wanted to wear my Joni Mitchell t-shirt today, but it's the same color blue as the carpeting in my room, so I'm having trouble picking it out amongst the piles of stuff I still haven't had time to put away since we moved in. I briefly consider turning on my super senses but decide against it. Since the whole portal, two-headed dragon, discovering I'm an Elemental thing, I struggle a bit with when and how to use my powers. My biggest fear is that I'll start to forget to be human and hurt someone I care about. It gives me a sick shiver in the pit of my stomach to think of that possibility, but I manage to shake it off. Right now, I am very human, just a teenage girl running late to get ready for school, and according to the mirror on my wall, having an intensely bad hair day. I give up on Joni Mitchell and switch to a Cranberries shirt (an authentic 90's hand-me-down from Eteri). I pull my hair up into a bun and shove in a couple of bobby pins, then grab my backpack and head out the door.

The sun blinds me when I step out onto the apartment's tiny porch. Another thing I'm not used to is how unbelievably beautiful the weather is in Mystikos when we aren't under attack. It's a perfect, crispy autumn day and I can smell a mixture of pancakes wafting over from the Wistful Willow and the scent of falling leaves.

A chorus of enthusiastic barks meet me the bottom of the porch stairs. Watcher and Sentinel dance around me, wagging their tails. "Don't worry. I didn't forget your treats." I reach into the pocket of my jacket and pull out two slices of apple. "Don't fight over them this time. There's one for each of you." I feed each dog their treat, then give them quick ear nuzzles.

"Pierogies for dinner tonight and vegan brats." Dave calls from the garage. Dave has pretty much moved into the garage full time now. He never wants to be too far away from Eteri and I don't mind. I've never had anything like a father figure in my life, but Dave is not only kind and a great cook, but a pretty cool dude too, with an incredible vinyl collection, so I'm ok if he's the one. We've fallen into the habit of Dave choosing the menu and me choosing the music to go with it every night. It's embarrassingly adorable and honestly, I love it.

"Sounds like a Tom Petty kind of night." I call back with a smile then hurry out of the garage yard gate.

As I cross the street to the café, I smile at the Volunteers busy rebuilding town. It will take a while to get things back to normal, but in Mystikos, everyone pitches in.

Opening the door to the Wistful Willow, I'm instantly enveloped in a hug of coffee and breakfast delights. The café is filled with the morning regulars and Eteri is making her rounds taking orders and dazzling customers with her friendly smile.

"Good morning, Sparrow. They're waiting for you."

I hurry through the café, my sneakers squeaking on the linoleum floor as I grab my mug from the regulars' wall. That wall was the first thing the Volunteers put back together after the big battle and my mug received the center spot as a special thank you from Roselyn and Fred.

"If I starve to death before you get here, I'm haunting you for the rest of your eternal life." Zion calls out from across the room. Several tables have been pushed together and my whole gang of friends are patiently (with the exception of Zion) waiting for me to arrive.

"The jury is still out on the eternal thing." I grab the last open seat, right beside Dell and sling my backpack around my chair. "I've got a lot of research to do at the library."

At the thought of my favorite place in Mystikos, I touch the small wooden figure that hangs from a necklace around my neck. While Julie rests, however long that might take, I'll be her protector.

"Who's getting what?" Roselyn cheerfully asks the table. "How about couple of everything? It's on me and Fred for a back-to-school present."

"You need fuel for your brains!" Fred yells from the kitchen.

The whole table gives Fred and Roselyn a round of applause, and with a curtsy and a wink, Roselyn heads back to the kitchen.

I turn to Sierra. She still has a red mark around her neck where she got choked by the tentacle, but it's getting lighter every day. She wears a Volunteers sweatshirt, and I point to the logo. "Nana and Pops let you out in that thing?"

"They're coming around. Nana said that as long as you and Eteri are here, the Volunteers are probably going to be in retirement anyway, so she's not too worried. She and Pops didn't even do a perimeter check before lights out last night."

This genuinely surprises me. "That's huge!" I turn to August, who's adjusting her prosthetic hand. "You found it again?"

"Mom's making me wear it. She says I ought to at least try since we spent so much money on it. I don't see the point when I have five good fingers and ten good toes."

"So, she's still "here?" I ask carefully. I don't want to upset my friend.

"She says something got jostled in her brain at the clearing and she thinks she might be back forever. Oh, and she told me to give you these." August hands over a tiny, folded packet. Inside are two shiny sewing needles. "She said to cross them under your pillow, and it will help with the nightmares."

I haven't mentioned that I'm still having nightmares to anyone (the only lingering damage from my ordeal in the portal), but Ellie Midwinter seems to have a way of knowing things.

"Did you sleep ok? Dell asks, giving me a kiss on top of my head. He has a way of knowing things too, at least when it comes to me.

"Mmmhmm." I squeeze Dell's knee and snuggle under his arm. He's my favorite hiding place whenever I need to remind myself that that I'm still normal.

#

We're all so full we nearly have to be wheelbarrowed to school as we walk down Mystikos' main avenue. I hang back a little bit behind everyone so I can watch. Part of me still feels like I need to make sure everyone is safe and part of me just wants to stare at how lucky I am to have such amazing friends.

When I look at Dell, my fingers began to tickle. I decide it's ok to play with my powers just a little bit, and with a quiet giggle, I allow a few tendrils of air to snake out towards Dell and pull him back to me by his belt loops.

"I wonder when I'll get used to that." Dell asks with a smile.

I let the tendrils touch the sides of Dell's face and pulled him to me for a kiss. "I like surprising you."

Noticing something out of the corner of my eye, I turn to look behind the building we're passing. A couple of imps have started a tiny fire and are dancing around it gleefully. I blow gently towards the imps and the fire goes out. They swear and stomp their feet angrily, but upon noticing me, they respectfully bow and run away.

"Do you think the Elementals will keep their part of the bargain?" Dell asks, bringing me towards him protectively.

"They're still plotting. I can feel them. But they're also scared. We'll find the rest of the ones like us. We have time."

Dell kisses me once more. I smile and grab his hand, pulling him towards the others. For now, things are perfect.